THE CONVENT'S SECRET

GLASS AND STEELE, #5

C.J. ARCHER

CHAPTER 1

LONDON, SPRING 1890

*M*att had walked to Lady Buckland's house, so there was no rumble of carriage wheels to announce his return to number sixteen Park Street, only the quiet click of the front door unlocking. The sound wrenched my frayed nerves and echoed through the deep silence of the small hours.

He was home, thank God.

I gathered my wrap around my shoulders and rose from the sofa where I'd given up trying to read an hour ago. I got no further than a few steps before his frame filled the doorway. The lamplight cast a soft glow over his face, highlighting his strong jaw and cheekbones, obscuring the signs of exhaustion. He should be resting, not breaking into the homes of well-to-do ladies.

"I saw the light," he said, prowling into the drawing room. It would seem that stealth, necessary for the night's burgling, had not yet rubbed off. He stole toward me without making a sound nor a hair on his head moving. The dark pits of his eyes threatened to swallow me whole. I couldn't tell whether his excursion had been successful or not, but I could read his desire. Or perhaps sense it.

Or perhaps I simply wanted it to be there.

Wanted it, yet did not at the same time. *Dared* not.

I was suddenly more anxious about being alone with him than I had been waiting for his safe return. "Well?" A whisper was all I could manage as panic set in. I really should have gone to bed. Tempting fate like this was a mistake.

"Well," he said, his rich voice sliding over me as thoroughly as his gaze. "You waited up."

"I was worried."

"There was no need. I've crept through houses while the occupants slept dozens of times. Mostly the occupants were armed outlaws, not old ladies." He stepped closer until we were barely a foot apart. He leaned forward a little and a small, crooked smile bedeviled his handsome features. "But I like that you were worried about me."

I clutched my shawl tighter and felt my heart flutter. It was definitely a mistake to stay up when no one else had. "But her servants…"

"Were asleep in their beds. Nobody stirred."

"They could have. Or her dog may have heard you."

"The dog is used to servants coming and going. Besides, I had treats." He pulled out a paper bag from his jacket pocket. I smelled the bacon before he showed me the contents.

I laughed, shedding the remnants of the worry that had weighed me down since he'd told me he would break into Lady Buckland's house.

"The others have retired?" he asked, pouring two brandies at the sideboard.

"They weren't as concerned." Duke and Cyclops had remained up until one. Willie had come home from her own nocturnal adventures half an hour later and had promptly retired to bed.

"They know me better." He handed me a tumbler and touched his glass to mine. "That side of me, anyway. You only know the respectable gentleman, not the outlaw."

"I've seen you in moments where you've shed your polished veneer." Like the time he'd fought off my attackers, the times he'd threatened Eddie Hardacre and Mr. Abercrombie, and the time he undid my corset laces.

He studied me over the rim of his glass, as if trying to determine which moments I meant. "And do you like those moments?"

I didn't answer him. That path led to treacherous waters. I sat on the sofa and sipped. The brandy steadied my nerves enough that I felt I could look at him again without falling into the depths of his eyes. "I know you well enough to know you're in a good mood. You were successful?"

He sat too, and the tension that had enveloped us since his entry broke. I sighed but wasn't sure if it was from relief or disappointment.

"I was," he said, a hint of triumph in his voice. "Tucked away in the hidden drawer of her escritoire was a document, from Mother Alfreda at the Convent of the Sisters of the Sacred Heart in Chelsea, stating that Lady Buckland agrees to give her child to the convent's care until such time as he can be given to a good Christian family to raise."

I closed my eyes and breathed deeply. We had another piece to the puzzle of Matt's magical watch. I'd been so afraid that our investigation would come to nothing. We'd opened old wounds and released painful memories for many people in recent days, including me, but I'd consoled myself with the thought that we were making progress. And we had. My grandfather, Chronos, had taught me the spell to combine with another magician's to extend their magic, and we had the doctor magician's spell too. It was written in Dr. Millroy's diary, now in our possession after we discovered who murdered him twenty-seven years ago. But the final piece of the puzzle had eluded us—a doctor magician to speak the spell. We only knew of one potential candidate: the illegitimate son of Dr. Millroy, who'd been given away by his mother all those years ago.

Now we had a place to begin our search for him. We were drawing so close I could taste the hope on my tongue, feel it thrumming along my veins. We would find him soon and combine our magic in Matt's watch to fix it.

I didn't dare think about what we'd do if we found him only to learn he hadn't inherited his father's magical ability.

"Did you find out anything else about the boy?" I asked.

"No." He drained the contents of his glass. For a moment, I worried he would pour himself another. He used to drink too much, years ago, but had curbed his excesses except for a minor relapse, the previous week, when he'd been with my grandfather in this very room.

Matt remained seated, the glass dangling from his finger-tips over the arm of his chair. He watched me from beneath heavy lids.

"Will we visit the convent first thing tomorrow morning?" I asked.

"Yes." At least he didn't correct my use of *we*. While there was no need for me to accompany him, we'd fallen into a pattern of investigating together. We worked well as a team, our strengths balancing out the other's weaknesses. That's what I told myself, anyway. It could be that he simply wanted my company.

"Then we should get some sleep." I glanced at the clock on the mantel but it was too dim to make out its face. I guessed it to be almost three.

He caught my arm as I passed. His fingers lightly skimmed my bare flesh and his gaze held mine. "India," he purred. "Stay. Talk to me. Tell me—"

"No," I said before he could ask me to tell him why I'd refused his offer of marriage. Only the day before yesterday he'd assured me he would find out. I wasn't prepared to broach the subject and defend my decision. "Not now."

"When this is over, then. When my watch is fixed and I have a future to look forward to."

I nodded.

"Unless I coax it out of you sooner." He smiled that crooked smile again, the one I found I wanted to capture and keep just for me.

He let me go and I headed up to my room, my heart in my throat.

* * *

"I HAVE to go out with Matt now," I said to Miss Glass, mid-morning. She sat in a rectangle of sunshine in the sitting room, reading her correspondence. She looked well, her eyes clear, but her frame seemed smaller of late, more frail. She ate very little, and I found I had to encourage her to finish her meals. "If I'm free this afternoon, shall we go for a walk? The day looks pleasant."

"Perhaps," she said. "I have letters to write and the latest editions of both the *World of Fashion* and *The Queen* arrived this morning. I'm thinking of having a new outfit made for the wedding, if there's time."

That was if the wedding between her niece, Patience Glass, and Lord Cox went ahead. So far, knowledge of Patience's past dalliance with a scoundrel had been kept quiet to insure her value as a society wife remained high; a gentleman such as Lord Cox prized virtue in a woman above all else. However, the knowledge had recently fallen into the hands of Sheriff Payne, the man who wanted to orchestrate Matt's downfall in any way possible. His latest attack had been in the form of blackmailing the youngest Glass sister, Hope, into stealing Matt's magic watch. Her failure to do so meant Patience's secret could be exposed any day now. Lord Cox was unlikely to want to marry her then.

"Ah, Matthew, there you are." Miss Glass held out her

hand to her nephew as he strode into the room. He took it and kissed her cheek. "Where are you two off to this morning?"

"A convent," he said.

Miss Glass lowered her correspondence to her lap and regarded her nephew as if he were mad. "Why do you want to go to a convent?"

"There's a matter I need to discuss with the mother superior."

"Oh my God. You're not..." She fanned herself with her letter. "You're not..."

"Not what, Aunt?"

"Not *Catholic*." The word burst from her like a violent sneeze.

Matt smirked. "No, I'm not."

Her gaze slid to me.

"Nor am I," I said. "We're hoping to find some answers about Matt's watch."

She knew Matt's magic watch kept him alive, but she didn't know the extent to which it was failing. We didn't know how long he had left, so we'd thought it best to keep her in the dark on that score. The problem was, she was cleverer than she seemed and may have guessed.

"That is a relief," she said. "But do be careful. They'll try every trick in the book to convert you."

Matt looked as if he were about to argue the point, but I quickly grasped his arm and squeezed. It was best not to give Miss Glass a chance to expound on her prejudices. My action brought us closer together and earned a narrowed gaze from Miss Glass. I let him go.

"Matthew," she said, "I'd like to discuss something when you return."

"Of course," he said. "May I know what, in case I need to prepare a defense?"

His light heartedness was met with an even narrower

gaze. "Securing interest in your future marriage before the wedding."

"Aunt," he said on a heavy sigh. "Not now."

She held up a finger. "The wedding may be a few weeks away, but we must at least have some viable prospects before then to use as ammunition against your Aunt Beatrice and Hope."

"You're likening marriage to war, Aunt. Doesn't that say something about the way you're approaching it?"

"It can be a battle to find the *right* wife, certainly. Fortunately you're better equipped for it than most men. You have a fortune *and* are the heir to a title and estate. It's enough to overlook your American mother."

His spine straightened. "I'm as proud of my American mother as I am of my English father. Now," he said when she opened her mouth to speak, "no more talk of marriage until after my watch is fixed, and then it will be on *my* terms, since I already have a wife in mind."

Her lips parted with her gasp. Then, realization dawning, her cool gaze slid to me.

I wanted to run off but I feigned ignorance instead.

"She simply needs to agree," Matt finished. "India?"

"No!" I cried.

He indicated his outstretched hand, angled toward the door. His eyes twinkled, damn him. "I was simply asking you to leave with me," he said.

I marched out but stopped at the top of the stairs. Cyclops and Duke leaned casually on the balustrade, but Willie scowled, arms crossed. She turned her scowl onto Matt.

"You look tired." She placed her hands on her hips. The movement pushed back her unbuttoned jacket, exposing the gun tucked into the waistband of her trousers. "You should stay and rest."

"Are you going to shoot us?" Matt asked, his good humor

still in play, despite the discussion with his aunt and now this delay.

"Don't be a dang fool."

"Willie's right," Duke said, pushing off from the balustrade. "You had a late night and could do with more sleep. Stay here and we'll go to the convent with India."

"And let Willie loose in a house of high principles and quiet contemplation?" Matt chucked her under her out-thrust chin. "That would be like asking a tornado not to spin."

"More like asking a stuck pig not to squeal." Duke chuckled but had to quickly duck to dodge Willie's fist.

Matt strode past them. "I'm fine. We won't be long, and I have the watch if necessary. India will also keep an eye on me."

"I don't like it," Willie said, "but I won't stop you. Just make sure you get answers. Nuns are a secret lot, and you can't rough 'em up like you can a cowboy to get answers."

I pressed my lips together but spluttered a laugh despite my efforts. Matt joined in, earning a glare from Willie.

"I'll drive you," Duke said, stepping aside to let us pass.

Cyclops laid a hand on Duke's shoulder and shook his head. "Let the new coachman do his job, and let Matt go to the convent. He don't need a nursemaid."

"Thank you, Cyclops," Matt said.

"Besides, we need to continue to look for Payne."

"We ain't never going to find him," Duke muttered. "This city's too big."

"And he's a slippery snake," Willie finished. "But we got to try. We ain't no use to anyone sitting around here sewing and reading."

"You're coming with us?" Duke asked, sounding surprised. "Don't you have someone to see at the hospital?"

Willie swanned off without answering, a smile teasing her lips. Duke stomped down the stairs. He was unhappy that she wouldn't tell him why she was visiting the London

Hospital most nights. Indeed, she wouldn't tell us if that's where she continued to go or if the time we'd seen her there had been a one-off. I suspected she was having a dalliance with a doctor or orderly and didn't want Duke to know. It worried me at first, as Duke was sweet on her and I didn't want to see his heart broken. But the more I thought about it, the more I suspected she didn't want to tell him because the dalliance meant nothing to her and was merely a temporary intrigue. He still had a chance, if that were the case.

Not that he saw it that way. The curiosity was eating him up, poor man, and Willie didn't help by maintaining silence.

"Do you think the mother superior will speak to us without an appointment?" I asked Matt as I settled in the carriage.

"I hope so," he said. "It would be better to have a letter of introduction from the police commissioner, though. She'll be more likely to give information if she knows it's for an official investigation."

Our investigation was not official, nor was it even related to a crime. Indeed, the more I thought about it, the less likely it seemed that the mother superior would tell us anything. We were going to ask her to hand over highly sensitive information—of course she wouldn't do it. Even the police would find it difficult to coerce her. If any institution thought themselves above the law, it was the church—Catholic *or* Protestant.

"I can't lie," I told him. "Not to a nun."

"Why would you lie?"

"Isn't that your plan? Perhaps tell her that the baby known as Phineas Millroy is your last surviving relative and you need to find him to make your family complete?" It was a story we'd used previously to extract the information that led us to this point. Matt was very good at playing different roles, and I was getting better. But it didn't feel right, now, not inside holy walls. "If you want to go that route, I'll support you by saying nothing."

"I'm not going to use that story," he said. "I'm going to tell her the truth, leaving out the parts about magic, my watch, and the boy being a magician."

I didn't think there was much of a story left after removing those facts.

"I'm also going to offer a sizable donation to the convent to use in any way they see fit." He winked. "I've never known a church to refuse money."

That eased my mind somewhat. "I'm sure they'll be grateful. Catholics are thin on the ground here in England, so donations must be too."

It made sense that Lady Buckland had taken her son to the mostly middle class area of Chelsea. It was far enough from her home in Mayfair that she was unlikely to meet anyone she knew, yet still respectable enough that her son would likely be given to a local family of adequate means and prospects.

The convent belonging to the Sisters of the Sacred Heart was everything my imagination conjured up. The original house was a perfectly symmetrical manor of soot-stained red brick with narrow arched windows. A gabled roof topped three levels and the door looked as if it had been carved from ancient oak and ravaged by enemies that had besieged the convent as far back as the Reformation. The building itself wasn't old, but I liked the idea of its blackened, worn door returning after centuries of exile to a less hostile country.

Matt tugged on the bell pull by the door and after a moment the panel slid aside and a woman's face appeared. She blinked back at us but did not speak. We hadn't checked if this order of nuns took a vow of silence. At least they weren't the cloistered variety. Silence was difficult enough, but access to a cloistered convent would be almost impossible.

"My name is Matthew Glass," Matt said in a pleasant voice, "and this is my friend, Miss Steele. We'd like to see the mother superior about a donation."

The hazel eyes widened then disappeared altogether. The panel slid closed and the door swung open. The hinges groaned.

"Welcome to the Order of the Sisters of the Sacred Heart," the nun said. It was difficult to tell her age with the bandeau covering her forehead and hair but I guessed her to be mid-thirties. "Come with me."

She led us toward the back of the house, passing a young nun carrying a mop and bucket. She gasped when she saw us and blushed profusely when Matt smiled, before hurrying on her way, head bowed. Our guide left us in a plainly furnished sitting room where the pope's portrait looked down at us from his lofty position above the fireplace. A large wooden cross with a crucified Christ hung on the wall, and a tapestry depicting him preaching to a flock of listeners occupied a prominent position on the opposite wall. We sat on stiff-backed chairs nestled around a table with a black leather-bound bible in the centre. The wooden floor was bare and the curtains didn't look particularly thick. It would be a cold room in winter.

I shifted on the hard seat, unable to get comfortable. "Do you think they consider cushions to be a sin?" I whispered to Matt. There was no one near to overhear us, yet I felt the need to keep quiet.

"Perhaps," he said, his attention focused on the view out of the large bay window. A simple rectangular building had been attached to the back and one side of the main convent building. It faced a courtyard paved in the same bricks as the house. Knotty roots from a large lime tree had erupted between the pavers and seemed out of place in this orderly, no-nonsense setting.

A bell rang, and a few seconds later, girls dressed in

simple gray dresses surged out of the doors leading from the attached building and into the courtyard. They giggled and talked and skipped in the sunshine until two nuns shushed them. The girls quieted but continued to talk eagerly, as if they'd been waiting an age to do so.

"Our pupils," said a nun standing in the doorway to the sitting room. I hadn't heard her enter, despite the lack of carpet. She moved as stealthily as Matt. "They're all from poor homes and are in desperate need of basic schooling to make them valuable members of society instead of a menace to it."

We both stood and Matt made our introductions. The nun introduced herself as Sister Clare, assistant to the mother superior. Going by the lines on her face and the sagging cheeks, I guessed her to be about sixty. She had kind eyes that smiled even when her mouth did not.

"I hope this isn't an inconvenient time," Matt said. "I'm sure you're very busy."

She removed work-worn hands from the voluminous sleeves of her habit and clasped them in front of her. "Sext prayers are at midday, so now is the best time. The sisters are all at work, either doing their chores inside or out in the garden, or teaching in the school." She glanced through the window. "The students are having a short break for morning exercise now."

The girls had formed several rows and proceeded to swing their arms back and forth at the instruction of the two nuns leading them.

"Do the students live here?" I asked.

"No, we're a day school," Sister Clare said. "The school opened only five years ago. Perhaps one day we'll take in those students with no homes, but we simply don't have the space currently."

She led us up a flight of creaking stairs and through a corridor and outer office paneled in dark wood that made the walls feel close. The door to an adjoining office stood open, and the nun behind the desk looked up upon Sister Clare's light knock.

"Reverend Mother, this is Mr. Glass and Miss Steele." Sister Clare smiled as she introduced us.

The mother superior did not return it. She indicated we should sit and clasped her hands on the desk in front of her. She was similar in age to her assistant, but that was where the similarities ended. Her face was gaunt, as if her cheeks had been scooped out between cheekbones and jaw, and her eyes were sunken inside their sockets. There were no jowls to speak of, and her eyes lacked sparkle. They were as gray as London's sky mid-winter.

Her office was just as unfriendly. An elaborately carved wooden crucifix hung above a bookshelf, but otherwise the walls were bare. The bookshelf housed some old books, and along with the desk, they made up the entire contents of the mother superior's office. The filing cabinets and a large dresser with dozens of small drawers were all in the outer office.

A simple cross hanging around the mother superior's neck bumped the desk as she leaned forward and appraised Matt. "You wish to make a donation."

"A sizable one for the continuing education of local girls in need," Matt said.

"Why?"

Behind me, Sister Clare made a small sound of protest.

"I know someone who was in need of your help some years ago," Matt said. "When I learned of her plight, and how this convent assisted her, I wanted to see if there was anything I could do as a show of appreciation."

"Ohhh," came Sister Clare's soft voice.

"Sister Clare, you have work to do," the reverend mother snapped. "Close the door on your way out." She waited for her assistant to leave before she said to Matt, "And who is this woman to you? A relative?"

"An acquaintance." Matt was not ruffled by the mother superior's brusqueness, although he was not using his charms to their fullest effect, either. He must have suspected they wouldn't work on her. "But the baby son she gave into your care is very important to me."

The mother superior's knuckles whitened. "I see. And you want to know what happened to him after he left here in exchange for your donation."

"You are very astute, Reverend Mother. That's precisely what I want."

"Then I cannot help you. Information about the children who pass through this convent is confidential. As a gentleman, I'm sure you understand that, Mr. Glass."

"It's in the boy's best interests that I locate him," Matt said. "And the best interests of at least one other God-fearing person."

"Then God will guide him to that person." For the first time since our entry, her eyes flared brighter. She enjoyed this verbal sparring.

"Sometimes God needs a helping hand from his earthly agents."

"It's not our policy to give away personal details, Mr. Glass." She did not take her gaze off him and he did not look away, either. Nor did Matt look disappointed. He expected this opposition, and he had come prepared for it. "The Convent of the Sacred Heart provides a confidential service to both the mothers who give up their children and the couples who want them," the reverend mother went on. "We cannot break that confidence and trust."

"What amount can I donate to convince you that it's in your best interests to give me his details?" Matt insisted.

The mother superior merely shook her head.

"Five thousand pounds?" he asked.

I held my breath. That was quite a considerable sum.

She stood. "No, Mr. Glass."

"Twenty thousand?"

Twenty thousand pounds!

The reverend mother unclasped her hands and flattened her palms on the desk. She stared at Matt yet seemed to be looking through him. Perhaps she was calculating all the improvements that could be made to the convent and school with a twenty thousand pound donation.

After a moment, she shook her head. "I'm afraid it's not possible."

"No one need know," I said. "We won't tell his mother or him that we learned his whereabouts through you."

"God will know, Miss Steele."

I gripped my reticule tighter. "Why don't *you* contact him on our behalf, Reverend Mother? He's an adult now and ought to be allowed to make up his own mind."

She didn't answer; she simply strode to the door and opened it. She moved so quietly that she caught Sister Clare listening on the other side. Sister Clare quickly scurried back to her desk where she pretended to read a document.

"It's a matter of life and death!" I cried.

Sister Clare lowered the document and gawped at us.

"Good day, Mr. Glass, Miss Steele," the mother superior said, not unkindly. She seemed a little sorry for us and not as severe. Perhaps my pleas were getting through to her. "I hope you understand that the poor mothers must be protected, and the children, too."

"Please," I begged, wanting to take her hand but not sure if touching a nun was allowed. "The mother wasn't poor, and as I said, her child is an adult now. Indeed, his mother was a noblewoman and Phineas Millroy would be a man of twenty-seven."

Sister Clare's gasp echoed around the bare outer office. The reverend mother's face paled.

"Twenty-seven years ago," Sister Clare whispered. "That was when—"

15

"Sister Clare!" the mother superior snapped.

The assistant clamped her lips shut and pressed her fingers to them.

The mother superior drew in a deep, shuddery breath. "Sister Clare, see our guests out." She retreated to her office and shut the door.

Sister Clare indicated we should walk ahead of her. Her outstretched hand trembled.

I waited until we'd reached the front door before stopping and rounding on her. "You remember him, don't you? You remember Phineas Millroy?"

Sister Clare gave the door a longing glance. "Please, Miss Steele. I should not answer your questions."

Should not was better that could not. "You must! A very dear friend's life depends on us finding him."

"How? I don't understand what you mean."

"India," Matt warned. "Let's go."

"But Matt—"

"We won't get any answers here today. It's all right."

It wasn't all right. It was very far from all right. If we couldn't get answers by offering a sizable donation or appealing to the nuns' consciences, then how would we get them? Aside from breaking in and rifling through their records in the night, I could think of no other way.

Perhaps Matt was desperate enough to break in, although I suspected he would hate himself for it afterward.

"Please, Sister Clare," I said. "The baby known as Phineas Millroy, who came here twenty-seven years ago, tell us where to find him."

"That's the entire problem," Sister Clare added in a conspiratorial whisper, "I don't know where he is. Listen. Twenty-seven years ago, something happened here that bothers me to this day. But it may or may not involve the child."

"Go on," Matt said.

She glanced over her shoulder then leaned closer. "We're a very quiet community here. We're not a cloistered order, but we keep to ourselves. We rarely go out into the world. There's simply no need, what with our own garden supplying us with most of our food, and a large kitchen to make our own bread. We have a little shop attached to the school, where we sell things we make to earn money to buy what we cannot produce ourselves. So when something of an unusual nature occurs, we tend to close up, not ask for outside help." She looked around again, and I was afraid she'd change her mind and stay silent.

"Sister Clare, are you asking for *our* help?" I asked. "We're good at solving mysteries, if that's what you require. And we are discreet."

"Extremely," Matt assured her. "Unburden your conscience, Sister Clare, and allow us to help if we can. What happened twenty-seven years ago that has you so worried?"

A nun walked past carrying a covered basket. Sister Clare nodded at her then ushered us outside to the porch and made as if she were sending us off. "The police got involved but nothing came of their inquiries."

Now I was intrigued. "Did a crime occur here?" I pressed.

"I'm not really sure. It has concerned me all these years, and I know we should keep our convent life to ourselves, but…this is different. This *could* be an earthly matter, not a spiritual one." She drew in a deep breath and gave a firm nod, as if she had finally convinced herself to leap off a high wall. "The previous superioress, Mother Alfreda, disappeared twenty-seven years ago. Here one day and gone the next, without telling a soul where she was going."

"Did she take any of her things with her?" Matt asked.

"We don't have things, Mr. Glass. We give up all worldly goods when we take our perpetual vows. She left with only the habit she wore."

"Did anything else of an unusual nature happen around

the same time?" I asked. "Any break-ins? Did she have a disagreement with anyone?"

She walked us slowly down the steps to our carriage, glancing left and right. "Something did happen at the time, but I didn't connect the two mysteries until later. And now here you are, asking about that baby after all these years. I remember his name very clearly because he was one of the children who disappeared around the same time as Mother Alfreda."

CHAPTER 2

"*D*isappeared!" I cried.

Sister Clare shushed me and glanced back at the open door of the convent. "It seems too coincidental for two babies to go missing and the mother superior to leave without a word. Don't you agree?"

"You remember that one of the babies was named Phineas Millroy?" Matt asked. "It was a long time ago."

"I have an excellent memory. I keep the records of all the abandoned children and where they go when they leave here. I created the records for those two babies when they arrived, then after they disappeared, I went to update them but couldn't find them."

"The records went missing too?" I asked.

She nodded. "I asked Mother Alfreda—our previous superioress, the one who disappeared—and she said one of them died in the night, but…it seemed unlikely. He was a healthy baby and, well, her answers were evasive."

"You think she took the children?"

"I don't know. The thing is, shortly after the second baby's disappearance, she too disappeared, and Sister Frances became our new Mother Superior."

Two nuns rounded the far end of the building, heads bent in quiet conversation, their gait ambling. Sister Clare bit her lower lip as she watched them approach. "I'm sure I'm worrying about nothing. I doubt anything untoward has happened. It's just that hearing the name of one of the missing children brought it suddenly back to me and I have been wondering all these years. I thought perhaps..." She shook her head then tucked her hands into her sleeves. "Never mind. It was a long time ago, as you say. Good day." She turned and hurried back inside.

Both of the approaching nuns looked up and paused upon seeing us. They looked old enough to have been here twenty-seven years ago. Matt must have had the same idea because he did not make a move toward our carriage.

Both nuns had friendly faces and warm smiles. One carried a wooden box by its handle and the other a basket filled with sewing needles, pins, fabric and cotton reels.

"Good morning," I said cheerfully. "Lovely day for a stroll."

"It is," said the one carrying the wooden box in a strong Irish accent. "Are you visiting the reverend mother? Can we fetch her for you?"

"We've just come from there." Matt gave them a little bow. "My name is Mr. Glass and this is Miss Steele. We offered the reverend mother a donation."

"Oh, how marvelous," said the one with the basket. "The school needs all the funds we can get. We're in sore need of more supplies for the girls to practice the domestic arts." She held up her basket. "It's difficult to teach them how to sew when we don't have enough cotton."

"Not to mention this old house needs some love and atten-tion," said the Irish sister with the box. "The window frames are rotting on the upper floors and the roof leaks. I'm too old to clamber over roofs now but we can't afford to pay someone to look at it."

"Our little shop doesn't bring in enough to cover such large expenses," the nun with the basket said.

"I'll take a look at the roof free of charge," Matt said. "It might be just a loose tile."

"Would you?" The Irish nun with the box brightened. "I'm Sister Bernadette and this is Sister Margaret. It's my job to see that the convent and school are well maintained, but it's difficult with limited funds."

"Not to mention your age," Sister Margaret teased.

"You're just as old as me," said Sister Bernadette. "Brings us closer to God, it does." She winked at us and I couldn't help smiling.

"Your donation will be greatly appreciated," said Sister Margaret to Matt.

"It wasn't accepted," he told them. "Your mother superior didn't like my condition."

I held my breath as the nuns' smiles faded.

Sister Bernadette swung the box in front of her and placed both hands on the handle. It was a toolbox, although I couldn't see what tools she had inside it thanks to the closed lid. "And why is that?"

"We asked nosy questions about a baby that disappeared twenty-seven years ago and she didn't like it," Matt said.

The nuns exchanged glances.

"Were you both here twenty-seven years ago?" he went on.

"Yes," said Sister Margaret, her gaze drifting away from Matt's.

"But we don't know anything about missing babies," Sister Bernadette said, her accent sounding even thicker. "If you'll excuse us, we have work to do." She shuffled her feet as though she wished to walk away.

Matt looked hopefully at Sister Margaret. "The boy we're looking for, and one other, disappeared from the convent's care around the same time the mother superior left without a word. You remember it, don't you, Sister?"

"Of course I do. Our life here is unvarying. Those few weeks were...an upheaval." She lifted the basket into her arms and clutched it to her chest. "It was a disconcerting time, what with Sister Francesca leaving too. She didn't disappear, just decided the convent life wasn't for her. She renounced her vows and went to live out in the world." She shook her head, as if this event was far more serious than the disappearances. "Silly thing, she was, but she'd been a kind friend to me when we were postulants and novices together."

"Sister Margaret," hissed the Irish nun. "Her leaving is no one else's affair."

Sister Margaret dipped her head and hurried after her colleague.

"Shall I come back this afternoon to look at the roof?" Matt called after them.

"That is for the Reverend Mother to decide," said Sister Bernadette.

We watched them disappear in the direction of the school then climbed into our carriage. "I'm sorry we didn't get any answers," I said as we drove off. "It seems as if we've hit another dead end."

"Not at all. Where is your optimism, India? We learned more than I expected to, and even better, we learned that Phineas Millroy's records are not where they should be."

"I fail to see how that is of benefit. We still don't know where his records are or, more importantly, where he is." I regretted pointing out our failure as soon as the words left my mouth. Matt looked enthused, not disappointed, and I preferred him that way.

"I didn't expect information on his whereabouts to be handed over to us today," he said. "At least now I know it will be futile to break in and search the filing cabinets."

He had been planning on breaking in after all. I swallowed down my gasp of surprise.

"You look shocked," he said, his crooked smile in evidence.

"Am I that easy to read?"

"To me, yes." His smile vanished. "I wouldn't have harmed anyone."

"I know that."

"And, if it helps, I'd feel guilty about it."

"I know that too. Pity you're not Catholic or you could have confessed and assuaged your guilt afterward with a few Hail Marys."

He laughed softly but it quickly died. He suddenly lunged forward, nudging me aside to peer through the rear window. "Stop!" He thumped on the roof. "Stop the carriage!"

The coach swerved to the curb and Matt jumped out before it stopped completely. He ran back the way we'd come, dodging pedestrians and traffic, and disappeared around a corner. I waited three minutes before I got out too—any longer and my nerves would have been shredded to pieces. He reappeared at the corner before I could go after him, however, and jogged back.

"What was it?" I asked as I climbed back inside.

"I think someone was following us in a hack, but I'm not certain." He climbed in too and thumped the roof for the coachman to continue.

"So what do we do now?"

Matt kept his gaze on the rear window as he answered. "We see what we can find out about the disappearance of the mother superior twenty-seven years ago. I think it's linked to the disappearance of Phineas Millroy. The timing is too coincidental for it not to be."

"Do you suppose she left to raise him and the other child?"

He simply shrugged.

"And what of the nun who renounced her vows?" I asked. "Sister Francesca. I wonder if she knows anything."

"It's worth questioning her. I suspect she'll be more willing to speak to us if she's left the convent life and its rules behind."

"True," I said. "She won't have the cadaverous Mother Frances glaring at her. But how do we find her? We don't even know her name."

Matt smiled. "First things first."

"Meaning?"

"Meaning we fix the convent's leaking roof."

* * *

DUKE WAS the first to return for luncheon, followed by Cyclops and Willie. I could tell from their long faces that they hadn't had any success. Matt didn't even ask how their search for Payne had gone; instead he immediately launched into what he termed "our success" at the convent and his plan to fix their roof.

"I want you both to go," he said to Cyclops and Duke. "The roof is steep and one of you will need to hold a rope attached to the other."

I expected Willie to protest that she was being left out but she said nothing.

"Tell the nuns I sent you," Matt went on, stretching his long legs under the desk in his study. "They'll be suspicious anyway because of your American accents and the fact that Sister Bernadette mentioned the roof to me only this morning. There's no point pretending we're strangers to one another."

"I weren't going to lie," Cyclops said, crossing his arms.

"Ask subtle questions," I told them. "Nothing too direct."

"Them two? Subtle?" Willie snorted.

Duke rolled his eyes at her. "What'll you do while we're working, Willie? Gallivanting off to the hospital again?"

"Depends if Matt needs me or not."

"I don't," Matt said, rising. "India and I are going shopping."

"We are?" I asked, also standing. "What are we buying?"

"A new watch."

Eddie Hardacre, also known as Jack Sweet, had crushed Matt's watch only days ago. It had been an ordinary time-piece, not his magical one, thank God. My insides recoiled as they did every time I thought about my former fiancé and how he'd duped my father and me for so long, and how he'd tried to kill Matt.

"Very well, we'll visit the Masons," I said. "But only after you rest."

"Of course."

Duke, Willie and Cyclops followed me into the corridor. "You got any messages for India to give to Miss Mason?" Duke asked Cyclops with a sly smile.

"You're begging for a hiding?" Cyclops shot back.

Duke chuckled, earning him a thump on the right shoulder from Cyclops. Willie, on Duke's other side, punched his left shoulder. "Ow!"

"Leave Cyclops alone," she said.

"You sure you want me to? If I leave him alone, then I might just ask you some awkward questions about your romance instead. You want me to do that, Willemina Johnson?"

Willie thrust her hands on her hips. "You're asking for trouble, Duke."

"Sure is," Cyclops said, his lips curving into a smile. "You want to go first, Willie, or will I?" He cracked his knuckles.

Duke raced down the stairs, his pounding footsteps echoing through the house long after he'd disappeared.

Cyclops laughed a deep, rumbling laugh. Willie grinned and put her arm around the big man's waist. "We got to get him a woman too before he drives us do-lally with his badgering," she said.

* * *

WHEN MRS. MASON saw us in her family's shop purchasing a

new pocket watch, she insisted we join them for tea. I readily agreed, grateful for the opportunity to reconnect with old family friends. Our relationship had become strained since they learned of my magical ability. I didn't blame them for wanting to distance themselves from me—or for trying to keep Catherine away. They were afraid The Watchmaker's Guild would look unkindly on the friendship and somehow punish Mr. Mason. Now that the guild and its master, Mr. Abercombie, admitted to knowing about my magic, the threat wasn't so pertinent. Of course, it helped that I declared I wasn't interested in setting up a shop.

Or so I thought.

"What will happen to the shop now that Hardacre has proven to be a fraudster?" Mr. Mason asked after pleasantries had been exchanged and tea poured.

"Papa," Catherine hissed. "Let India and Matt enjoy their tea." My friend had joined us along with her parents, leaving her brothers to keep shop.

"It's all right," I said. "I don't mind the questions. I know you're worried, Mr. Mason, so let me assure you that I have no intentions of fixing or selling timepieces even if the shop returns to my family."

"India doesn't yet have possession of the premises anyway," Matt added. "The process will need to pass through the courts to determine who it belongs to."

"It'll be an injustice if Eddie keeps it," Catherine bit off. "Or whatever his real name is. I still cannot believe the lengths he went to for revenge on Chronos, or that we all fell for his lies."

"Nor can I," I muttered.

"He was very good," Matt said gently. "Everyone was taken in."

"It's not just his duplicity working in your favor though, is it?" Mr. Mason said. "It's the fact that your father's will is invalid because he died before your grandfather, who is very much alive." He looked at me as if I were to blame for that, when I'd only learned about Chronos recently too.

"Papa!" Catherine lowered her cup to the saucer with a clank and glared at her father. I liked that she'd developed a spine where her parents were concerned, although I shouldn't be surprised. She visited me several times without their knowledge. She'd grown braver and smarter in recent weeks.

"Mr. Mason," his wife snapped. "Must you talk of death? India and Mr. Glass are our guests."

"It is another thing in my favor," I told Mr. Mason. "Chronos wrote a new will while he was here, leaving the shop to me, so there is that, too, should he pass away. The case is in the hands of lawyers now, so we can only wait for a judge's verdict."

"But your grandfather is not dead," Mr. Mason said. "So rightfully he still owns it, which means *you* must manage it, India."

"He told me I can do what I want with it. I will probably lease the premises," I said, wanting to assure him that I wasn't a threat to his family business. I was, after all, the only known timepiece magician in the city, so it made sense that he would seek that affirmation. "It may not even be to anyone in the watch and clock trade. If that turns out to be the situation, I'd like to offer you first right of purchase to any stock at a discounted rate, since we are good friends."

"I...I..." Mr. Mason blinked at me then turned to Matt.

"Don't look at me, sir," Matt said. "Any business dealings involving India's property have to go through her. She'll have the use of my lawyer, of course, if she wishes."

"Good," Mrs. Mason declared. "That's settled. India, can you assist me in the kitchen for a moment? You stay, Catherine," she added when her daughter rose.

I followed Mrs. Mason into the kitchen where her maid was slicing carrots for the evening meal. Mrs. Mason asked her to check on the laundry in the copper in the rear court-yard. Once she was gone, Mrs. Mason turned to me.

"I know you and Catherine have been seeing one another these past weeks," she said, "despite our express wishes that she avoid you."

I opened my mouth to protest, but found I couldn't lie, so closed it again.

"That isn't important," she went on. "Perhaps it wasn't fair of us to ask it of either of you. Anyway, it's not why I wanted to speak to you." She glanced at the door and the corridor beyond. "Does Catherine have a paramour?"

Her question was so unexpected that it took a moment for my wits to return. "No," I said with certainty. "She doesn't."

It was not a lie. While Cyclops and Catherine liked one another, Cyclops refused to explore their feelings and see if they could develop into something deeper. It wasn't so much his color that worried him—although it probably played a factor for him, though not for Catherine—but more his past in America. A powerful and wealthy mine owner was hunting him after Cyclops told the authorities how his employer used cheap materials, causing a mine to collapse and kill several miners. The hunt had meant a hard life for Cyclops, constantly on the run and in hiding. Matt and the others had helped him to a certain extent, but it was still no life to take a woman back to. Cyclops was adamant that he would return home, however, along with Willie, Duke and Matt.

A lump rose in my throat at the thought of them leaving. It wasn't just Matt I would miss but all of them. They'd carved out a place in my heart that would be difficult to fill when they left. The space reserved for Matt was the biggest.

"Then what is upsetting her of late?" Mrs. Mason asked. "She's so listless, ever since she ended her liaison with Mr. Wilcox. I do wish she had not cast him aside."

"They were not suited," I said. "He was much too staid for her. Catherine is lively and adventurous, and she requires a husband who will take her places, not tie her by the apron strings to the kitchen."

Mrs. Mason choked and pressed her own apron to her lips. I instantly regretted my insensitivity. Mrs. Mason was a wonderful wife and mother. Her home was her sanctuary and her family was her entire life. She didn't understand Catherine's hankering for something different.

I squeezed her arm. "You've brought up a spirited young woman who is kind, competent, and full of energy. You should be very proud, Mrs. Mason. Catherine is a wonderful person, thanks to the fine example you and Mr. Mason have set."

She dabbed the corner of her eye with her apron. "Yet she will leave me. I know she will. If not soon, then one day."

"We must all leave our parents eventually."

"You did not. You never abandoned Eliot. You were a good daughter, India, and you're a good girl still. I wish Catherine was more like you, more content with her lot in life instead of always looking for more."

I wanted to tell her there was nothing wrong with wanting more, that we should all strive to improve ourselves in some way. But I suspected she didn't want to hear more hard truths. Besides, Catherine wasn't going anywhere in the foreseeable future. She may be adventurous but she lacked the means and knowledge to go adventuring on her own. Her life must be shelved until someone with the means and knowledge could show her the world.

I suddenly felt immeasurably sad for her. It wasn't fair that she couldn't do the things she wanted to do without securing a husband first. It drove home how much we women relied on finding a husband who matched our sensibilities, dreams and values. If we did not, life became an endless slog.

I put on a smile for Catherine as she walked us to our carriage with her parents, but she saw through it.

"What did my mother want?" she whispered, eyeing Mrs.

Mason's back.

"My assurance that I wouldn't lead you down a dark, magical path," I lied.

She rolled her eyes. "I wish I had some magical ability. How exciting it would be."

"To hide it from the world and not be yourself? I don't think you want that."

"It's not all that different to what I'm doing now, is it?" She sighed. "Hiding my feelings for Nate is growing harder each day. I find myself thinking about him all the time."

"Then you need to find something else to occupy your mind. Why not visit museums or learn everything you can about a topic that intrigues you?"

She laughed. "You're an odd creature sometimes, India. Only you would think museums are interesting. Now," she added. "Tell me, how is Nate?"

"He's well. Will you come and visit him?"

"Perhaps." She nodded at Matt up ahead, holding the carriage door open for me. "Is Matt all right? He looks ill."

"He is," I said simply.

I studied Matt anew on the way home. Being with him every day meant I didn't always see the subtle changes in his face. But now that Catherine had pointed it out, I noticed the deeper and more numerous lines radiating from his eyes, the dark smudges under them, and the grayer pall of his skin. It was a mere two hours since he last used his watch and rested. I didn't like that short timeframe. Didn't like it in the least.

"Why are you looking at me like that?" His crossed arms and narrowed gaze told me he already knew why, and he didn't appreciate my concern.

"Like what?" I asked, attempting innocence.

"Like you pity me. Don't pity me, India."

"It's not pity, it's sympathy."

"Don't do that either."

I crossed my arms too and arched my brows. "What would

you have me do, Matt? Not look at you? Not think about you? Well I can't."

One side of his mouth kicked up. "I'm glad you finally admitted it, but I wish it didn't come with a side of pity."

"Sympathy, not pity. And admitted what?"

"That you think about me." The corner of his mouth lifted too in a genuine smile. "I can even ignore the sympathetic looks if it means hearing that I do occupy your thoughts after all. I was beginning to wonder, since you're so adamant that you won't marry me. But now I can be a little more confident that you'll come around."

Heat rushed to my face despite my efforts to think cooling thoughts.

His smile widened. "You're even prettier when you blush."

"Matthew Glass, that's enough, thank you." I turned to the window, but it was futile. There was no avoiding one another in the close confines of the carriage.

"Why? Are you afraid of what else you'll reveal to me? Perhaps you might even tell me what silly notion is stopping you from accepting my proposal, since you claim it's not my health."

"How did I fall into this conversation?" I muttered to my reflection.

"You admitted that you couldn't stop looking at me or thinking about me."

"I'm quite sure that's not how it happened."

"Tell me, India." He leaned forward and rested his elbows on his knees. "Tell me what it is about me that you dislike in a husband."

"There's nothing. Everything. It's…complicated. I don't want to discuss it now."

"Afraid I'll change your mind?" There might have been a teasing layer to his voice, but underneath it was very serious. He was testing the waters, testing *me*, before he pressed too hard.

He was afraid of being rejected. Matt was as vulnerable as —well, as me.

The stunning realization hit me like a slap to the face. I hadn't expected the foundations of this confident, desirable man to shake, or that I was capable of shaking them. It should make me feel powerful, but it didn't. I felt utterly miserable.

After a few moments of staring at me, he leaned back in the seat. We didn't speak for the rest of the journey home.

The first words he spoke to me were to call me back as I headed up the staircase. He'd remained behind in the entrance hall to read the mail Bristow handed to him.

"There's a letter from my lawyer," Matt said, catching up to me to on the stairs. "It's regarding your cottage."

He handed me the letter and I read it through. "It's leased," I said. "That was fast."

"No point in waiting. So it seems you're stuck here now. I hope you can bear to be in the same house as me."

"I've managed so far."

He caught my hand. Being a step above him meant we were almost the same height, and looking him in the eye played havoc with my nerves. I couldn't quite catch my breath.

"Why are you being so cruel?" he murmured, searching my face.

I couldn't think of an answer, or of how to extricate myself without giving one. And I certainly did *not* want to give one.

Rescue came in the form of Miss Glass. "India!" she cried shrilly from the landing above. "India, I need you. Come at once."

Matt let my hand go only to lightly brush his fingers along mine. I could have easily moved off but didn't. "I will get my answer from you after I'm better," he said. "Yes?"

I nodded. "Just get better, Matt, and I will have any conversation you wish. Just please get better."

CHAPTER 3

e remained home only long enough for Matt to use his watch and rest again. Not wanting a lecture, I avoided Miss Glass by reading in my room. The afternoon had grown long by the time Matt and I arrived at New Scotland Yard, and the shadows cast by the palatial orange and white building stretched across Victoria Embankment to the Thames.

Usually we visited Commissioner Munro at the police headquarters, but not this time. Matt wanted to speak to Detective Inspector Brockwell, a plodding yet thorough policeman whom Matt admired. I couldn't decide what to make of him, however. While I appreciated his dogged determination to get to the truth, I worried that he saw Matt as an outlaw and would arrest him one day. The police arrested him before, almost costing him his life when he couldn't access his watch in the prison cell. I didn't trust them not to do it again. With Sheriff Payne whispering in the commissioner's ear about Matt's misdeeds in America, my concerns were justified. So far, the commissioner had chosen to believe us when we told him that Payne couldn't be trusted, but for how long? How many times would he overlook our tendency to attract trouble, particularly when we couldn't explain it thanks to the secrecy surrounding Matt's magic watch?

"What can I do for you?" asked Detective Inspector Brockwell. We sat in his small, windowless office at the back of the building. It was nothing like Commissioner Munro's office on the top floor overlooking the river. Aside from the lack of view and space, it also lacked orderliness. Like Brockwell himself, his office was untidy. Papers were scattered across the desk and chair and spilled onto the floor. A lopsided portrait of the queen hung on the wall with a map of London pinned beneath it. The bookshelf was largely empty, yet books piled up in the corner of the room.

Matt plucked the papers off one of the chairs and offered me the seat. I took it and he placed the stack near my feet since there was nowhere else for them to go. He remained standing at my side.

"India and I are investigating a case of a missing nun from the Convent of the Sacred Heart in Chelsea," Matt began.

Every word saw the inspector's eyebrows rise higher until they almost met his hairline at the mention of the convent. "You're investigating a crime? Why?"

"One of the nuns asked us to look into it. It's been bothering her, and she'd like a resolution after all these years."

"How many years?"

"Twenty-seven."

"Twenty-seven," Brockwell repeated flatly. "That number again."

"Pardon?" I asked.

"It seems to come up frequently, of late. Dr. Millroy's death occurred twenty-seven years ago, after he was involved in a suspicious death, also at that time." He scratched his bushy sideburns with deliberate strokes that I was convinced he slowed on purpose to annoy me.

It did not seem to annoy Matt. "I doubt the good nuns

from the Order of the Sacred Heart had anything to do with those crimes," he said.

I pressed my lips together to suppress my smile.

Brockwell stopped scratching. "I don't believe in coincidences."

While Brockwell knew the specifics surrounding Dr. Millroy's death, he did not know the wider story of the doctor's magical abilities or how his illegitimate son may have inherited those abilities and might be the only person alive that could save Matt. Brockwell had made it very clear he did not believe in magic. A non-believer wouldn't understand our desperate need to find Phineas Millroy. He might even get in the way of us finding him if he thought Matt guilty of the crimes Sheriff Payne accused him of. It was best if Brockwell was kept in the dark as much as possible.

"Then you're a fool," Matt said.

I closed my eyes. Calling the inspector a fool when we required his help wasn't a good idea.

"How so?" the inspector asked.

"Coincidence can be understood by the study of probability theory. Mathematically speaking, it's not unlikely that two disparate events will occur in the same years when taking into account the ages of the nun, Millroy, and anyone else involved in both cases."

Brockwell put up his hands in surrender. "Get to your point, Glass. What do you want from me?"

"I want you to check the police archives for any reports of the mother superior's disappearance from the convent twenty-seven years ago. According to Sister Clare, it was out of character and she did not tell anyone where she was going. She has not been seen or heard from since."

"And this Sister Clare came to you and asked you to investigate?"

"Yes."

"Why?"

"I was there to make a donation and happened to mention that I'm a private inquiry agent," Matt said without hesitation. "Perhaps it was the first opportunity she's had to discuss it with an investigator in all this time."

Brockwell scratched his sideburns again. "Or perhaps something triggered her memory while you happened to be at the convent offering a donation. Sizable, was it?"

"I don't like your tone," Matt said darkly.

"Will you help us, Inspector?" I asked before he could get even closer to the truth. "There's no need for you to trouble yourself beyond a quick check of the archives. It's unlikely to be a police matter."

"You think the mother superior left of her own accord?"

"It seems the most likely scenario."

"You will inform me if you suspect something illegal." When Matt didn't respond, Brockwell added, "Miss Steele?"

"Of course," I said. "Are your archives kept in this building?"

"Some, but this might be a case for the local Chelsea branch."

When he didn't rise, Matt said, "We can wait while you check."

"I'll send word when I've found a record of the investigation, if there is one."

"By the end of today?"

Brockwell checked his pocket watch. "It's almost five, Mr. Glass. Hopefully I'll have something by tomorrow."

"Midday."

Brockwell gave a non-committal grunt then walked with us out of his office. "Jack Sweet's trial will be soon," he said. "If he pleads not guilty, you will both be called to testify. I am sorry for the trouble and anxiety, Miss Steele."

"I'm happy to testify if it helps," I said. "I'm not worried about being called to speak in front of a jury."

"You are very brave." He suddenly grasped my hand and

patted it. The intimate gesture took me by surprise, as did his smile. This serious man hardly ever smiled. "I've never met a woman with such steely nerves as you, pardon the pun."

I smiled back. "Thank you, Inspector. It must seem odd that we attract more trouble than most, but it's a relief to know that you don't think us guilty of anything untoward. Sheriff Payne would have you believe otherwise, but he cannot be trusted."

"As you say."

"Good day, Inspector," Matt said briskly. He put out his arm for me to take then led me back through the building and outside. "What a nerve!"

I frowned at him. "Brockwell?"

"I don't like the way he smiled at you."

"It was just a smile," I said, stepping into the carriage.

"He patted your hand. That makes it more than just a smile."

"It's called flirting, Matt. You should know all about it, considering you're quite the expert."

He settled on the seat opposite. "I am not."

"You are and you know it."

He tugged on his cuffs and stared out the rear window. I thought the matter ended, but as we neared Mayfair, he said, "Next time we visit Scotland Yard, you're staying home."

* * *

DUKE AND CYCLOPS arrived home just before dinner and reported on their success in the sitting room where Matt and I sat with Miss Glass. She had insisted we tell her about our day as she was tired of looking through magazines.

"We fixed the roof," Duke said, rubbing his shoulder. "There were a few broken tiles. We found some spares in the outbuildings. It weren't too much trouble and Sister

Bernadette was real grateful. She didn't want to climb up there herself."

"I'm surprised she doesn't think God will stop her from falling," Miss Glass said with a sniff.

"How grateful was she?" Matt asked. "Did you manage to get any more information out of her?"

"We didn't want to be too nosey, as you suggested," Cyclops said. "But we did learn something that might be useful. The priest who takes their confessions is the same one from twenty-seven years ago. If one of the nuns knew something, or did something, they might have told Father Antonio in the sanctuary of the confessional."

"He's unlikely to tell us anything he heard in confidence," I said. "It'll be sacrosanct."

"Aye, but Matt's good at reading people. If he asks the right questions, he might learn something."

I sighed. "It's better than nothing."

"He can be found at St. Mary's in the same street as the convent," Duke said.

Matt lowered his head into his hand and ruffled his hair. When he straightened, he did not smooth his hair back into place. I sat on my hands so as not to do it for him.

"You look tired, Matthew," Miss Glass said. "Why not rest before dinner?"

"I don't need to."

She cocked her head to the side. "You tell him, India."

"Give me the watch." I held out my hand. "Let me speak Chronos's spell into it and see if I can extend the magic again."

He heaved a sigh but complied. I caressed the back of the case, stroking the smooth silver with my thumb as I spoke the extending spell. It warmed and a faint purplish light flared before extinguishing. I handed it back to Matt.

"Use it in your room then lie down for a little," I said.

"Don't argue," I added when he opened his mouth. "You're not needed here."

"Bully," he muttered, tossing me a tired smile.

I watched him go then sank into the armchair.

"He's getting worse," Cyclops said.

Miss Glass's hand pressed to her chest and she blinked damp eyes. "My poor boy."

I stood and crouched before her. "We're very close to finding someone who can help him. Very close." I did not mention the possibility that Phineas Millroy might not have inherited his father's magic, nor did I mention the very real possibility he could be dead or out of the country. I couldn't bear to discuss either of those scenarios; Miss Glass's delicate mind might shut down altogether.

She gave a small nod and returned to the magazine on her lap.

Cyclops and Duke left to clean up before dinner. I raced out after them, catching up to Cyclops on the stairs. "I saw Catherine Mason today," I said. "She asked after you."

His step slowed but he forged ahead without glancing at me. "Ain't no concern of mine."

"I can see that you're pleased she enquired about you so don't try to hide it. She's unhappy. She feels stifled at home, and she can see her life stretching out before her in a monotonous stream of housekeeping." I tapped his arm. When he didn't respond, I poked him. "You have the capacity to make her happy—and yourself at the same time."

"I told you why I can't," he snapped. Cyclops never snapped. I'd hit a raw nerve.

"I don't like your reason. I don't agree with it. If you're worried about her safety in America, then don't return."

"Easy to say, not so easy to do."

"I disagree. You have a choice, Cyclops. One of them easy, and one of them is hard but not impossible. Don't shy away from the hard one when it will make you both happier."

He stopped and rounded on me. I folded my arms and glared right back. "Seems to me you're taking the easy way too, India."

My arms dropped to my sides and I stared at his back as he walked off up the stairs. It wasn't until he'd disappeared from sight that I thought of a retort.

I heard the front door open and Bristow greet Willie. I decided to join her instead of dwelling on Cyclops's words.

"India," she declared with a smile. "How was your afternoon?"

"Fine, thank you. I see from your good mood that yours went well."

She handed her battered cowboy hat to Bristow, who took it between thumb and forefinger. "Well enough, and that's all I'll say. Don't try to get anything out of me because you won't."

I held my hands up as I joined her, then leaned closer. "I don't need to question you since I know you have a lover," I whispered.

Her smile vanished. "What do you know?"

"That you're always happy lately and that you're blushing now."

She slapped her hands to her cheeks. "I am not!"

"And that your hair is down when you left with it pinned up earlier."

She touched her hair at her shoulder. It tumbled down her back in long, thick tangles.

"You have the look of a woman who has recently had a fumble in the hay with a fellow. Or perhaps a store room at the hospital."

Her cheeks lost some of their heat and her shoulders relaxed. "How would you know? You ever taken a turn with a lover in a storeroom?"

"I've never had a lover," I shot back, not in the least concerned what she thought of me. "Eddie doesn't count."

"He sure don't. That little turd ain't worthy of you. He ain't worthy of any woman. I reckon he wouldn't even know what to do with one if he got her into a storeroom."

"Probably ask her to fetch a broom and clean up the mess he made of his life."

We both laughed. Then she put her arm around me and dragged me into the library.

"I need a drink. Come and have one with me and shut the door, India. But one more mention of lovers and hospitals and I'll call Bristow and tell him you've been drinking before dinner again."

"Please, spare me his lecture."

* * *

MATT COULDN'T SETTLE the following morning as he waited for word from Brockwell. He paced into and out of rooms, stared out the front windows to the street, and struggled to make conversation. It worried his aunt, so I offered to walk with her in Hyde Park as a distraction. Hopefully by the time we returned, Brockwell's information, or lack of, would be known.

But it wasn't Brockwell we saw upon our return to the Park Street house. It was Lord and Lady Rycroft, alighting from their carriage. While Matt's aunt visited from time to time with her daughters in tow, his uncle rarely did. His presence didn't bode well.

"Let's keep walking," Miss Glass said. "Perhaps they'll leave if I'm not at home."

"Or perhaps it's Matt they wish to see," I said. "In which case, we ought to be there to support him. I suspect they'll want to discuss Patience's situation."

"I do want to know if Lord Cox has found out about her indiscretion." After a hesitation, she quickened her pace.

"You're right. We cannot leave Matthew to bear the brunt. Come along, India."

We met them in the entrance hall where Bristow was in the process of taking Lord Rycroft's hat and walking stick. They greeted Miss Glass formally and even spared a brisk "Good morning," for me, although neither met my gaze.

"Is Matthew at home?" Lady Rycroft asked. "We must speak with him urgently."

"Come through to the drawing room," I said since Miss Glass made no move to invite them to stay. "Bristow, have tea sent in. I'll fetch Matt."

I didn't have to look far. He met me on the stairs as I went up. "Your aunt and uncle are here." I reached out to straighten his tie then quickly pulled back. "Have you heard from Brockwell?"

"No. I was considering going to him instead."

"After this meeting."

"You are joining me in there, aren't you, India?"

"If you wish."

"I most certainly wish it." He gave me a wry smile. "With you there, they might restrain themselves."

"Do you think they're here because of Patience and Lord Cox?"

"I have no doubt about it."

Miss Glass's head was bowed when we entered the drawing room, her hands demurely folded in her lap. Lord Rycroft stood over her, the fat beneath his chin folded into thick layers as he scowled. They could not be less alike. She was thin where he was broad; she had gray hair and most of his was still black; she was submissive while he was domineering. It was easy to forget they were brother and sister.

"Do you understand, Letitia?" Lord Rycroft demanded.

She gave a small nod.

"Say it. Say you understand so that I know you heard me."

"Rycroft," Matt cut in with a scowl of his own for his

uncle. "Aunt Letitia doesn't appear to be up to your questioning. May I help?"

Lord Rycroft regarded Matt down his nose. Since Matt was taller, it meant he had to tilt his head back quite a way. "It's of no concern to you."

"When you're in my house and my aunt looks afraid, it becomes my concern."

Lord Rycroft continued to glare at his nephew and Matt glared right back. It took the arrival of Bristow with tea things to break the standoff. I poured and handed out cups, hardly breathing until Lord Rycroft finally sat.

"Richard ordered me to travel with Beatrice and the girls to the estate in preparation for the wedding," Miss Glass said, looking up from her lap. All the color gained from our walk had drained from her face, and her eyes had lost their brightness.

"Do you want to go with them or come later with me?" Matt asked.

"She doesn't have a choice," Lord Rycroft said, setting down his teacup without taking a sip. "She's going with Beatrice. It's for the best."

"For whom?"

"For everyone! She's Patience's aunt. She'll be needed."

His wife rolled her eyes. "It's the best place for *her*," she said. "You can't keep an eye on her here, Matthew. You're too busy. She needs companionship and security or she'll just wander off again like last time."

"Last time she wandered off, she was with you," Matt shot back. "She returned here, as I recall."

Lady Rycroft sniffed. "Yes, well, it just goes to show that she must be watched at all times."

"She doesn't wander off when she's here alone, and she has India for company a lot of the time."

Fortunately Miss Glass did not dilute his argument by mentioning I was rarely at home lately.

"She's no trouble," I added.

Lord and Lady Rycroft ignored me. "Very well then, stay here," Lady Rycroft mumbled into her cup.

Her husband turned his icy glare onto her. "Beatrice," he hissed. "We agreed."

"It's all well and good for you, Richard, you're coming later. You're quite happy to saddle me with the responsibility of caring for her in the meantime. What if she wanders off again? She could go into the woods or the lake. Imagine if she turns up in the village talking nonsense. I'll never live it down."

"If you force me to leave London with you, that's precisely what I'll do," Miss Glass said with a pinched smile for her sister-in-law.

I wanted to applaud her for speaking up. Alas, her courage was short lived. She bowed her head again when her brother snapped, "That's enough, Letitia."

"So it's settled," Matt said. "Aunt Letitia will travel with me. We'll arrive the day before the wedding."

"Oh no," Lady Rycroft said. "You must come at least three days before. My girls will be desolated if you deprive them of your company, Matthew."

He looked slightly panicked at the prospect. I wasn't sure whether to smile or be panicked too.

"That's if there *is* a wedding," she added with a loaded glance at her husband.

"That brings us to the main reason for our visit," he said, puffing out his barrel chest. "But I won't discuss it in front of the companion." He didn't look at me so I felt no compulsion to leave the room.

"India stays," Matt said. "If you have something to say to me, say it in front of her."

Lord Rycroft's lips puckered and pursed with his indignation. When Matt didn't back down, he clicked his tongue. "Hope told us everything about a certain sheriff acquaintance of yours and his attempt to blackmail my family. I will not stand for it, do you hear me? I will not stand for it. Clean up your mess before word gets back to Lord Cox."

"I cannot control what Sheriff Payne does or says," Matt said.

"You can and you will! Do as he demands, for God's sake!"

"He has made no demands of me. If I knew where to find him, I'd attempt to convince him to stay away, but I don't know where he is."

"Then find out." A vein in Lord Rycroft's neck bulged. His collar looked far too tight, all of a sudden. "The situation is precarious. Patience is hardly a fine catch at her age, but for some reason, Cox wants to marry her. Suppose it has something to do with his children needing a mother, although that's nothing a good governess couldn't solve."

"Perhaps he loves her and will overlook her past," Matt said.

Lady Rycroft's nostrils flared. "Don't be absurd," her husband muttered.

I had often thought myself less fortunate than the privileged Patience Glasses of this world, but listening to her own parents speak about her made me glad I wasn't born to that class. She was nothing more than a tradable object to them, as expendable as a horse unfit for racing.

"You must fix this, Matthew, before it's too late," Lady Rycroft said. "This family is counting on you."

"I'll do my best, but I can't stop Payne if I can't find him."

"Try harder! If the wedding is called off, all the girls will suffer. Even Hope will find it difficult to secure a husband if the scandal gets out. They'll all be ruined. The girls won't be able to show their faces in London for at least two seasons, and by then it'll be too late!" She set down her teacup and pressed the edge of the turban at her temples. "This situation is unbearable, and it's *your* fault, Matthew."

"It is not," Miss Glass said huffily. "Patience should have

been more careful. A young lady's reputation is her most valuable possession. Lose it and lose her chance of a secure future. Patience was gullible enough to believe that reprobate cared for her, but she was young. As her mother, *you* ought to have warned her about such men, Beatrice. It is your fault that she's in this predicament now, not Matthew's."

Lady Rycroft's features contracted so tightly her lips almost disappeared altogether. "*You* dare to accuse Patience of not being careful with her reputation! *You*, of all people! Are you going to let her speak about your daughter like that, Richard, when she is no better?"

Miss Glass's fingers splayed on her lap. She looked away. "Patience's situation is not the same as mine."

"Isn't it?" Lady Rycroft grasped the chair arm and leaned forward. "You both had intrigues with unsuitable men. At least Penelope saved *your* reputation before you could do anything too foolish."

Penelope. That was the friend Miss Glass had been visiting with Lady Rycroft last week when she had a turn and walked away without telling anyone. And to think, Miss Glass had a liaison with an unsuitable man yet she didn't like the notion of Matt and me being together. Well well.

"Enough!" roared Lord Rycroft. "Do you really need to air your dirty laundry in front of our nephew, Letitia?"

Miss Glass blinked quickly then took up her teacup and saucer. Her hands shook as she sipped.

Lady Rycroft shot a triumphant look at her sister-in-law, which only made Miss Glass blink harder. Poor thing. I wished I were sitting next to her to offer comfort and show Lady Rycroft that Miss Glass had supporters.

"I have to ask you both to leave," Matt said. "You can't come here and insult Aunt Letitia—"

"She insulted me first!" Lady Rycroft declared.

"Listen," Matt said, his voice strained. "I am sorry for

Patience, but I can't stop Payne from speaking to Lord Cox. Perhaps he loves her and will forgive her."

Lady Rycroft made a scoffing sound. "How can he marry her if the indiscretion becomes public?"

"Precisely," her husband said. "He'll be ridiculed if he goes through with it. No one will think ill of *him* for ending the engagement, not even me."

"A little indiscretion in a woman's past shouldn't taint her future," Matt snapped.

"Clearly things are different in America," Lord Rycroft said with a vehemence that set all of his chins wobbling. "We English have morals. And Patience is not merely a woman, she is a *lady*. There is a difference."

Matt squeezed the bridge of his nose. He was tired and frustrated, and he clearly wanted his relatives gone. I wished I knew how to get rid of them for him, but I was at a loss. They wouldn't listen to me.

"If Payne tells Lord Cox about my daughter's past," Lord Rycroft said, "then *you* must set it to rights. Do you understand? If her future is lost because that man wishes *you* ill, then you have a responsibility to her, Matthew. Is that clear?"

He sighed. "It is. And I agree."

"Richard," Miss Glass said carefully, "in what way are you expecting Matthew to set it to rights?"

"Recompense will be discussed if and when the need arises." Lord Rycroft stood and buttoned up his jacket. "Come, Beatrice." He almost walked out ahead of his wife, but stopped at the door to allow her to go through first.

We three did not follow. The front door closed then Bristow and Peter the footman quickly collected the tea things. No one spoke until they left.

"Do you think Payne is cruel enough that he'll ruin Patience to get to you?" I asked Matt.

He nodded. "It's a cowardly, low act so yes, he would. I expect him to go to Lord Cox soon, unless…"

"Unless what?" both Miss Glass and I said.

Matt merely shrugged.

"If you could stop him, you would have already done so," Miss Glass said. "My foolish brother ought to understand that. The real question is, what will Richard do when Lord Cox breaks off the engagement?"

"*If* he ends it," I told her. "He might love her too much to let her go."

"Dear India, your idealism does you credit, but the truth is, Lord Cox is not marrying Patience for love. Love within a marriage may be a possibility where you come from, but not for us. It's simply the way it is."

It didn't have to be, I wanted to grumble at her, but I held my tongue.

"I'll set up Patience and the other girls if necessary," Matt said, standing. "I'll even give them the estate to live in, if I ever inherit it."

"You certainly will not," Miss Glass said, also rising. "The estate is for Lord Rycroft, and you will be Lord Rycroft one day."

"Perhaps."

"Don't talk like that. Your health *will* improve." She stalked out of the drawing room, leaving behind a sense of hopelessness. Despite what she said, she was worried.

The entrance of Cyclops with a letter was a welcome distraction from my grim thoughts. "This just arrived," he said, handing it to Matt.

"It's from Brockwell, finally." Matt read on, then added, "He found a report on the missing mother superior."

"Good," I said. "That's something. What did the police do?"

"Nothing. The statement was retracted and the disappearance was never investigated."

"Retracted by whom?"

"Father Antonio, the priest for the parish then and now."

He showed me the letter. "He reported Mother Alfreda missing the day after she disappeared."

"Sister Clare went to him," I said, reading ahead. "She's the mother superior's assistant. She expressed her concerns that Mother Alfreda had not been seen since nine PM. She did not appear all the next day and was not in her cell. They searched the convent and grounds, but there was no trace of her and no one knew where she'd gone."

"Then, the day after he reports her disappearance," Matt went on, "he told the police that the nuns heard from her. Apparently she sent word explaining she needed to leave the convent for personal reasons and would not be returning."

"She broke her vows." Cyclops shook his head slowly. "Must have been strong reasons."

"You think it's the truth?" I asked him. "You think she really did just leave of her own accord?"

"He's a priest, he ain't going to lie to the police."

Matt took back the letter and scanned it again. "Then why did Sister Clare not know about Mother Alfreda being found? Why did she mention the disappearance to us and not state that Mother Alfreda sent word later that she'd left of her own free will?"

I sat heavily on the sofa. Cyclops sat beside me, staring unblinking at the carpet. "The priest lied," he murmured. "That ain't right."

I squeezed his arm. "He must have had his reasons."

"But he's a priest."

"And human," Matt said. "Humans are not perfect."

I tried to catch his eye to determine if he was upset about something other than the priest lying, but he didn't meet my gaze. He sank into an armchair with a deep sigh and rubbed his forehead.

"We'll pay Father Antonio a visit after luncheon," I said. "Hopefully we can get some answers out of him."

"Don't know why a lying priest will suddenly tell us the

truth," Cyclops mumbled. "I ain't Catholic, but I always thought them upstanding folk who don't lie or cheat." Clearly he didn't have a good grasp of European history.

"You're right," Matt said. "If Father Antonio lied all those years ago, he won't tell us anything now. What about the nun who left the convent around the same time? If she left because she was unhappy or had a falling out with the other nuns, she might be more amenable to talking to us."

"An excellent idea," I said, warming to it. "Sister Francesca, her religious name was. She'd go by her given name, now. How do we find her if we don't even know her name?"

"We ask the convent," Cyclops said. "We say we're her relatives and need to find her to give her news of an inheritance or something. Send Willie, since they already know the rest of us."

"You'll lie to the nuns?" Matt teased. "And you such a God-fearing man."

"If it's good enough for their priest to lie on a police report, then it's good enough for me." He crossed his arms and gave an emphatic *humph*.

"Willie isn't here and she also has an American accent," I said. "They'll know she's associated with us."

"I'll go." Miss Glass swanned into the room, her fierce mood of earlier nowhere in evidence. "They don't know me, and I'm not Catholic, so it's all right if I need to tell a false-hood to save your life, Matthew."

"I don't know," Matt hedged. "It'll require steely nerves."

"I am quite capable, thank you. Now, off to your room with you. You look terrible."

He kissed her cheek as he passed. "Thank you, Aunt. I'm glad you're on my side in this."

"I am on your side in all things."

His gaze flicked to me and his lips flattened before he strode out. Miss Glass looked as if she would upbraid me, as if Matt's disinterest in discussing marriage to suitable ladies was my fault. I suppose it was, in a way.

I quickly excused myself and left the room before she decided to speak.

* * *

MISS GLASS PERFORMED ADMIRABLY and returned to the carriage with a name and address for the former nun known as Sister Francesca. We drove her back to Park Street and then continued on to Bermondsey across the river. I smelled the tanning and leather factories before I saw them. Thick black smoke spewed from their chimneys, making the sky darker and grittier here than Mayfair. The faces we passed were just as dark and gritty with dirt and soot. It must be impossible to keep clothing, houses and skin clean, and I felt a pang of sympathy for housewives and their endless laundering. Imagine having to work all day in one of those factories then come home and face the cleaning. I wouldn't blame them for not bothering.

Bermondsey didn't look like a kind place for a friendless former nun who suddenly had to make her own way in the world. At least she was used to hard work and meager living, but the putrid smell smothering the streets would take time to get used to.

According to the convent, Miss Abigail Pilcher rented a room in a two up, two down row house on Spa Road. As with the rest of the houses lining the street, it was simple, functional and in need of repair. Two children sat on the stoop. Their hair resembled abandoned nests and their feet were bare. They stopped drawing in the mud with their fingers to watch our arrival through wary eyes.

"Does Miss Abigail Pilcher still live here?" Matt asked them.

The boy shook his head.

"Damn it," Matt muttered.

The children didn't so much as blink at his foul language.

"Is your mother home?" I asked.

Both shook their heads.

"Are there any adults here now?"

The door behind them opened and a woman with a bent back and whiskery chin peered out. "Get away from my grandchildren," she snapped.

"We don't want your grandchildren." Matt plucked a coin out of his pocket. "My name is Matthew Glass and this is Miss Steele. May we speak with you?"

She palmed the coin but did not invite us in or offer her name. "Are you lost?"

"We're looking for Miss Abigail Pilcher. She used to live in this building twenty-seven years ago."

The woman's eyes screwed up and she leaned forward to study Matt's face. "Are you that priest?"

"Which priest?"

"The one what used to visit her."

"I'm not a priest, merely a relative searching for her. My parents lost contact with Cousin Abigail when she entered the convent. They didn't agree with her choice, you see, being C of E themselves."

"Rightly so too. I never did trust Micks, and after I learned she used to be a nun, well, I trusted 'em even less. That's what happens when you pick the wrong side."

Matt held up his hands for her to slow down. "What do you mean, that's what happens? Did something terrible happen to Abigail? Is she dead?"

"Could be, by now. She moved on about ten years ago, when her son got himself a supervisor's job at a factory."

"She has an adult son?" I asked, hope surging. Why hadn't we considered that *she* had taken Phineas and passed him off as her own? "How old would he be now?"

The woman's mouth twisted this way and that. "Twenty-seven, if you say that's how long ago she moved in. She was close to her time when she came here."

My heart sank. "She was pregnant? The baby wasn't already a few weeks old?"

"She had her babe two or three months later." She chuckled a brittle laugh, revealing more gum than teeth. "Question is, how does a nun get in the family way?"

CHAPTER 4

"*A*bigail was a good way along when them other nuns got rid of her," the old neighbor said with a wicked flash in her eyes. She seemed delighted to impart such salacious gossip to us. "That's what I'm trying to tell you. Bad things happen when you choose the wrong side. A wiser girl wouldn't have chosen to be a Mick nun; she'd have picked C of E. Them dirty Micks ain't a good lot, that's what I always say. Look what happened to her there."

How *did* one become pregnant in a convent? Not that it mattered to us. Abigail's predicament seemed to have nothing to do with Phineas's disappearance. What did matter was where she could be found now. We still needed to talk to her.

Matt asked the crone but she merely shrugged. "Well I don't know, do I? She left here 'bout ten years ago, when her son got a good job."

"At a factory," Matt reiterated.

"Aye, making hats. Abigail used to do finishing work in her garret to pay the rent and buy enough food for the two of 'em. She were a good worker, at it day and night, putting silk covers and bindings on fine top hats. The pay weren't good but she got by. Real fast, she was, and they gave her plenty to do. More than me and my daughter, and there were two of us. Don't know how she got through her lot *and* slept. The gov'ner at the factory liked her so much he gave her son a job working the machines when he were still a boy. Few years later, they made him supervisor and he and Abigail moved out, lucky buggers. They just up and left without a goodbye. Dirty Micks never did belong here." She spat into the mud. "Abigail thought she were better than us, even though we're good Christian folk too." She squinted at Matt and once again eyed him up and down. "You her cousin, eh? Well, well."

Matt took out another coin. "What's the name of the factory where the son works?"

She licked flaky lips and didn't take her gaze off the money. "Christy's Hats in Bermondsey Street."

Matt gave her the coin and thanked her. I lifted my skirts and flicked off the mud clinging to the hem before climbing back into the carriage. Matt gave instructions to the coachman and joined me.

A few minutes later we walked through the arched entrance beneath the warehouses of Christy's hat factory on Bermondsey Street. It was like stepping into a noisy, bustling village. An enormous engine hissed and whirred at the end of a long avenue, its chimney adding more filth to the miasma smothering this part of the city. Workers wheeled carts laden with crates and boxes between buildings, and a man shouted orders over the rhythmic *clack clack* of machinery. I expected the stench of the leather and tanning factories to be overpowered by more pleasant smells but if anything, they seemed stronger here, and I asked Matt why that would be.

"The furs for the hats have to be removed from the carcasses," he said. "They must do it on the premises." He shot me a worried look. "Do you want to return to the carriage?"

"It won't help. That smell is in my clothes and hair now."

He placed a hand at my lower back. "This won't take long."

He stopped a man carrying a clipboard and asked if he knew of a supervisor named Pilcher. He did not but directed us to the clerks' office. The sounds of the machines were louder inside the office and Matt had to raise his voice to speak to the bespectacled man behind the desk.

"I'm looking for a fellow named Pilcher. I was sent here by his old neighbor who told me he was a supervisor on the factory floor. Do you know him?"

The clerk frowned a moment then his forehead cleared. "I recall the fellow. He left some years back."

My heart plunged, although I'd prepared myself for this outcome. At least leaving voluntarily was better than being dead.

"He didn't last long after he got promoted," the clerk added. "He used to work as a machinist in the silk-hat room, then as supervisor. He was an excellent employee, so we moved him to the japanned hats department, with a view to training him in all areas of the business so that he might rise through the company. But he didn't take to it, or to beaver hatting either. We tried him in other departments too—shellac, wool carding and blowing, among others—but he never did show the intuition we saw on the silk hat floor."

"Why not move him back there?" I asked.

"He resigned before we could."

"Do you know where he works now?" Matt asked.

The clerk shrugged. "I don't recall."

"What about his mother, Abigail Pilcher? She used to do piece-work for Christy's from her home."

"I don't remember all the piece-workers. They come and go."

"Apparently she was very good and got her son the job here."

"Mr. Danver is in charge of the piece-workers." The clerk called out to one of the other clerks passing by and asked him if he knew Abigail Pilcher.

"She hasn't worked for us in years," Mr. Danver said. "Pity. She was fast and did good, clean work."

We thanked the clerks and returned to our carriage. Matt gave the orders to drive us to St. Mary's church in Chelsea. He sat opposite me and tipped his head back before closing his eyes and drawing in a deep breath.

"We'll find them," I told him.

"Does it really matter if we don't? She may know nothing about the disappearances. Her leaving the convent at that time could be a coincidence."

"You don't believe in coincidences."

He cracked open his eyelids and smirked. "Did I say that?" He folded his arms and closed his eyes again. "This does seem rather a large coincidence and less likely."

"We will find her," I said again. "But at least we know where to find the priest."

He didn't answer me and I remained quiet for the journey back across the river so he could rest. It was not a long drive, however, and we arrived at the church in good time. It was near the convent but far enough away that we would not be seen by any nuns who happened to be peering out of windows.

Father Antonio wasn't in the church or at home in the rectory, and his housekeeper didn't know when he would return. We left a message saying we needed to speak with him, but I doubted he would go out of his way to contact us. The nuns had probably already informed him of our impertinent questions.

We didn't discuss this delay but I could tell it weighed on Matt's mind as it weighed on mine. He was not his cheerful self and went straight to his rooms to retire upon arriving home. I was glad I didn't have to order him to rest and bear the brunt of his frustrations.

I found Miss Glass and Willie in the sitting room, talking

quietly and, of all things, knitting. Well, Miss Glass was knitting while Willie tried to untangle a ball of white wool.

"If she was here, she'd be warning you too," Miss Glass said.

They both looked up as I entered.

"You tell her, India," Miss Glass added. "Tell Willie that her own mother would be warning her to be careful of strange men."

"My ma wouldn't care." Willie gave me a sad smile. "We were just talking about our lovers, India, and how they don't always turn out to be what they promise."

"That's certainly a conversation I can contribute to," I said wryly. "Indeed, I'm quite the case study."

"Eddie Hardacre were just one," Willie said. "I've had more disappointments than I can count." She glanced at the door as if expecting Duke to be there, ready with a sarcastic comment.

I gave her a sympathetic look. "Has your current fellow turned out to be a disappointment?"

"I ain't never said I got me a fellow."

"We're not blind, Willie."

"You sure about that? Anyway, Letty were just about to tell me about *her* lover."

"I was not." Miss Glass clicked her tongue as she dropped a stitch. "You're not holding the wool properly, Willemina."

"Go on, Letty. Tell us about him." Willie leaned in and whispered, "Your secret'll be safe with us girls, eh, India? We won't tell a soul, cross our hearts." She crossed her heart, earning a scowl from Miss Glass for jerking the wool.

"Do tell us," I pressed, unable to help myself. I got the feeling a gentle nudge would get her to divulge the story.

"Go on, out with it," Willie said. "We young ladies need your guidance, Letty. Without it, gosh, we'll be prey for all manner of bad men. Look at what happened to India."

Miss Glass set down her needles in her lap and took the wool from Willie. "It's more of a tale about my former friend,

Penelope, and how she…" She lowered her head, but her back remained ramrod straight. "She's the worst kind of woman. A wart on humanity."

Willie blinked at her, suddenly serious. "She hurt you, didn't she?"

"She reminds me of Lady Buckland," Miss Glass went on. Lady Buckland had been Dr. Millroy's lover and the mother of his child, Phineas. Even in old age, she seemed rather lecherous toward her young footman.

"A mistress?" I asked.

"A husband stealer."

Willie and I exchanged glances. Miss Glass had never married, but perhaps she'd come close and Penelope had lured her intended away. If he could be lured then she was better off without him.

She put her knitting in the basket at her feet. "I'm going to dress for dinner. You two should as well."

"Why?" Willie asked. "We expecting guests?"

"No, but guests or no, your day clothes are not for evening wear. Honestly, Willemina, you're quite the cowboy. India will change, won't you, India?"

"If it's what you prefer," I said.

"Good girl." She patted my shoulder as she passed.

"'If it's what you prefer,'" Willie mimicked in a high voice once Miss Glass was out of earshot.

"What's eating you?" I asked. "You seem out of sorts."

"Nothing's the matter." She shot to her feet and strode to the window where she drew the curtain on the darkening street. "Nothing at all," she added, quieter.

"Nonsense. I'm not as blind to reading the signs as some people think. Has your man said or done something to upset you?"

She snorted as she drew the other curtain. "You got it wrong, India. I'm just frustrated. I ain't patient like some."

I sighed. "I understand entirely. Our lack of progress is

frustrating me too, and Matt, although he pretends not to be affected. I know he's worried though, particularly with his watch slowing even more."

She plopped down on the sofa and buried her face in her hands. "God forgive me, I'm selfish. I've been so distracted lately, I weren't even thinking of Matt."

"Then what were you talking about?"

Duke and Cyclops entered, looking bored. "So this is where you two are hiding," Duke said. "Thought you were out, Willie."

"I got home a while ago. Where've you been?"

"Library," Cyclops said.

"You two? Reading? What's the world coming to?"

"Don't change the subject," Duke said. "Why'd you come home early? And why the long faces?"

She crossed her arms. "Ain't no business of yours."

"Your lover quit, eh?" He chuckled. "Got tired of you spouting off about this and that?"

She sprang up and ran at him, teeth bared. Thankfully she didn't make a sound to alert the servants. Duke caught her and, with Cyclops's help, held her at bay.

"Calm down!" Duke snapped. "It was just a lark."

She shoved Duke's chest and both men let her go. She stormed back to the sofa where she sat with a flounce and petulant frown.

"Stop it, the lot of you," I said. "You ought to be ashamed of yourselves. You're supposed to be friends."

Duke retreated to the mantelpiece, not taking his wary gaze off Willie. Perhaps he thought she'd charge again. "You're right. Sorry, Willie."

She looked up, surprised. "Accepted. I'm sorry too, but you got no right, Duke. I ain't putting up with your lip no more."

Cyclops caught my eye. He arched his good eyebrow in question.

I sighed. "Everyone is a little testy this evening," I told him. "It's the lack of progress that's doing it. I ought to warn you that Matt's nerves are stretched thin too. We continue to meet delays in our investigation. Indeed, the more we investigate, the further away from finding Phineas Millroy we get. At least, that's how it seems."

"You got to stay strong for him, India," Willie urged. "Be his anchor."

That was all well and good, but who was going to be *my* anchor? I felt all at sea, drifting further and further from shore.

"We all do," Cyclops told her. "Lumbering it all on India ain't fair, considering she and him aren't…" He coughed and looked away.

"Getting married," I offered. "No, we're not. I've made it clear to him, and I'd like to end any speculation and gossip here and now. Matt and I are not together and never will be."

"I'm glad," Willie said. "On account of him needing to go home to America when this is done. But does he know it? Because it don't always look like he does."

"I've told him."

She huffed. "Being told and knowing ain't the same thing."

"No," I said quietly. "They are not."

* * *

Dinner was a strained affair, and I was glad when it ended, even though most of us retired to the drawing room. Miss Glass went to bed early, easing the tension somewhat. Although she knew all our magical secrets, somehow it was easier to discuss them without her there. Nobody wanted to worry her more than she already was.

Matt poured brandies, and Willie pulled out a cigar from her breast pocket. She slid it beneath her nose and drew in a deep breath.

"You are not going to smoke in here," I said. "Miss Glass will smell it in the morning. Go to the smoking room."

She took her glass from Matt and stormed out without a word.

"Is it just me or is she upset about something?" Matt asked, watching her go.

"Her lover's had enough of her irritating ways," Duke said.

"You're the only one who finds her irritating," I told him. Everyone just looked at me. "You're right, that's not true. But I do think Duke is partly right and the problem is with the gentleman she's been seeing at the hospital."

Duke grunted and drank the entire contents of his glass in one gulp. "Another," he said to Matt.

Matt hesitated then obliged. "Did India inform you how our afternoon went?"

"Aye," Cyclops said. "You ain't getting far."

"We still have the priest to talk to yet," Matt said. "I think we'll learn a great deal from him."

"How?" Duke accepted the glass. "He ain't going to tell you what he heard in the confessional."

"We might be able to convince him."

"How?"

Willie strode back in, holding the unlit cigar and tumbler in one hand and a newspaper in the other. She thrust the newspaper into Matt's chest. "Bristow just got the evening papers. Read it." Her gaze slid to me.

That was enough to have me crowding around Matt along with Duke and Cyclops to get a better look. My insides tightened when I read the masthead—*The City Review*. A journalist from that newspaper had teamed up with the Watchmaker's Guild master, Abercrombie, and threatened to print an article demonizing magicians. While I hadn't forgotten their threat, I'd set it to the back of my mind as we searched for a medical magician.

The page was opened to the article in question. A quick scan of the first three paragraphs proved that they were not going to hold back in their judgment. "Evil," "sinful," and "un-English" they called magicians, drawing on their readers' religious and patriotic fervor to stir up hatred and fear.

"Lies," Duke spat. "All damned lies."

"They're drumming up sympathy for tradesmen and shopkeepers," Matt said quietly.

"'Depriving honest, hardworking people of their livelihood,'" Cyclops read. "'And starving their children in the process.'"

As if that wasn't bad enough, the article took an even more serious turn by mentioning the death of Wilson Sweet at the hands of two magicians, Dr. Millroy and my own grandfather, Gideon Steele. I clamped a hand over my mouth to stifle my whimper but forced myself to read to the end. The journalist, Mr. Force, mentioned how the two men had colluded to experiment on the "humble" Mr. Sweet to "play God and extend his life, only to end it instead."

Although the article stated that Dr. Millroy was a medical magician and Chronos a horology one, it did not specifically mention that magic was only fleeting unless that horology magician used a specific spell. Some readers—namely, magicians—would read between the lines, however, and realize that had been my grandfather's role in the experiment.

I sat down with a groan. "Anyone who didn't suspect I was a magician will now connect Gideon Steele to me. My secret is out."

Matt touched my shoulder. "Not everyone will believe this."

"Enough will. Many more will wonder. Matt, I'm sorry. This is all my fault; that article is in retaliation to Oscar Barratt's, and he wouldn't have written it if I hadn't gone to him that day. And now I've brought suspicion to your door too simply by living in the house."

"If you think that means you ought to leave, think again." He squeezed my shoulder, as if his stronger grip could keep me there.

"I'm not thinking it," I assured him. I didn't add that I had nowhere to go, with the cottage now being leased.

"Don't worry about us," Cyclops told me. "We can take care of ourselves. But you be careful, India. There might be some watchmakers who resent your magic."

"But she ain't a practicing watchmaker!" Willie declared. "It's not them she has to worry about anyway. It's magicians thinking she can extend their magic. Those folk will come looking for her, mark my words."

"And that will stir up trouble with all manner of artless craftsmen and the guilds," I added heavily. "Not just the watchmakers."

Matt's fingers tightened. "Enough," he said to his friends. "You're frightening her."

"Better she's frightened and aware than ignorant and exposed to danger," Duke said.

"The question is, what do we do now?" I asked.

"Nothing," Matt said emphatically. "A counter article will only lead to another response from *The City Review* and that will only serve to keep the story alive. The sooner it dies, the better."

I agreed, in part, but I wasn't sure Oscar Barratt could leave it alone.

I was right. The man himself arrived at our door a mere half hour later. He strode into the drawing room ahead of Bristow, still carrying his hat. "Have you read it?" he asked without so much as a greeting.

"We have," Matt said, a hard edge to his tone beneath a calm shell. "Hand your hat to Bristow or he'll think himself superfluous."

Oscar hesitated then did as told and Bristow left with the hat, shutting the door behind him.

"Drink?" Matt asked our visitor.

Oscar nodded and took the seat I offered him. He stroked his short goatee beard and rested his injured arm on the armrest. He still wore it in a sling. He'd been shot in the shoulder by Mr. Pitt, the man who'd killed Dr. Hale, but it had not hindered him too much. Indeed, his work had only intensified after his article exposing magic appeared in *The Weekly Gazette*. The last time I'd seen him, he'd told me of all the correspondence he'd received from the public. I'd been furious with Oscar for exposing magicians, but he'd managed to soften my stance a little with his solid reasoning and desire for we magicians to live a normal life, free to practice our magic. His heart was in the right place, at least, and I couldn't remain angry with him for that, particularly when I agreed, in principle. Not that I would tell Matt. He was vehemently opposed to exposing magic.

Matt handed Oscar a glass of brandy then tossed the newspaper in his lap, open to the page with Force's article.

Oscar flinched. "What do you make of it?" he asked.

"What do we make of it?" Willie pushed out of the chair and stood over Oscar. His eyes widened and he pressed back into the chair. "It's all your fault, Barratt, that's what we make of it."

Oscar picked up the newspaper and placed it on the table near the lamp beside him. "I didn't mention India in my article. I didn't name any magicians. Nor did I mention that magic is fleeting. This…" He tapped the newspaper. "This is not my doing. It's Abercrombie's and the reporter, Force. If you're looking for someone to blame, blame them."

"Be assured," Matt hissed, "they will not escape my wrath either."

Oscar swallowed heavily.

"But *you* started it, Barratt," Willie said with a pout. She stomped back to her chair and threw herself into it. "You should take some responsibility for that. A real man would. God damned men," she muttered into her chin.

Duke and Cyclops exchanged grimaces.

"I'll fix it," Oscar said. "I'll write another—"

"No!" Matt slammed the heavy tumbler on the table beside Oscar. Luckily it was empty or the contents would have splashed out. "You will not write another thing about magic. Is that clear?"

Oscar's jaw hardened. "I'll write what I see fit to write, Glass. As long as my editor wishes to publish my articles about magic, I will continue to write them. It's not up to you."

Matt glowered back at him, his jaw equally uncompromising. It was like watching two gladiators circle one another in the ring, taking the other's measure, looking for weaknesses. Physically, Matt was the stronger of the two, particularly with Oscar's arm in a sling, but I knew from experience that Oscar could not easily be swayed. Not only did he dig in when he set his mind to something, but he refused to even consider alternatives.

"When your articles bring danger to my door, and the people I care about, it becomes my business," Matt said. "And if you think I can't stop you writing another article, think again."

Oscar tugged on his sling. "Are you threatening me?"

Matt picked up his glass but did not fill it. He sat beside me on the sofa and smiled at Oscar. It was a friendly, open smile that seemed to throw the journalist off balance. Only I could feel the anger vibrating off Matt.

"Have you spoken to Mr. Force?" I asked Oscar in an attempt to diffuse the tension.

"I tried to but he wouldn't see me. I left a written message for him at *The Review's* office, telling him how irresponsible it was to name names and mention the murder of Wilson Sweet."

"A written message, eh?" Duke rolled his eyes. "That ought to fix it."

"Words are powerful, sir."

"My name's Duke, not sir. And words are only powerful when they say something the reader is willing to hear. I don't know Mr. Force, but I do know Abercrombie, and he won't care that magicians will be harassed now thanks to that article, and India in partic'lar. He won't care one bit."

"If anyone bothers you, India, tell me immediately," Oscar said. "Perhaps I can help."

I paused, waiting for Matt to scoff or say something but he did not. "Thank you, Oscar," I said, "but I don't see how you can."

"You can help by not writing anything more on the subject," Matt said. "Let the topic be forgotten."

Oscar shook his head. "I can't. You know that."

"You've stirred up enough trouble."

"I can't let that piece of rubbish be the last word on magic." He sipped and set the glass down on the newspaper. "No magician can." He lifted his brow at me.

I glanced down at my lap but felt everyone's glare bore into me, Matt's being the hardest. "I agree with Oscar," I said.

Matt shot to his feet and stalked to the sideboard. He poured himself a large brandy and drank half in a single gulp. "We agreed it was best to leave the matter alone, India."

"No, we did not. Oscar's right. We can't let Force's vile piece be the last word. He calls magicians all manner of horrible things, and people will believe it. We have to print a rebuttal and show magicians in a favorable light."

He turned his back to me and leaned a fist on the sideboard. If we'd been alone, I would have touched his shoulder and tried to reason gently with him, but I couldn't do it in front of the others.

I appealed to Oscar. "Be sure to mention that all the magicians of your acquaintance regularly attend church, have families, and simply wish to live peaceful lives as the artless do. Don't use the word artless though. It implies a lack in character. Use mild, conciliatory words, nothing too clever."

Oscar's face lifted with his smile. "I do know how to write persuasive pieces, India."

"Yes, of course. I am sorry, but this is an important article and it needs to be exactly right."

"Be sure and say that magic don't do anyone any good," Cyclops chimed in. "Remind folk that it don't last."

"Cyclops!" Willie spat. "Whose side are you on?"

"I ain't on anyone's side, but he's going to write that article no matter what. Seems this way we get some say in what he puts in it. Being all cut up about it will get us nowhere."

We all looked at Matt's powerful back, slightly hunched as he towered over the sideboard. He slowly turned to face us.

"Don't mention India's name," he said, his voice as dark as his eyes.

Oscar looked to me. "I'd like to. Your grandfather has already been mentioned so—"

"No," Matt snapped.

Oscar didn't take his gaze off me. If Matt's raging ruffled him, he didn't show it.

"Don't mention me," I said. "Only those who know me well will know my grandfather's name. Acquaintances do not and hopefully haven't made the connection."

"Say you agree, Barratt," Matt said.

"If it's what India wants, then I agree."

"Maybe write how Chronos was forced by Dr. Millroy to experiment on Wilson Sweet," Willie added.

"I can't say that since it's not true and is unfair to the memory of Millroy. But I will write how both magicians involved in that sorry event regretted their actions and never tried it again."

My swallow sounded loud in the silence. We all averted our gazes. Thankfully Oscar didn't seem to notice. Matt's past and his life-giving watch were the only thing about magic that I'd kept from him, and I wanted to keep it that way.

"I'll note that one is dead and the other thought to be overseas," Oscar went on. "Does that suffice?"

"Yes," I said quickly. "I think so."

"As long as India isn't named," Matt said again.

"Or any other magicians," I added.

"Except myself." Oscar smiled over the rim of his glass as he sipped. "Don't look so shocked, India. It's time I put myself forward as a magician. It's the best way for these articles to be taken seriously, otherwise questions about their authenticity will continue to arise."

"But you'll be inviting all manner of judgment on yourself," I said. "Are you ready for that?"

"Yes."

"Are your family?" He had a brother who ran the family ink production business. Like Oscar, he was an ink magician.

"Let me worry about my family. Besides, a reminder that magic is fleeting should dampen the outrage of my brother's business rivals. I'll use the ink trade as an example of what magic can and cannot do. Once I describe the pretty effects I can create with ink yet the utter uselessness of the magic, no one will continue to feel threatened. My brother will be furious at first, but he'll calm down when he sees that nothing will change."

"You think nothing will change?" Matt went to take another drink but found his glass empty. If he tried to fill it again, I might be compelled to take the glass off him. But he did not. "You're a fool if you believe that, Barratt. A damned fool."

Oscar finished his drink and bade us goodnight. I couldn't blame him for making a hasty retreat in the face of Matt's hostility. Perhaps I should have retreated too, but I remained, along with the others, in the drawing room. I had one final point to make before retiring to bed.

"Another favorable article from Oscar could be the very thing we need," I told Matt after Oscar left. "It could flush out Phineas Millroy."

Matt leaned back in the armchair and stretched out his legs. He closed his eyes and expelled a long breath. "What's done is done. The article will be written. Let's leave all discussion about it alone now." He opened weary eyes and looked at me. "I don't like arguing with you."

I returned his soft smile. "I don't like arguing with you either."

"But she's right," Willie said. "If the Millroy bastard suspects he's a magician, he could contact Barratt hoping to learn more about himself." She pressed her hand to heart. "I want to state how sorry I am, India. I didn't think about that before. It's a good idea. You're right to get him to publish another article, and I was wrong."

"You should get that in writing, India," Duke said.

"Then frame it," Cyclops added.

Willie threw a cushion at Cyclops but he caught it and tossed it back. "I'm going to bed," she said, setting the cushion on the sofa again. "Goodnight."

"You not heading out tonight?" Duke asked, following her.

"Nope."

"Why not?"

"Because I don't want to."

"Something happened between you and your lover, didn't it?"

She didn't respond or slow down as she made for the door. Duke caught her arm and she rounded on him. Her eyes flashed. "What do you want, Duke?"

"I want you to know you can talk to me," he said quietly. "We've been through a lot together, and I'll always be around if you need a shoulder to cry on. No judgment, no giving advice if you don't want it, just to talk."

Her features softened and, for a moment, I thought her

face would crumple and she'd cry. But she rallied and even managed a distorted smile for him. "Thanks, Duke. Appreciate it. But I don't want to talk. I just want…" She shrugged. "I don't even know what I want."

They left together, and Cyclops filed out after them with a speaking glance at Matt. I was suddenly alone with him, precisely where I did not want to be. I picked up my skirts and hurried toward the door.

"I want you to know that I don't entirely blame Barratt," Matt said from his chair. He did not try to stop me leaving or ask me to stay, but I stayed anyway—at a safe distance and in sight of Bristow, who hovered outside the drawing room.

"That's not how it seemed," I said.

"Barratt had a hand in inflaming the situation, but I can see his intentions are good."

"You should tell him that, not me."

"I care more about your forgiveness than his."

"Matt." I took a step toward him but stopped again. I clasped my hands behind me. "There's nothing to forgive."

Lounging in the dim light cast by the lamps, he'd never looked more youthful. The signs of exhaustion were hidden by shadows and he had a way of looking at me that was not quite looking but pretending to be focused elsewhere. My heart thumped loudly in response.

"When is your birthday?" I asked.

His mouth twitched. "July nine. Why?"

"Sometimes it's hard to believe you're not yet thirty."

He laughed. "It's hard for me to believe too. I feel like an old man, some days. In many ways, I'm lucky. I've lived a full life. If it all ends—"

"Don't." My voice cracked. "It's not going to end. No way in hell, Matt, so you can stop talking like it is."

He chuckled. Chuckled!

"I fail to see what's so amusing about the turn of this discussion," I bit off.

"It's just that you and Willie are sounding more alike every day. Do I need to be worried about you carrying a gun?"

I snapped my skirt and spun around. "Only if you say something that offends me. Goodnight."

"India! Come back and talk to me. I desire your company."

"Goodnight, Matt," I said over my shoulder, my anger already fading but my resolve to leave even stronger. I hurried out before it faded too.

* * *

To everyone's surprise, Matt was gone before breakfast. He'd left the house alone. Not even Bristow knew where he'd headed.

"He didn't inform me," Bristow told us as he replaced the empty teapot with a full one. "He took the coach."

"Damn it," Willie muttered, sitting down hard on the chair. "If he's gone out without telling anyone, it's somewhere bad."

"Aye," Duke muttered. "You sure he didn't leave a note under your door, India?"

"Quite sure." If he didn't want a single one of us to know then I had to agree with Willie. It was somewhere bad. Somewhere he knew we'd object to him visiting.

I ran the previous night's conversations through my head, and for a moment, I suspected he'd gone to see Oscar Barratt to order him not to write the article after all. But Matt must know that was a futile exercise. So if not to see Barratt, where else would he go? The office of *The City Review*? But it was too early and it wouldn't be open. He didn't know Mr. Force's home address so he couldn't have gone there.

But he did know where Mr. Abercrombie lived, and Matt had told Oscar that Abercrombie and Force wouldn't escape his wrath.

I sprang up. "I know where he is!"

Duke, Cyclops and Willie all rose too. "Where?" they chimed together.

"Confronting Abercrombie." I snatched up a slice of toast and marched out of the room, my skirts snapping at my heels. "Bristow! Bristow, I need a hansom!"

"Make it a growler to take all of us," Cyclops added from behind me. I turned to see him surging out of the dining room, a slice of bacon sandwiched between two pieces of toast. He shoved it in his mouth and signaled to the others to hurry.

"What are we going to do if Matt's there?" Willie asked me.

"Stop him from saying or doing something that will land him in trouble."

CHAPTER 5

*A*ccording to the footman who answered our knocks, Mr. Abercrombie was not at home. He had business to attend to at the Watchmaker's Guild hall before opening his shop. It wasn't far and we arrived at the Warwick Lane building by eight-thirty. There was no sign of Matt or his carriage.

I tipped my head back to peer up at the coat of arms above the door. Old Man Time looked somewhat ridiculous in nothing but his loincloth, and the emperor reminded me of the arrogant and overbearing men I'd met from this guild, chiefly Abercrombie and Eddie. *Tempvs Rervm Imperator: Time is the ruler of all things.* That may be true, but the Worshipful Company of Watchmakers no longer ruled me as it once had. I felt no connection to it anymore, no indignation that I hadn't been invited to become a member. I used to. When I thought their exclusion of me was because of my gender, I'd been angry. But I'd also felt a burning need to be recognized for my skill then, and the guild monopolized the awards and other means of recognition. Now, I knew their exclusion was based on something else entirely, and that my skill could never be compared to that of the members. It was liberating to not care.

The porter with the white bushy beard opened the door. He sighed upon recognizing me. "What do you want this time, Miss Steele?"

"Is Mr. Abercrombie here?"

"He's indisposed."

"Nonsense."

"Is Mr. Matthew Glass here?" Duke asked.

The porter's flinty gaze narrowed. "No. Why?"

Duke pushed past him, bumping his shoulder. "You sure about that?"

"Excuse me!" the porter cried. "I say, excuse me, you can't just barge in like this."

Willie and Cyclops followed Duke, and I trailed behind them. "We'll be but a moment," I said.

"This is outrageous! I expect it from Americans, but you, Miss Steele, are a good English girl from a good English family. I knew your father—"

"Do be quiet or I'll be forced to say something very un-English that I might regret later." I didn't spare him another thought as I followed the others through the guild hall.

We peered into the sitting room, a meeting room, dining hall and even the back of house. All except the service rooms were vacant. Despite the search, it was Mr. Abercrombie who found us. He came down the staircase as we were about to climb up.

"I should have known you'd be at the root of such a hubbub, Miss Steele," he said down his equine nose. He remained half way on the staircase, not proceeding further. I suspected the presence of three angry Americans at the base of the stairs was the reason for his reluctance.

"Is Matt here?" I asked.

"No."

"Have you seen him this morning?"

"Lost him, have you? Well, it was bound to happen sooner or later, him being what he is and you being, well…" His meaning was not lost on me, particularly because he accompanied his acidic tone with a sneer.

Willie surged up the staircase. "You better not be lying."

Mr. Abercrombie stumbled back a step. "I'm not."

Willie placed her hands on her hips, revealing the gun thrust into the trouser band.

"Miss Steele, control your...whatever this person is...or I'll summon the constables."

"Come on, Willie," Duke said. "Matt ain't here."

Mr. Abercrombie stretched out his neck and tugged on his jacket lapels. He did not take his gaze off Willie. "Why would he be?"

"To speak with you about the article in *The City Review*," I said, climbing the steps. "It was irresponsible of you and Mr. Force to write so negatively about magicians. You ought to be ashamed of yourself for treating innocent people so cruelly."

"Innocent! You are no innocent, Miss Steele, and neither is the rest of your ilk. You're a wolf in sheep's clothing, and wolves do no belong in the flock. They're a danger. Magicians are a danger. Look what happened to Wilson Sweet!"

"That was a tragedy and won't be repeated. Chronos regretted it, and Mr. Barratt will say as much in his upcoming article."

He screwed up his nose in distaste. "You're a fool to put your trust in him. But you're not very good at trusting the right sort of man, are you?"

"I seem to recall *you* believed Eddie's story too," I shot back.

"I wasn't referring just to him." His gaze skipped from Duke to Cyclops. His mouth twisted into a grimace of disgust.

With his attention pre-occupied, he didn't see Willie's fist. It slammed into his jaw with a sickening thud. He reeled backward, only to stumble over the steps and land heavily.

He lay sprawled over the staircase, moaning and clutching is face.

"Mr. Abercrombie!" The porter ran past us to reach his master.

Abercrombie shoved him away. "Get out!" he spat. "Get out, *witch*!"

I led the way outside, only too glad to leave him behind. Despite my determination not to let the man affect me, my nerves shook. I took Cyclops's offered hand and allowed him to guide me into the coach.

"So if Matt ain't there, where is he?" Willie asked, inspecting her knuckles. They were red but not cut or bruised.

"Do you want to go home, India?" Duke asked.

I nodded and he gave the driver directions before climbing into the cabin and shutting the door.

"You look troubled," Cyclops said quietly to me. He sat beside me, my shoulder rubbing against his arm. He took up quite a lot of space and seemed uncomfortable in the close confines. His knees hit Willie's, opposite.

"I've punched Mr. Abercrombie a thousand times in my imagination, but I'd never dream of doing it." I looked at Willie. "How can you be so calm about it?"

"Practice," she said.

"He deserved it," Duke added, shrugging. "Where we come from, people like him get punched all the time. It's called Wild West justice."

Willie rolled her eyes. "He just made that up."

"True, but I like it." Duke grinned. "Good shot, Willie. Maybe you can retire the Colt and just use your fists from now on."

"Not on your life, Duke."

We arrived home a mere five minutes before Matt returned. The four of us presented a united front when he entered. No wonder he hesitated just inside the door, faced with a wall of crossed arms and scowls.

"The Inquisition has arrived, I see." He handed Bristow his hat and gloves and indicated we should enter the library ahead of him.

Willie was the first to speak after he shut the door. "Where have you been?"

"That's not your business." He held up a finger upon her protest. "You, of all people, should respect my right to privacy."

That thoroughly doused her fuse before it began to even flare. She sat with a pout and a grumble.

I wouldn't be put off, however. "Did you visit Mr. Force?"

"No."

"Mr. Barratt?"

His gaze narrowed. "Enough questions, India. You won't get the answer out of me. I had business to attend to. That's all I'll say."

I sat with a huff too.

Duke took over. "We already know you didn't visit Abercrombie."

Matt frowned. "How do you know?"

"That's not your affair," I said before anyone else could tell him how we'd spent the morning. I didn't want to avoid answering out of spite—well, not entirely out of spite—but because I didn't want the lecture.

His lips flattened but he sat too and the matter was dropped. "One thing I can tell you," he said, "is the temperature of public opinion. Every conversation I overheard was about Force's article in *The City Review*. The city is humming with gossip and speculation, and it's still early."

"What are they saying?" I asked. "Do they believe it? Do they agree with Force's views?"

"Some but not all. Sides have been picked and people are defending their choice vehemently."

I hoped those who chose the side of the magicians didn't find themselves persecuted for their choice—or accused of being witches, as Abercrombie accused me. I suddenly wished I had my watch with me to feel the familiar smooth case, the magical warmth, and the faint throb of each tick. It usually comforted me.

"They also want to know who among them is a magician," Matt went on. "Names of craftsmen and manufacturers are being bandied about."

"In hatred?" Willie asked. "Fear?"

"Merely in curious tones."

"The hatred and fear comes later," Cyclops said heavily.

Duke grasped his friend's shoulder. "It may not happen that way."

The weighty silence that followed was broken by the entrance of Bristow with the mail. He handed a thick envelope to me. It was sealed with red wax.

"It's from Lord Coyle," I said, opening it. "He has invited me to a dinner party he's having on Saturday." I re-read the invitation then folded it again. "How odd. I hardly know the man. Why would he ask me?"

"Because he collects magical objects," Matt said darkly. "And thanks to Abercrombie and Force, he now knows your grandfather is a magician and therefore you are most likely one too."

"I think he already guessed after witnessing my watch capture Mr. Pitt."

"Perhaps, but the article must have confirmed his suspicions. The timing of his invitation coming the day after the article is too coincidental." He rubbed his forefinger lightly along his lower lip. "Damn it. This is what I was afraid of."

"It's just a dinner invitation," I said. "Anyway, I'm going to decline. I have far too much on my plate to bother with a nobleman I hardly know. I'll write a response now. When I'm done, shall we visit Father Antonio again? Or is that where you went this morning without me?"

"I wouldn't dare." He gave me one of his mischievous smiles. "I'm only half the investigator without you."

"I'm glad you realize it."

* * *

FATHER ANTONIO MADE us wait in the church for sixteen minutes before he met with us.

"You know that staring at your watch doesn't make time go faster," Matt said while we sat on the third pew from the front.

I snapped the watchcase closed and returned it to my reticule. "I need to look at something to soothe my nerves."

"You're surrounded by beautiful stained glass windows and are sitting beside a handsome man. Isn't that enough?"

I bit back my smile and made a show of glancing at an elderly parishioner in the pew across the aisle. He was either asleep or deep in prayer. "He is quite handsome, isn't he?"

Matt was saved from answering by the arrival of Father Antonio. The priest couldn't have been more than mid-fifties in age, making him quite young twenty-seven years ago. For a reason I couldn't remember now, I'd expected an elderly, cantankerous fellow who'd send us on our way immediately upon meeting us, but Father Antonio was all pleasant smiles and warm handshakes. The eyes behind the spectacles were equally warm.

Matt didn't try to hide the fact that we'd visited the convent and had some questions about events that had happened there in the past.

"You're the American they warned me about," Father Antonio said. "Mother Frances told me to send you on your way if you came here."

My heart sank. Could we not have one conversation in this investigation without being blocked at every turn? I shifted my glare from Father Antonio to the effigy of Christ in the sanctuary and back again.

"Please, Father, just hear what we have to say before you dismiss us," Matt said.

"I'll speak with you on one condition." Father Antonio leaned forward and lowered his voice. "Don't tell Mother Frances." He winked and sat on the pew in front of us. "You wish to know about a particular baby brought to the convent many years ago. I am sorry, but I know nothing about the infants taken there, and even if I did, I'd be sworn to secrecy. Most of the adopting couples prefer anonymity. I'm sorry your journey here has been wasted."

"We have other questions," Matt said. "About the missing Mother Alfreda, for one thing."

A blink was the only change to the priest's features. "I know nothing about that either. It was a long time ago."

"You're on record claiming she wrote to say she left the convent of her own free will, and yet we know she wrote no such letter. Her departure is still shrouded in mystery. Why did you lie to the police?"

Matt had spoken in hushed tones but the priest still glanced toward the elderly parishioner, the only other person in the church. "Come with me," Father Antonio said.

He led us to the rectory next door and into a sunny sitting room at the front of the house overlooking the street. From here, he could see the comings and goings at the church, the convent, and many of the houses. He adjusted his cassock and sat in a chair by the window. The sunshine bounced off his bald head and picked out the golden stubble on his chin.

I wondered how much he'd been told. If only the mother superior had warned him and not the other nuns, Matt's question about the missing Mother Alfreda would have come as quite a surprise. Yet he had shown very little sign of being ruffled. Perhaps a man in his position had heard a great many odd things over the years and was used to not giving away his thoughts.

"How do you know what was reported to the police?" Father Antonio began. "Do you work for them?"

"I consult for them on occasion," Matt said.

"On this occasion?"

Matt settled into the chair and smiled at the priest who smiled back. It was a battle of pleasantness with no clear winner—yet. "We're looking into the departure of the previous mother superior on behalf of an interested party."

"Who?"

"Someone who does not wish to be named. Can you help us?"

"I'll certainly try." The priest's smile slipped a little and his gaze lost focus. He was trying to think who could have tasked us with finding out what had become of Mother Alfreda, and what, if anything, it had to do with our inquiry into baby Phineas.

"The mother superior was reported missing by you," Matt went on, "and you retracted the statement the following day. However, no correspondence was received from her by anyone at the convent. They're still under the impression she did not leave of her own accord. Why did you retract your original police statement?"

I held my breath and watched Father Antonio very closely. It wouldn't be often that he was called a liar, yet he managed to keep his features schooled. "It's true that no correspondence was received, but I retracted my statement anyway. You see, the convent is securely locked at night. No one from the outside can get in without great commotion. There were no signs of a break in, no evidence of an intruder, and Mother Alfreda's cell was as it should be. There were no signs of foul play, as the police put it. After contemplation and prayer, I decided it wasn't worth upsetting the rest of the nuns by having police crawling over the convent. Some of them are young and very naive about the world. It would upset them greatly to think something awful had happened to their beloved reverend mother, and I wanted to spare them that. Please understand, sir, that if there was evidence of something having befallen Mother Alfreda, I would have been the first to invite the police in. But there was not. All evidence pointed to her having left of her own accord during the night. That alone was disruption enough for the good sisters, but to upset them further by involving the police, when there was no cause, would have been irresponsible of me. Without a mother superior, I was their only spiritual guide, their parent, if you like, and it was my responsibility to take care of their wellbeing. So yes, I made the decision to retract the statement. I never regretted that decision."

It sounded plausible, if somewhat patriarchal, yet I wasn't sure I entirely believed him. Surely he must have been as worried about the mother superior's disappearance as Sister Clare and the other nuns?

"Do you have any inkling why she left?" I asked.

"No. She seemed devoted to her work. It came as quite a shock. That doesn't mean I think she was met with foul play, just that I didn't know her all that well."

"Didn't you ask the sisters if it was out of character?" I went on.

"I spoke to them," he said tightly.

"So did we, and it seems Mother Alfreda wasn't the sort to just leave without word."

His only answer was a small shrug.

"The nuns you spoke to about her," Matt said, "what did they say to you?"

"I cannot tell you that. Surely you understand my position, Mr. Glass, even if you're not Catholic."

Matt inched forward on the chair. "They spoke to you about the matter in the confessional?"

Father Antonio clamped his mouth shut and forced a

smile. Another shrug told us his answer to that question. Someone had spoken to him in confession, but he was not able to say more. Why would one or more of the nuns have something to confess if they were innocent?

"How convenient," Matt murmured, sitting back again.

"Did you look for her?" I asked.

"No," Father Antonio said. "If she wanted to be found, God would have guided me to her."

"Her disappearance occurred around the same time two babies disappeared from the convent," Matt said. "They were not given away for adoption and their records also disappeared. Do you know anything about that?"

The priest adjusted his cassock again and crossed his legs. "No. Are you suggesting that the reverend mother's disappearance is linked to theirs?"

Matt spread out his hands. "I'm not suggesting anything, merely stating facts."

"Are you sure you're not a policeman? You sound like one." Father Antonio's eyes crinkled at the corners. When Matt didn't return the smile, the priest sobered and adjusted his spectacles. "As I said earlier, I know nothing about the babies that go through the convent. That's something organized entirely by the sisters."

"You must know the families who adopt them," I said. "Aren't they your parishioners?"

"I'm not at liberty to say, Miss Steele. I hope you understand."

I sighed. We were getting nowhere. Apparently Matt thought so too because he changed the subject. "There was a young nun who left the convent around that time. She's not missing; she left of her own accord. Her religious name was Sister Francesca, her real name Abigail Pilcher. Do you remember her?"

Father Antonio pursed his lips, steepled his fingers, and shook his bald head slowly. "I don't believe I do."

"Are you sure? You visited her in Bermondsey several times after she left the convent."

The priest's gaze sharpened.

"Before and after she had the baby," Matt went on.

The priest's face suddenly cleared. "Ah, now I recall. She was a silly girl, quite unsuited to convent life. She was far too…" He waved his hand in the air and searched for the right word.

"Worldly?" I offered.

He pointed at me. "Precisely, Miss Steele. Too worldly to be a nun. I wasn't particularly surprised that she left under such circumstances."

"I thought you said it was difficult for outsiders to get into the convent. How do you think she got pregnant?"

"The sisters aren't locked in. They could leave, although it wasn't encouraged. Clearly Abigail chose to come and go as she pleased."

"Or perhaps just the once," Matt said.

"Why do you want to know about her?"

"She might be able to shed some light on Mother Alfreda's disappearance."

He blinked. "I doubt that. It was nothing to do with her. She left because of her condition."

"Are you sure? Did you ask her on one of your visits to her home?"

The priest looked away. "Did she tell you I'd visited?"

"She's no longer at the same residence. She moved ten years ago. You didn't know?"

Father Antonio face flushed. He adjusted his cassock over his knees again. "Of course not. Why would I? I only visited her once or twice after she left the convent to make sure she settled into civilian life. As I said, I feel responsible for the nuns, even after they leave my care."

"Yet we had to remind you of her name moments ago," I bit off. The man was beginning to grate on my nerves. He was clearly hiding something, and I suspected it was the identity of the father of Abigail's baby. I didn't want it to be him. I really didn't. But he was the most likely option.

"I've never been very good with names," he said. "Look. I don't know where she is now. She asked me not to return again, so I didn't. I didn't even know she'd moved out of that awful garret."

"You stopped going?" I pressed. "Just like that, even though you say you felt responsible for her? She was an unwed woman with a newborn baby. As if that's not difficult enough, she had no friends or family to help her. It's a miracle she survived at all."

He bristled. "She not only survived, she was thriving the last time I saw her. Indeed, she had more savings than me! I didn't worry about her, Miss Steele, because Abigail had work from the hat factory. She was making a good sum, despite the low pay. Indeed, she enjoyed the work. It seemed to fulfill her, somehow, in a way that being a nun never did."

"How do you mean, fulfill her?" I hedged. The use of that term piqued my curiosity. It wasn't one I would have used to describe a piece worker forced to do menial labor for low wages.

"She told me she enjoyed working with the silk. She spoke about the way it felt against her skin, how lovely it looked when it caught the light." He stared out the window and smiled wistfully. "She was drawn to it," he murmured, his voice distant. "That's the word she used—drawn. Like a gentleman to his lover." His face suddenly turned scarlet and he dismissed his comment with a chuckle. "Or so I'm told."

Fulfill. Drawn. I looked at Matt. He looked at me, his eyes bright with the same realization. Abigail Pilcher was a silk magician.

CHAPTER 6

"Silk is a natural fiber," I told Matt as we drove home. "But working it is where the magic comes into play."

"Like gold and wood," he added with a nod. "Abigail must be a magician. I'm convinced of it. Her son must be too. That's why he was good in the silk hat department at Christy's but not the other areas. He had an affinity for it."

"We should be looking at factories that work with silk to find him."

"He could be in a shop, not a factory. Any draper or dress-maker would do. And there must be a thousand of those scattered through the city."

"Not so many high-end ones, and silk is definitely high-end."

My reasoning seemed to rally him a little. "Does London have a silk trade?"

"Spitalfields used to be full of pure silk weavers, but the trade has suffered in recent times, and I don't think there are many left. They used to work from their homes for manufacturers that required silk for their goods, rather like Abigail did for Christy's. That's all I know of the business."

"Then it seems more likely we'll find Abigail's son working for one of those manufacturers rather than as a weaver. Ready-made gowns, hats, undergarments...can you think of anything else that requires silk?"

"Silk flowers, waistcoat lining..." I absently stroked my thumb along the padded fabric covering the door as I thought —the *silk* covering. "Coach interiors."

I pulled out a notepad and pencil from my reticule and jotted down all the trades we could think of that required silk, but I didn't know where to begin looking for the factories that produced them. Many wouldn't even be made in London these days. Bristow might know.

We told the others of our discovery when we returned home. While Duke and Cyclops considered it a significant finding, Willie wasn't so sure. "Why does it matter that Abigail Pilcher is a magician?" she grumbled. "It don't mean she'll know what happened to Phineas Millroy."

"Or it may mean she sensed magic in the baby and knew he had to be cared for by people with a knowledge of magic," Matt countered. "*She* could have squirreled him out of the convent."

"It's worth finding her and asking," I said.

"S'pose," Willie grumbled into her chest.

"She's been like this all morning," Duke whispered to me. "Best to leave her alone or she'll bite your head off for talking."

Willie glared at him, as if she knew what he was saying even though she couldn't have heard from the other side of the drawing room.

"What did Father Antonio have to say about Miss Pilcher?" Cyclops asked. "Did he know who the father of the baby was?"

"I suspect so," I said with a glance at Matt. I didn't want to upset Cyclops with my suspicions. He was already disappointed to learn that the priest had lied to the police.

"He didn't say it, but I think *he's* the father," Matt said, obviously devoid of the same qualms. "What do you think, India?"

"I tend to agree. I am sorry, Cyclops, but Father Antonio shouldn't be held up as a fine example of the priesthood."

Cyclops shook his head and sighed.

"To be fair," I added, "I believe he may have cared for Abigail. He seemed sad when he spoke of her."

"It was as if he'd lost something," Matt said. "I felt a little sorry for him. The life of a priest can't be all that easy for a man such as him."

"You mean one with urges?" Willie asked.

"I was thinking along the lines of a man in love. Urges seems appropriate too."

We fell to discussing our next course of action, and with Bristow's help, I noted down several London manufacturers that worked with silk. It felt immensely satisfying to have a course of action and the rest of our day planned.

A plan that couldn't be put into immediate action, thanks to the arrival of Lord Rycroft. At least his wife wasn't with him. Somehow she managed to turn every discussion into an argument, particularly with Miss Glass. Lord Rycroft insisted on speaking to Matt and Miss Glass alone, and I was happy to go for a stroll with Willie to Hyde Park.

Willie, however, was not much of a stroller. "Walking's for getting places when a horse ain't available," she said as we entered the park. "And for folk with nothing better to do."

"We're folk with nothing better to do at the moment," I said, slipping my arm through hers. "Or are you going to tell me you have an invitation to be elsewhere?"

She eyed our linked arms as if it were a chain to keep her from running away. "Not today."

"That letter wasn't an invitation to meet a friend?" I attempted innocence but failed miserably if her withering glare was an indication.

"You saw that?"

"It's not the first message you've received in the last day or so. Are they from your lover?"

She lifted her chin. "I ain't saying."

I stopped and took her hands, forcing her to stop too. She didn't meet my gaze. "Willie, why won't you share your secret with me? Or if not me, then someone else? We care about you, and you're clearly unhappy at the moment. Perhaps I can help."

"You can't." She pulled away and stalked off along the path, bypassing a nanny pushing a perambulator and almost getting in the way of a rider on horseback.

I picked up my skirts and had to trot to keep up. "Very well, I respect your wish for privacy."

I let the matter drop. I let all matters drop. I didn't start another conversation and she didn't attempt to, either. After five minutes that felt like thirty, she still hadn't given in, and I found she'd steered us back to Park Lane. Another five minutes later we were home again, the briefest and most awkward stroll having ended.

Thankfully, Lord Rycroft had already left. "He wouldn't even sit down," Miss Glass said as I joined her and Matt in the drawing room.

It wasn't my place to ask what he wanted but I was terribly curious. I suspected Matt would have told me in private, away from his aunt, but Willie couldn't wait. "So what did he want this time?"

"He insisted I go with Beatrice and the girls to the estate," Miss Glass said. "It was my last chance, he told me. Overbearing, insufferable ogre. He always has been, even before our father died. It's no wonder your father left, Matthew. No wonder at all. I should have gone with Harry, like he asked me to. I could be married to an Italian count by now."

Matt sat beside her and sandwiched her hand between

both of his. "You wouldn't want to live in Italy, Aunt. It's far too hot in summer."

She smiled at him but there was no joy in it.

"Don't wish yourself married, Letty," Willie said, lounging against the window frame. "It ain't always a good state for a girl to get herself into. She's got to choose the right husband, and there ain't a lot of men out there like Matt. Many of 'em are just hogs dressed in trousers."

"Poor Willie." Miss Glass rose and clasped Willie by the elbows. Eyes, wide, Willie swayed back until the window pane got in the way. "You haven't been exposed to many gentlemen so it's no wonder you have that attitude."

"I've been exposed to plenty of gen'lemen in my time, and they're just as bad, sometimes worse. They're just hogs in finer clothes. You're better off here, Letty, with Matt and India and the rest of us. You can do all the strolling and visiting you want. Ain't that a peach?"

Miss Glass kissed her cheek. "It certainly is. Thank you, dear Willemina."

Willie watched her leave with a puzzled expression. "She's lost her marbles again. She called me dear."

"That's definitely a sign of madness," Matt agreed then grinned when his cousin glared at him.

"What did you say to your uncle?" I asked Matt.

"I didn't say anything. Aunt Letitia did all the talking. She told him she'd make a very public scene if he forced her to go with Aunt Beatrice and the girls." One corner of his mouth lifted. "She raised her voice and everything. He decided not to test her."

"Why did he come back and try her again? I thought he'd accepted her decision the other day."

"I…I couldn't say."

I cocked my head to the side. "Matt? What aren't you telling me?"

Willie shook a finger at him. "Don't you keep secrets from us, Matthew Glass. I ain't asking you where you went this morning because a man has a right to his privacy, but you got to answer India now. This concerns all of us, don't it?"

"Not all." Matt cleared his throat and finally met my gaze. "He'd read *The City Review*."

I'd suspected as much but felt no victory in being correct. I plopped down on a chair. "And he connected my name with the Gideon Steele involved in the death of Wilson Sweet. He didn't want Miss Glass associating with me."

"Can't imagine he wants any of his family associating with you," Willie added. "Sorry, India, but you know it."

"I do."

Matt crouched before me and rested his hands on my knees. The gesture was far too intimate, yet I didn't shift away. "Don't worry about my uncle and aunt. I don't care what they think, and nor does Letitia."

"Are you sure she doesn't?" As far as Miss Glass was concerned, I wasn't good enough for her nephew. While that had nothing to do with my magic—and everything to do with my lowly status—I thought she might use the opportunity to remind Matt how unsuitable I was for him.

"Quite sure," he said gently. "You should have heard her defend you. She told my uncle that you possessed more lady-like qualities than his daughters, and she'd rather have you as a companion than anyone else. She adores you, India, and admires you greatly."

Yet that apparently wasn't enough. Nothing I did ever would be.

* * *

THE FIVE OF us split up to conduct our search of silk manufac-turers, weavers, and any shops we could think of that traded in bolts of silk. We had to disregard sellers of products made from silk, however. There were simply too many hatters, tailors and dressmakers in the city.

I wasn't too keen to be separated from Matt. What if something happened to him and he couldn't use his watch? Who would know to place it in his hand if he fell unconscious? He gave me no choice, however, as he got out of the carriage at the area allotted to him and ordered the coachman to drive on with me inside. We were away the moment the door closed.

The section of the city assigned to me was one I knew well. I'd lived in St. Martin's Lane, near Covent Garden, my entire life, and it was there that my search began. After the coachman deposited me outside the shop that had been mine, then Eddie's, and was almost mine again, I traversed the neighboring streets on foot. Being familiar with the shops and workshops, I was able to target specific streets and not venture down others. Even so, it took me all afternoon to cover my zone, since it contained the main shopping precincts south of Oxford Street.

I returned to Park Street without a shred of information, however. All I had to show for my efforts were sore feet and sweat-soaked underthings. Not a single shopkeeper had heard of Abigail Pilcher or her son. I tried not to let it worry me as I freshened up in my room, but it was impossible not to think gloomy thoughts about the Pilchers' fates.

By the time I ventured downstairs again, the others were back, waiting for me in the library. And they were smiling.

"You found him?" I asked Matt.

"Duke did."

"Found him *and* Abigail, actually," Duke said, pouring the tea. "She's a dressmaker, working at Peter Robinson's, in the workroom."

"Peter Robinson the draper on Oxford Street?" I said, accepting a cup from him. "His shop grew quite large once he began stocking more than fabric. Did you speak to her?"

"The seamstresses had just clocked off when I got there.

The supervisor wouldn't give me her details but said to come back first thing in the morning. He praised her a lot. Said she was a good worker and helped the other girls, most of 'em much younger. The finishing work is given out to piece workers who work from home, but the main manufacturing is done in the workroom above the shop."

Cyclops accepted the teacup from Duke and slapped him on the shoulder. "Well done, old friend."

"What about her son?" I asked. "You said you found them both."

"Antony Pilcher works for Peter Robinson's too," Duke told me. "But he ain't in London much on account of his work takes him overseas a lot. He's a buyer for the company. Travels to China, apparently."

"China has the best silks," Matt said.

"Antony?" I arched a brow. "That sounds a lot like Antonio to me."

"It does indeed," Matt said. "It does indeed."

* * *

WE ATE A LATE, informal dinner in the dining room after Matt rested. The servants served then left us alone to talk, but instead of waiting until we'd vacated the dining room to collect the plates, Bristow entered just as we were getting up from the table. He placed a hand on my elbow and bent his head to mine.

"I need to show you something, Miss Steele," he whispered. "Come to my office when you can get away."

With such an intriguing carrot dangled before me, I decided to "get away" as quickly as possible and made my excuses. I made sure no one followed me as I snuck down the service stairs. I passed the kitchen, where the maids and cook were too busy to notice me, and went immediately to Bristow's small office. The door stood open and he ushered me inside. He shut the door.

"Sorry for the subterfuge, but I didn't want Mr. Glass blaming me for telling you." The butler was usually a stickler for the proper order of things, so it must be important for him to keep a secret from Matt.

"Telling me what, Bristow?"

"It's more like showing, not telling." He handed me a newspaper. It didn't sport a single crease so he must have been ironing it when he spotted the thing he needed to tell me about. "Look in the classifieds."

The paper was neither *The City Review* nor *The Weekly Gazette*, but *The Times*. I skipped to the classifieds section and scanned the pages. I knew which item Bristow referred to immediately upon seeing the large bold face type of the first line: ATTN SHERIFF PAYNE.

I read the brief advertisement then folded up the newspaper. I forced a kind smile for Bristow's sake, despite the blood boiling in my veins. "Thank you for bringing this to my attention, Bristow. You did the right thing. Don't worry about Mr. Glass. He'll probably realize you showed me this, but he won't admonish you for it."

"Why wouldn't he, if you don't mind me asking, Miss?"

"Because he's going to be too busy dodging my temper."

I marched out of his office and up the stairs. I found Matt with his aunt, Willie, Cyclops and Duke in the drawing room. Conversation halted upon my entry.

"India?" Matt asked. "What's the matter? Your face is flushed and your lips are pursing so hard they've almost disappeared." His gaze fell to the newspaper under my arm. "Bloody Bristow."

I smacked the newspaper into his chest. "Don't blame him. He's worried about you, and knew you'd done a foolish thing as soon as he saw it. Bringing it to my attention was the only thing in his power that he could do."

"India?" Miss Glass said crisply. "What's come over you to speak to Matthew like that?"

I snatched the newspaper off Matt and passed it to Miss Glass. Duke, Cyclops and Willie crowded behind her and read over her shoulder. I did not take my glare off Matt. He glared right back.

"I had to do it," he said. "It was the only way."

"It was not!" I snapped. "You are not responsible for Patience's mistake."

"And what of *my* mistake? I shouldn't have let Payne manipulate my family like he has. I should have dealt with him earlier. I should have posted that advertisement sooner, before he got the upper hand."

"Matt!" Willie exploded. She took the paper off Duke and waved it in front of Matt's face. "This is the stupidest thing you've ever done. You invited Payne to meet you and talk! He ain't going to talk. He's going to kill you."

"If he wanted to kill me, he could have done so already."

"He tried!" My shout reverberated around the room and I lowered my voice. "Bryce died in that accident after Payne fired at us. If it hadn't been for your watch, you would be dead too. When Payne realized the watch was keeping you alive, he tried to steal it. I agree with Willie. He's not going to simply talk with you. He'll try to kill you."

"Try being the most important word in that sentence. He won't succeed."

"You god dammed arrogant saphead!" Duke spat. "You ain't immortal. Sorry, Miss Glass, but sometimes a man's got to use strong language to get his point across."

Miss Glass didn't seem to hear him. She'd gone quite still and peered off into the distance. Perhaps she'd slipped into her own world to get away from the heated conversation in this one.

Matt appealed to Cyclops for support, but Cyclops

crossed his arms over his massive chest and scowled. Matt stood with a sigh and headed for the sideboard and its decanter.

I beat him to it. "Don't turn to drink now. You need your wits about you."

"Just one, India." When I didn't move, he put up his hands and sat again. "Go on, then. Get it off your chest. You'll feel better."

"Don't patronize us. We're worried about you enough as it is, without adding this to the mix." I indicated the newspaper. "You've given Payne permission to get close to you, and if he gets close to you, he will strike."

"Not directly. He's too much of a coward."

"He's desperate now," Cyclops said. "He hasn't been able to kill you or discredit you. Desperate men are more dangerous. You know that."

Matt's eyes briefly fluttered closed before he reopened them. "I had to do something. Patience's life will be ruined because of me. Payne *will* follow through on his threat to tell Cox, and if he's the sort of man they say he is, he'll end the betrothal."

"Worry about it if and when it happens," Willie wailed.

"It'll be too late then."

"Hopefully Payne don't read the classifieds in *The Times*," Cyclops said.

Several voices chimed in agreement, but not Matt's.

"India's right," Duke said. "Patience ain't your responsibility, Matt. She made her bed, now she must lie in it. You don't have to protect her."

"I disagree," Matt said. "Setting aside the fact it'll be my fault if Payne talks to Cox, I am the heir to the Rycroft title and estate. That puts me as the head of the family after my uncle dies."

"He ain't dead yet!" Willie cried.

"And you don't even care about the title," I said hotly. "Nor about the estate or the way the system of inheritance and entailment works here. So you claim." I could no longer look at him. All this time he'd told me the customs associated with the English upper classes didn't matter to him, and yet now he claimed the opposite. Did that mean it mattered that I was beneath him after all? Was he lying about me being his equal? I was too confused and angry to think clearly on the subject.

Matt shot to his feet and grasped my elbows. "India," he purred. "I know what you're thinking and—" He cut himself off and glanced at his aunt. "We'll discuss it when we're alone."

I jerked free and turned my back to him. Needing something to do, I poured myself a brandy then drank the entire glass. The liquid warmed my chest, but did nothing to calm the emotions roiling inside me.

"Matthew is correct," Miss Glass said, proving she had been listening after all. "Patience and the girls are his responsibility. My brother Richard is their primary guardian, of course, but as his heir, Matthew has a duty to see that he plays a part in situations like this. They will be, after all, his burden to bear if they don't marry before he inherits."

"Just like you're Lord Rycroft's?" Willie said, brows arched.

"Willie," Matt snapped. "That's not fair."

She muttered an apology. Miss Glass accepted it with a curt nod. "My point," Miss Glass went on, "is that Matthew has a responsibility to stop this from happening if it's within his power to do so."

"But to expose himself like this," I said to her. "Surely you can see that he's putting himself in danger by inviting Payne to meet with him."

"I do see it, and that's why I can't agree to it."

Willie threw her hands in the air. "Then what *are* you saying?"

"That Matthew must be prepared to make amends if Lord Cox backs out of the arrangement."

"Fair enough." Willie tilted her chin at Matt. "You've got money enough to give her. Hell, you've got enough to give to her sisters if they're affected too."

"Which they will be," Miss Glass noted. "It's not financial recompense I'm referring to, however."

I suddenly felt the need for another drink and turned back to the sideboard. My vision blurred and my hand shook as I poured the brandy.

"Then what are you referring to?" Willie asked carefully.

"No," Matt said, also catching on. "Don't even think it, Aunt."

"Think what?"

"Are you talking about marriage?" Cyclops asked. "As in Matt marrying Patience?"

"God damn," Duke muttered.

Willie burst out laughing but it died just as quickly. I felt all their eyes on me but I didn't turn around. Couldn't. I didn't want to face Matt.

"All three girls will be affected if Lord Cox ends the engagement," Miss Glass said. "Their reputations can only be rescued if one of them marries well, but who would have them once the scandal erupts?"

"Patience is the only one who put herself about," Willie said. "Not the other two."

"It won't matter. The scandal will stick to all of them. At least for long enough to ruin their chances of making swift and good marriages."

Willie scoffed. "I don't believe it."

"Why can't one of them make a good marriage?" Duke asked. "The middle one's got a few matches missing from the box, but the youngest, Hope, ain't so bad. She's pretty, too. Some lord or other could fall in love with her."

"How, when she won't be invited anywhere?" Miss Glass

asked. "She won't get to meet any suitable gentlemen, closeted within the walls of Rycroft House. Besides, she's not that easy to love. Believe me, I tried. None of the girls are."

I expected Matt to admonish her for being unkind, but he remained silent. Too silent. I hazarded a glance at him only to see him watching me, a small frown forming a line between his brows.

Miss Glass emitted a small sigh. "What gentleman of quality will love a damaged girl?" she murmured.

"This is absurd," Matt said. "I am not marrying one of my cousins. I'm meeting Payne and resolving this once and for all."

"Aye, with your death," Duke muttered. "That's the only thing that'll satisfy him."

"I don't want to hear any more about it. Is that clear?"

Duke and Cyclops stormed out, shaking their heads. Miss Glass touched her fingers to her temple and declared herself too tired to discuss it anymore. She followed them out.

"I'll come with you," I said.

"India, wait," Matt said. "Stay a few minutes."

"I'd rather not."

"Please."

How could I refuse when he injected so much vulnerability into that one word? I waited as Willie gave him a final dressing down over the subject of him meeting Payne then left too. She shut the door. I wished she hadn't.

"Don't try to sweet talk your way out of this, Matt," I said as he moved toward me. "I'm still angry with you." He drew closer, his gaze intense beneath heavy lids. I backed up against a chair. "Surely you must see how foolish it is to meet with Payne. He's not going to—"

He touched a finger to my lips. "I meant it when I said I don't want to discuss it."

That simply wasn't being fair. He had no right to cut me off from voicing my opinion a second or third time. I pushed his finger away and stamped my hands on my hips. "Then why did you ask me to remain here? And do not say to kiss me. I am *not* kissing you. Either we talk or I leave."

"Very well." His mouth flicked up on one side. "You're beautiful when you're angry."

I crossed my arms. "Is that it? Are you done?"

"Not in the least." He backed away and indicated I should sit before doing so himself. The distance between us allowed me to catch my breath but my nerves remained brittle. "I want you to know, without a shadow of doubt, that I intend to marry *you* if you'll have me. No matter what my aunt says, I will not be marrying Patience, Charity or Hope. Only you."

I simply stared at him. After a moment, I realized my mouth was ajar and closed it. "Now is not the time," I said, rising. "Considering Sheriff Payne might kill you, you won't be marrying anyone. Let's see if you live, first."

I regretted my quip the moment I said it. How could I be so thoughtless? If Payne didn't kill Matt there was a good chance he'd die anyway if we couldn't fix his watch.

"You're right," he said. "And yet I wanted you to know my feelings."

"I am aware of your feelings," I murmured, my face heating.

"Are you?" He crouched before me. "Because sometimes I don't think you understand the depth of them. India, I—"

"No, Matt. Please. We agreed to leave this discussion until after you're better."

"I've decided I can't wait for then. I want you to know now. I want to kiss you now. I want to have you now."

I blinked at him.

He smiled and brushed the hair off my forehead. The sweet gesture almost undid me. I felt the sob rise in my throat and swallowed it down.

"But I'll wait for that," he said. "The kissing, however…"

I put a hand to his chest. "There will be no kissing. There

will be no more suggestion of anything between us, including marriage."

He sighed. "Until after I am better, yes, I know and agree."

"No, Matt." I pushed myself up and strode to the door, away from him. "Enough pretending. The conversation tonight has only driven home to me how much you and I cannot be together."

He rose too, slowly, and regarded me levelly. "Because I'm the Rycroft heir? That's the reason for your rejection of me? Come now, India, you know that means nothing to me. I don't care if you're a kitchen maid. I've fallen in love with you."

My heart lurched painfully in my chest. I pressed a hand to my stomach and concentrated on what I had to say and not the curious look in his eyes and the vein throbbing in his throat. It was not time to give in to my desires, but time to be a sensible adult and lay out the reasons why I couldn't marry him.

"I don't want a life where the people I see every day consider me unworthy," I said.

"They won't."

"Hear me out. I finally feel as though I'm standing on my own two feet, out of the shadow of my father, and even of you. And I like it. I like being in control of my life, knowing my future is an open book, waiting for me to write the words. Me, Matt, not a father or husband, or even sons." A lump rose in my throat at that. I wasn't just giving up Matt but any future children I may have had with him. "Marrying you will see that all disappear. Not because you want it to be that way, but just because it will. That's the way of the world. I will be *your* wife, not *me* anymore. Not my own person."

"That's not true. Many married women make their own mark on the world. I'm not going to imprison you. I don't want you to not be yourself. Marrying me won't be the end of your freedom, India. It'll simply mark the beginning of a new phase."

I blinked back the tears threatening to well. He was right; I knew he would never smother me if we married. Yet I forged on. I didn't really know why, when every argument I threw at him was as thin as paper and my resolve crumbled with every word.

"Your own family will treat me as inferior," I went on. "They'll think I am marrying you for your money and title. It will drive a wedge between us, and I'll lose Miss Glass's friendship."

His face softened. He took a few steps toward me and skimmed his thumb down my cheek. "Aunt Letitia will come around. She likes you more than she likes her friends. If they want to make an issue of it then she'll refuse to see them. As to Uncle Richard and Aunt Beatrice, I simply don't care what they think, and I doubt Aunt Letitia does either."

My breaths came in short, sharp bursts and my skin felt hot, tight. I shouldn't allow him to seduce me with words. Shouldn't want him to seduce me. Yet his deep, rumbling voice wrapped around me, and I couldn't get free.

"They'll be determined for you to marry Patience if Lord Cox breaks the engagement," I said, feeling sick at the thought of him marrying anyone but me.

"Don't worry about that. I'll think of something, if it comes to pass."

A bubble of nervous laughter escaped. "You have an answer for everything."

"Almost." He searched my eyes then his gaze fell to my mouth. "Almost." He kissed me lightly on the lips then suddenly pulled away.

I grasped the back of a chair for balance and blinked at him. He stood by the door, a wicked smile on his lips and heat in his gaze.

"I told you I'd wait to have you," he said, thickly. "So you'd better go."

I slipped past him and hurried up to my room, not

entirely sure if I'd accepted his proposal of marriage—or if he'd even offered one. I wasn't entirely sure of anything anymore, except that we needed to fix his watch soon and resolve what lay between us, one way or another—whichever way that may be.

CHAPTER 7

*A*bigail Pilcher and her supervisor weren't keen for her to take a short break when Matt and I showed up at the workroom of Peter Robinson's Oxford Street shop. Matt had to slip the supervisor some money and use all his charm on Abigail before she agreed.

We left the workroom and its dozen seamstresses bent over their noisy sewing machines, making our way out through the shop and into the street. The day had already begun to warm, and the dense early morning traffic had thinned to the usual mid-morning bustle.

"You're the American what asked about me yesterday," Abigail said, a wary eye on Matt.

"That was my friend. I'm Matthew Glass, and this is Miss Steele, my…friend."

My face heated, despite the innocuous description. Matt and I had not spoken of the previous evening's conversation. There was simply nothing more to say. But it made the walk to Oxford Street a little awkward.

"What do you want?" Abigail asked. She was a sturdy woman, like me, although her girth was wider and her cheeks as round and rosy as apples. The rosiness began to fade the longer we remained out of the stuffy workroom. Despite the ravages of a difficult life imprinted on her face, she wasn't old. She must have been quite young when she left the convent.

"I want to buy you and Miss Steele *gelati*." Matt indicated the brightly painted cart where a man with a heavy Italian accent was trying to drum up business to little avail.

"I can't be gone too long," Abigail said, glancing back at the shop as a customer left, a parcel under her arm.

"Then you'll have to eat your ice cream quickly." Matt spoke to the seller in a language I assumed was Italian. The seller beamed and the two of them fell into a genial conversation as the seller filled two glasses with the confection stored in the iced depths of his cart.

Matt returned and handed a glass and spoon to each of us. Abigail accepted hers with an even warier gaze. I didn't blame her for her caution; I knew how odd it felt to have a gentleman suddenly pay you a lot of attention.

"We have some questions for you about your time at the Convent of the Sisters of the Sacred Heart," Matt said.

Abigail stopped licking her spoon and stared wide-eyed at Matt. She removed the spoon slowly from her mouth. "How do you know I was there?"

"Sister Margaret told us. She says you were friends."

Abigail's shoulders relaxed and a wistful smile touched her lips. "She remembers me?"

"She not only remembers you but she misses you," I said. "She was sorry you left."

"I never told her why." Abigail toyed with her ice cream. "I couldn't."

"We know why," I said gently. "We know all about Antony."

Her head snapped up. "How?"

"We're investigators. Finding out things is what we do. For example, we know you're very proud of your son." It was a guess but not a very difficult one. Most women would be proud of a son who'd been born in a filthy Bermondsey tenement and risen to become an importer for a growing business enterprise.

She smiled. "I am. I miss him when he's away, but he's got to make his own way in the world." She scooped up a spoonful of ice cream and popped it into her mouth. "So that's what you want? To know who Antony's father is?"

"We already know," Matt said.

She went very still. "He told you?"

"Not in so many words. But it was easy to put the pieces together and see Father Antonio's reaction when we spoke to him about it."

She lowered her gaze. "So you know my shame."

"It's not yours," I said quickly. "He took advantage of your naivety and his position."

"It wasn't like that. I was naive, yes, but he and I…" She huffed out a half-laugh. "I like to think he loved me but loved God more."

"I think he did love you," I said gently. "Perhaps still does. We won't tell anyone your secret, Miss Pilcher. That's not why we're here. We want to ask if you know why Mother Alfreda disappeared."

She shrugged. "No. Why would I?"

"Did she leave the convent before or after you?" Matt asked.

"About a week before."

"Do you think she left of her own accord or did something happen to her?"

She licked ice cream off her lower lip as she thought. "I don't rightly know. Her disappearance came as a shock, I'll tell you. None of us knew what to think. Seems strange she'd just up and leave without a word, but if she didn't…well, it means something happened to her, don't it. Something happened to her right inside those convent walls." She smirked as she scooped out more ice cream. "Maybe one of them done her in. Can't blame 'em. She was a dragon."

"Any ideas who might have...done her in?"

"Could be anyone. I had good reason, but it weren't me, if that's what you're thinking."

"We weren't," I assured her. "Was she cruel to you after learning of your plight?"

She nodded. "Not just after. She hated me all along. Sister Margaret said it was because I was too pretty and spirited. I don't rightly know, but Mother Alfreda didn't like me before, and she thought even less of me when she learned I was with child. She called me all sorts of terrible things. I didn't think I'd hear words like that inside those walls. It got worse because I wouldn't give her the father's name."

"She asked you to leave?"

"No, that were the new mother superior what done that. Mother Frances."

"She took over the role immediately?" I asked.

"She couldn't wait. She'd been eyeing off that office for years, so the older nuns said. Apparently she'd wanted to become mother superior before but missed out and they gave it to Mother Alfreda. Once she was gone, the next in line was Sister Frances. She was a bitter, nasty old thing too. Don't s'pose she's dead now?"

"No," I said.

"Pity."

"What about the other nuns?" Matt asked. "Did any of them have reason to dislike Mother Alfreda?"

She lifted one shoulder in a shrug. "There was always something. One sister complains of working too hard, another thinks she should be allowed to keep a book given to her by her family, that sort of thing. Just petty problems."

No reason to "do her in," as Abigail put it. Only Mother Frances had reason enough—if a power struggle could be considered a good reason. It may have been the motive for countless murders of political rivals over the centuries but not within convents.

"What do you know about the missing babies?" Matt asked.

She slowly lowered the spoon she'd been licking to the empty bowl and wiped her mouth with the back of her hand. "You know about them?"

"Yes. As do you."

She nodded. "Sister Clare told me. She's the mother superior's assistant and kept the records. She told me one day that a baby had disappeared and then another a short time later. Their records were also missing."

"Was one of the babies named Phineas Millroy?"

"I don't know."

"Did you ever see either of the babies?" I asked. "Touch them?"

She frowned. "Why?"

I drew in a deep breath to steel myself then stepped closer to her. "Because you're a magician," I said quietly, "and so was —is—Phineas Millroy. We thought perhaps you might be able to somehow identify the magic in him."

She looked from me to Matt then back to me again. "I don't know what you're saying."

"Yes, you do. I'm also a magician, Miss Pilcher."

"Don't be scared," Matt assured her. "We just want answers, nothing more. We don't care about your magical connection to silk."

Her throat jumped with her hard swallow. "What kind of magic do you do, Miss Steele?"

"Watches," I said. "I can make them run on time. You can work silk easily, can't you?"

"Quick and easy," she said with a hint of pride. "I can make a dress in half the time it takes two girls. I can make the prettiest, most delicate flowers and decorations. I even made a dress for a princess, last year. It were the loveliest thing you ever saw, all golden yellow with butterflies flitting between flowers on the skirt. Mr. Robinson himself says I might get another royal commission soon. Imagine that, eh? Me, thrown out of the Sisters of the Sacred Heart for being a bad girl, making dresses for princesses. I bet Sister Margeret'll be tickled. You'll tell her for me, won't you?"

"Of course," I said with a smile, "but I thought you were friends."

"We were, in a way. Friends but rivals too." She leaned forward and whispered, "She had an eye for Father Antonio too. We used to make up silly stories about him admiring our bright eyes and taking a fancy to us. They started as just girlish fantasy but when he took notice of me for real, she stopped being so friendly to me."

Matt cleared his throat. "Back to the missing babies," he said. "You say Sister Clare told you they'd disappeared."

She nodded. "I used to help her in the office, sometimes. She was new to the assistant position then, and the records were in poor order. I worked with her to get them right, and that's when she told me. I saw one of the babies in the nursery but I can't recall if I touched him. Anyway, you can't feel magic in another magician, Miss Steele, only in what they work on. You should know that."

"I do," I said on a sigh. "I suppose I was just clutching at straws, wondering if perhaps the baby had touched someone and—" I cut myself off before revealing that Phineas potentially had the power to heal. "Anyway, he was just a baby. If he did possess magic, he couldn't have practiced it without speaking a spell."

"And babies don't talk." She handed the empty glass and spoon to Matt. "I better get back."

"Of course," Matt said, taking my glass too.

"One last question," I said. "Did anyone at the convent know about your magic?"

"No. I kept that part of me hidden. The church don't look

kindly on magic, Miss Steele. Mark my words, some of 'em think the devil's in us magicians. Be sure and keep it a secret from any religious folk."

"I will," I assured her. "But are you saying that you never worked with silk while you were a nun?"

"Silk ain't common in a convent, but there was one time. A silk handkerchief were donated by a toff lady. We got donations from time to time that we sold in our little shop for extra money. Well, the handkerchief were a bit frayed so I offered to fix it up all nice to sell." Her face took on a glowing reverence, as if recalling a divine experience. "It were a fine piece and I loved feeling it. It had been an age since I'd touched silk. I knew about my magic but I didn't think I'd miss silk until I could no longer feel it. I missed it so much that I wasn't all that upset when the reverend mother threw me out. I just wanted to work with silk again, see. But no one at the convent knew about my magic. No one saw me fix that handkerchief, and no one there could even recognize magic heat since they were all artless."

"Are you quite sure?" Matt asked.

"Y-es. I think so."

She didn't sound all that sure to me. "You don't think that's why Mother Alfreda disliked you?" I asked. "You say she hated you for no reason, but perhaps she knew, somehow, and thought you did the devil's work."

"Then why didn't she say? Why didn't *she* throw me out? It was Mother Frances who threw me out, not Mother Alfreda, and because of "my mistake," as she called it, not my magic. No, I don't think she knew. I don't think anyone knew."

But she didn't sound positive.

We thanked her and she re-entered the shop while Matt returned the glasses and spoons to the ice cream seller. They were in the midst of a conversation in Italian when Matt paused. He stood on his toes and peered over the heads of passersby. Then he suddenly ran off.

I lifted my skirts and followed. Or tried to, but he was too fast. I caught a glimpse of him through the crowd ahead before he vanished. Had he gone into a shop? Or into the side street? I was about to enter the nearest shop, a millinery, when I heard him call my name.

He hurried toward me from the side street, caught my arm and walked me briskly back past the ice cream seller.

"You saw Payne?" I asked.

"I saw a fellow lounging against the wall," he said. "I can't be sure, but his stature reminded me of Payne. His hat was pulled low over his face so I couldn't see it. You shouldn't have followed me."

"You shouldn't have tried to confront him."

He wisely kept his mouth shut.

We avoided narrow back streets and kept to the busier thoroughfare as we walked home. I wondered if Matt would have been as cautious if he were alone. I didn't ask, not wanting to stoke the embers of our argument.

Instead, I steered clear of sensitive topics altogether. "Do you think it odd that Sister Margaret drew our attention to Abigail Pilcher in the first place, considering they were such good friends?"

"In what way?"

"She mentioned Abigail's departure out of the blue when we spoke to her at the convent. She didn't have to, and if they were friends, I'd expect her to protect Abigail from our prying questions. Yet she set us down the path of seeking Abigail out. Why?"

"Perhaps she was genuinely interested in her friend's welfare and couldn't check on her herself."

"There's no reason Sister Margaret couldn't visit Abigail."

"Visiting a disgraced former nun is probably strongly discouraged by the mother superior. Putting that aside, what are you suggesting? What would be Sister Margaret's purpose in setting us on Abigail's trail? To find answers that she couldn't give us? If so, it wasn't a successful strategy. We didn't learn anything about Phineas's disappearance, or that of Mother Alfreda."

"Or was Sister Margaret's intention to send us on a wild goose chase, perhaps to throw suspicion onto Abigail and away from the guilty party?"

He frowned at me. "So…they weren't friends?"

"It seems you don't know as much about women as I thought you did."

"I'm hardly the expert, India. The female of the species manages to constantly surprise me, and you in particular. So explain what I've missed."

I wasn't entirely sure if he'd paid me a compliment or not. I decided not to dwell on it. "Women are not always kind to those who've broken the bonds of friendship, and I do believe the bond that existed between Sister Margaret and Abigail was broken when Father Antonio began to take notice of one and not the other."

"Ah, jealousy. That I understand. But you think Sister Margaret would set aside their friendship out of jealousy? Jealousy over a man who could not belong to either of them, I might add."

I sighed. "I don't know. Perhaps. But it does feel a little as if Sister Margaret deliberately steered us toward Abigail to put us off."

"Or to help us. She didn't know Abigail was pregnant. She may have thought she left for a reason related to Mother Alfreda and the babies' disappearances."

I wasn't convinced that Sister Margaret and the other nuns were oblivious to Abigail's condition. With very little else to do in the convent except gossip and observe, it seemed likely the more observant of them would have guessed.

"The real question is," I said, "did anyone at the convent

know Abigail was a magician? She didn't think so, but perhaps she was wrong."

"In particular, did Mother Alfreda know? Was that why she hated Abigail?"

"And if she did know," I added, "how did she find out? Because *she* was a magician too? Or because someone else was and told her?"

Matt's pace slowed and I glanced at him. He appeared lost in thought, his gaze unfocused.

"What is it?" I asked.

"I'm trying to work out what connection there might be between Abigail's magical ability and the disappearances from the convent. I can't think of one. If Abigail knew Phineas was magical, then perhaps she let it slip to someone who then squirreled him out of the convent, but she says she didn't know."

"She may have lied to us."

* * *

WE DECIDED to visit the convent after lunch and yet another rest for Matt. I no longer had to order him to retire to his room in the middle of the day; he simply went after using his watch's magic. That meant he must be exhausted. The others noticed too, and a heavy silence weighed us down as we waited for Matt to wake and rejoin us. I couldn't settle and found no joy in reading. Cyclops, Willie and Duke, being more active, also couldn't sit still. The men finally left to go to the stables, where they could at least do something, but Willie remained in the house. She paced into the entrance hall and back up to the sitting room again, over and over. I realized after half an hour that she was waiting for the mail.

"Have you heard from your grandfather, India?" Miss Glass asked while Willie was out of the room.

"No, nor do I expect to. It's too much of a risk for him to

write. While *I* don't expect the police to monitor my correspondence, it's something Chronos would expect them to do."

The clearing of a throat behind me had me spinning around and my face heating. Police Commissioner Munro stood there with Willie. He regarded me through narrowed eyes.

"Commissioner!" I said. "To what do we owe the pleasure?"

Willie looked like she would argue with me about it being a pleasure but thankfully kept her mouth shut. She occupied a position by the mantel, as Matt often did when he was in the sitting room, and regarded the commissioner with cool indifference.

"I must discuss a matter with Mr. Glass," he said.

"You remember Mr. Glass's aunt, Miss Glass," I said.

"Of course." The commissioner bowed with great formality. He was a stickler for the proper order of things and for order in all things around him. His office was the neatest I'd ever seen, and his uniform never had a thread out of place or a dull button. Even his curled mustache was always trimmed and his white hair oiled into place.

That's why it had always seemed so odd that he would do something quite out of the ordinary for a policeman of high standing and have a child with his mistress. His son had died at the hands of an apprentice mapmaker out of jealousy, but I had not seen the commissioner show emotion over the loss. Indeed, it was hard for me to reconcile this man with the sweet natured mother of his son, Miss Gibbons. They just didn't seem suited. Perhaps they were no longer together and their relationship had ended years ago.

"Is Mr. Glass here?" The commissioner addressed Miss Glass.

"I told you," Willie said. "He's indisposed."

"When will he be available?"

"Soon," I said. "Is there something I can help you with? Is

it regarding our investigation?"

"That's what you call it? An investigation?" He grunted. "I've had complaints about the two of you, Miss Steele. You must cease your questioning. It's simply not right to pester members of our community whose reputations are beyond reproach."

"Are you referring to the nuns?" I asked.

His mustache wiggled with the pursing of his lips. "Father Antonio says your harassment of the good sisters is interfering with their peace and prayer."

"Good lord," Miss Glass muttered. "If they have done something wrong, they ought to be held accountable."

"What have they done wrong?"

I tried to signal to Miss Glass to keep quiet, but she paid me no attention. "Cavorted with the priest, for one thing."

His bushy brows inched ever so slightly up his forehead. "Is that a crime?"

"No, but it is immoral. Honestly, they consider themselves higher than the rest of us, yet they're no better." She placed a hand to her chest. "Now, *I* don't mind what they get up to. But I can't abide them looking down their noses at those who try to be good and fail on occasion when they themselves are not perfect. Can't abide it at all."

"I see your point, Miss Glass."

I'm sure he did. He wasn't exactly a moral member of society, and no doubt he'd felt guilty for his indiscretions, particularly in church, even if it wasn't known that he'd had a child by his mistress.

"Won't you sit down, Commissioner?" I asked.

"I haven't the time. Please inform Mr. Glass that I was here and asked him not to bother Inspector Brockwell again with matters that do not involve the police. And tell him that I'm watching him. I'm not satisfied that he has the public's best interests at heart on this matter. Not satisfied at all. If I find out it has something to do with the madness for magic that's

116

sweeping the city, he can expect to hear from me and perhaps endure another stint in the lockup."

"The lockup!" I cried.

Willie pushed off from the mantel. "What the blazes for?"

Miss Glass clutched the lace collar at her throat. "Oh dear. Oh dear, oh dear."

I marched past the commissioner, hoping he would follow me out. Fortunately he did. "Please do not upset Miss Glass like that," I hissed. "She has a delicate constitution."

"My apologies." He did not look apologetic. He looked somewhat triumphant at ruffling our feathers. "But consider yourselves warned. No more upsetting the church, no more wasting my men's time, and no more magic nonsense. I won't have you and Mr. Glass inflaming the situation." He leaned closer. "Magic must be kept quiet. It's dangerous for the public to know about it. You ought to understand why, Miss Steele."

My anger suddenly faded. His visit was fueled by worry about magic becoming public knowledge—worry for Miss Gibbons and her father. It was too late for his son, but he could protect the rest of his mistress's family. Or he could try.

"I do understand," I said gently. "Thank you for stopping by."

I walked him down the stairs and watched him leave. The mail had arrived and Bristow handed me a letter to pass to Willie. The handwriting was distinctly feminine. I returned to the sitting room where Willie sat alone in a chair by the window.

"Where's Miss Glass?" I asked.

"Went to her room."

"This arrived for you."

She snatched the envelope and tore it open. She quickly scanned the contents and folded the letter up again. She slumped into the chair.

"Is it bad news?" I asked.

"No," she said with a sullen pout.

"It must be. You look upset."

"I ain't upset. I'm...disappointed." She waved the letter. "My friend won't see me no more."

I almost asked her if she meant to say her lover, not friend, but held my tongue. This was the most I'd learned from her, and I didn't want to frighten her back into her shell. "Tell me about her."

She gave me a sharp look but did not correct my usage of "her." So I was right. Willie had been seeing a woman, not a man. As to what their relationship entailed, I could only guess. I'd heard about women being in a romantic relationship but had never actually known any.

"She's a nurse at the hospital," she said. "That's how we met, when I was there looking for answers into Dr. Hale's death. We liked each other straight away. There was a connection between us and she was—is—special. But when I tried to...advance our friendship to something more, she wouldn't do it. She acted all shocked and said she couldn't." She held up the letter. "She can't take that step. That's what she says in here. She's too afraid to see me anymore. Seeing me makes her want to let her true nature free, and that scares her. She thinks it ain't right."

"It is a large step to take, Willie, particularly if she hasn't experienced a relationship with a woman before." I squeezed her shoulder. "So Duke really never had a chance with you, did he? Does he know?"

"Aye, he knows. Don't worry about Duke. We tried to be together years ago and it didn't work. He won't try again. We're better as friends."

"You were together? Even though you're not...interested in men?"

"I was interested then. Still am, for the right man."

"Now I'm really confused."

She huffed out a humorless laugh. "Don't try and understand it, India. I've tried and failed. The thing is, me and Duke didn't work then and we won't work now. He was good to me when I needed it after…after a bad experience with a man. He helped me feel better about myself again, helped me trust men again. I needed him then, but I moved on. He knows it, but he just don't always accept it." She elbowed me. "He likes to think he's the most important person in my life. Came as a shock when Matt arrived in California and we got close, but Duke adjusted eventually. But I don't think he'd like getting put down another rung on the ladder."

"Do Matt and Cyclops also know that your lover from the hospital is a woman?"

"They might. They know I sometimes like women."

"I can't believe Matt didn't tell me."

She smiled sadly. "He wouldn't tell a secret, not even if you and he were married."

"So let's see if I have this right. You've been seeing a woman and you'd like your relationship to be something more than friendship, but you're not entirely averse to a romantic relationship with a man either."

"You got it." She gave a sheepish shrug and chewed on her lower lip. I'd never seen her quite so uncertain before. Perhaps she was worried about my reaction. "The thing is, India, I just like people I like. It don't matter what sex they are. I don't understand it, but that's how I feel."

I smiled at her, trying to reassure her this revelation didn't change anything between us. "Thank you for confiding in me. I suspected I was missing something but I couldn't think what. I'm glad you cleared it up for me."

"Wish it would become clearer for me. Being like this, liking both men and women, it gets complicated, sometimes."

A bubble of laughter escaped. "I'm sure it does. But it's not easier liking just men. Take it from me, I've made quite a mess of things, and I've only had one paramour."

"That's because you're a bad judge of character. I'm good

at it. I know a good person when I see one." Again, she held up the letter.

I leaned down and hugged her. "Then you must not give up on her. Turn on that Johnson charm and make her see what she's missing."

Finally I got a genuine laugh out of her. "The Johnson charm only works on cowboys and criminals. But I won't give up. Not yet."

* * *

MATT and I waited at the school gate instead of the convent, hoping to catch Sister Margaret as she saw the children off at the end of the day. I felt rather conspicuous, standing beneath the shade of a tree on the footpath, when Sister Bernadette spotted us. The nun marched toward us, her toolbox swinging with each long stride.

"You two again," she said in her thick Irish accent. "What is it you want now?"

"We wish to speak with Sister Margaret," Matt said.

The school bell tolled and girls began spilling out of the classrooms in chatty groups. We searched for Sister Margaret but couldn't see her.

"What do you want with her?" Sister Bernadette asked.

"That's not something we can divulge," I told her.

"We have no secrets here."

I merely smiled. She was quite hostile; she had been ever since we'd asked prying questions of her and Sister Margaret on our first visit. It seemed ungrateful, considering Matt was responsible for sending Duke and Cyclops to mend the convent roof.

"How is the roof?" I asked.

Matt's gaze slid to me and a small smile touched his lips.

"It stopped leaking," Sister Bernadette said, her tone damper. "I suppose I have you to thank for that, Mr. Glass.

But don't expect me to answer your impertinent questions now. It changes nothing."

"I'll keep that in mind," Matt said, "for when we have impertinent questions for you."

Her mouth clamped shut but she was in no hurry to leave. She followed Matt's sharpened gaze to the school. Sister Margaret emerged and, seeing us, joined us at the gate. Her cautious smile quickly faded as Sister Bernadette intercepted her.

"You don't have to speak to them," Sister Bernadette said.

"We only have a few quick questions," Matt said. "It won't take long but they are a little sensitive. Perhaps we can go somewhere quieter where there are no children."

Sister Margaret exchanged a glance with her fellow nun then looked toward the convent. "I…I…don't know."

Sister Bernadette sighed. "They won't give up. Come to the school hall." She headed off, clearly determined to be part of the conversation whether we wanted her there or not.

Sister Margaret tucked her hands into the sleeves of her habit and followed.

The hall was situated behind the school building. The scent of oiled wood came from the large cross hanging on the wall, and several children's drawings of Christ hung on the opposite wall. We sat on chairs arranged in a circle beneath the cross. Both nuns regarded us levelly, if somewhat nervously. Neither looked comfortable meeting us like this, but I took it as a good sign that they were willing to speak with us at all.

"We found Abigail Pilcher," Matt began.

Sister Margaret gasped then covered her mouth with her hand.

"Who?" Sister Bernadette asked.

"Sister Francesca," Sister Margaret told her. "You remember her. She left when…" Her face flushed and she returned her hands to the sleeves of her habit.

"Sister Francesca!" Sister Bernadette blurted out. "But what does Mother Alfreda's disappearance have to do with her? Are you saying *she* knew something?"

Sister Margaret made a small sound of protest.

"That's what we wanted to know," Matt said. "Her leaving at the same time seemed too coincidental, but after speaking to her, we don't think she had anything to do with it."

"Are you sure?" Sister Bernadette shook her head. "She wasn't a good girl, if I remember rightly. Don't you agree, Sister Margaret?"

Sister Margaret looked like she would burst into tears.

"Why did you mention her to us?" I asked gently. The nun looked troubled and not at all like she had cruel intentions toward Abigail. "Did you suspect she knew something? Or were you motivated for a different reason?"

Sister Margaret's lower lip wobbled. She squeezed her eyes shut and pressed her lips together, holding her emotions in check.

I leaned forward and touched her arm. "Tell us what you know about Abigail Pilcher," I urged her. When she didn't speak, I added, "Did you know she was with child?"

She nodded. Neither she nor Sister Bernadette seemed surprised. If they both knew, perhaps the entire convent did.

Something black fluttered just outside the door. It could have been a bird, but was more likely a nun's habit. Someone was eavesdropping.

I sat back and glanced at Matt, lifting my eyebrow. He nodded, encouraging me to go on. I drew in a deep breath. "Did you know that Abigail is a magician?"

Sister Margaret's eyes flew open and she crossed herself. Sister Bernadette pressed the crucifix hanging around her neck to her lips. Her face turned as pale as her wimple.

Behind and above me, something cracked and wood grated against wood. I turned and looked up just in time to see the large cross plunging toward me.

CHAPTER 8

$\mathcal{M}$att dragged me to the floor a moment before the cross smashed into the chair I'd been sitting on. The backrest splintered and the chair collapsed under the weight of the cross.

I lay on the floor, half beneath Matt's body, and stared at the spot where I'd sat moments ago. The cross was intact, but the chair was destroyed.

"Are you all right?" Matt asked, helping me to sit up.

My heart hammered but I was unharmed. I nodded, knowing I could not yet speak without my voice shaking. I'd never been an overly devout person, although I was a regular church goer, but the timing of the cross falling on me as I mentioned the word magic…it was too coincidental. As Matt often said, he didn't believe in coincidence. Nor did I.

"Do you see now?" Sister Bernadette said, her accent thick despite her trembling voice. "Magic is the devil's work, and God does not approve of you coming to his house and questioning his faithful daughters about it."

Sister Margaret clutched her friend's hand in both of hers. The two nuns held one another, clearly shaken by the incident.

As was I. My body trembled uncontrollably. Matt must have felt it as he helped me to stand. He eyed me closely and I offered him a smile that I knew wasn't convincing but it was all I could muster.

"You should go now," Sister Margaret said, rising. "The sign is clear—God doesn't want you here. He doesn't want us to talk to you about the devil's work."

"Magic is not the devil's work," Matt growled.

Both nuns looked to the cross now lying dormant where it had fallen.

"If God didn't want people to possess magic then why did he give it to some?" he went on. "Why are some born with it?"

"I don't have all the answers, Mr. Glass," Sister Margaret snapped. "But if Sister Francesca—Abigail—is a magician, then there is your evidence. She was not a good Catholic girl. One sin begets another and another."

I clasped Matt's arm, digging my fingers into him. There was no point in arguing with the nuns. He could not change their minds.

Even so, he continued to try. "She made a mistake," he said tightly. "And it wasn't entirely her fault. The baby's father had a role to play in her predicament."

"*She* seduced *him*! Father—" Sister Margaret bit her lip and glanced at Sister Bernadette.

But Sister Bernadette was still staring at the cross and didn't appear to have heard. She bent to pick it up and Matt let me go to help her. Together they righted it and leaned it against the wall. Matt inspected the wall and the nails that had held the cross in place. They were badly bent and one had snapped in half.

"Thank you," Sister Bernadette murmured. She was not the same fiery nun who'd scolded us at the church gate. Her face remained pale and her hands still shook.

Sister Margaret stood by the door, arms crossed, and scowled as we departed.

Matt and I crossed the courtyard, meeting the mother superior inspecting one of the window frames on the school building. If she'd been there a few minutes ago, she would have seen the person who'd come to the hall's doorway. She would also have heard the cross falling.

I planned on slipping past her, but Matt had other ideas. He greeted her with a tip of his hat.

"Does it need repair?" Matt asked, nodding at the window frame. "I can have my friends look at it."

"In exchange for information? No, thank you, Mr. Glass." She flaked off some paint with her finger and clicked her tongue.

"Sister Bernadette can't do it all on her own," he went on. "She's aging and this place is getting older too."

"She doesn't complain."

"I'm sure she doesn't, but that doesn't mean she's not struggling to keep up."

"I told you," the mother superior ground out through a hard jaw, "I will not pay the price you ask."

"Reverend Mother!" came a sing song voice from the convent side of the courtyard. "Reverend Mother, are you out here? Oh." Sister Clare, the mother superior's assistant and the one who first alerted us to the missing babies, stopped upon seeing us. She looked torn as to whether she ought to return inside or join us.

"What is it, Sister Clare?" the mother superior asked.

"There's a matter requiring your attention. It can wait until you're finished with Mr. Glass and Miss Steele."

"We are finished." The mother superior arched a severe brow at Matt, waiting for him to concede and depart. Clearly she had a lot to learn about him.

"We spoke with Abigail Pilcher, known as Sister Francesca when she lived here," he said.

Mother Frances showed a flicker of surprise but schooled

it quickly. Sister Clare, however, gasped. "How *is* she?" the assistant asked.

"She's well, and so is her son," Matt said.

"She has a son? How marvelous."

The mother superior glared at her and Sister Clare bowed her head.

"Do you have a point, Mr. Glass?" Mother Frances asked.

"Abigail told us that she was forced to leave the convent," Matt said. "She claims you forced her to go soon after you took over the role of mother superior here."

"She was wholly unsuited to being a nun. I would have thought the condition she was in upon her departure was proof enough of how unsuitable. Mother Alfreda should have overseen Abigail's departure but she was too weak to do anything about it."

"So you didn't force her to leave because she was a magician?" Matt asked.

Sister Clare gasped again. She stared wide-eyed at Matt. "Magic," she whispered with reverence.

"Magic doesn't exist," the mother superior said in cold, clipped tones. "I would appreciate it if you didn't come here and say otherwise, sir. Magic is harmless fantasy for children but it's irresponsible for adults to perpetuate the myth of its existence. Believing in magic does more harm than good."

"But the newspapers," Sister Clare murmured. "At least one is saying magic is real."

"Journalists will say anything to sell more copies of their publications. You've been taken in, Sister Clare. You all have."

"Sister Clare," I said to the assistant, "were you aware that Abigail was a silk magician?"

"Silk?" she whispered.

"Stop this nonsense!" the mother superior spat. "Sister Clare, you ought to know better."

Sister Clare bowed her head. "Yes, Reverend Mother."

"We have work to do, Mr. Glass, Miss Steele. Good Christian work that requires our complete devotion."

Matt held up his hands. "We're going."

I couldn't leave like this, with the mother superior thinking the worst of us for mentioning magic. Imagine what she'd say if she knew about me. "We are not your enemy, Reverend Mother. We respect your values and rituals. We only wish to find the man known as Phineas Millroy, who was given into the convent's care twenty-seven years ago. It's absolutely vital that we find him. He has the power to save someone very dear to me. We know he disappeared from here under mysterious circumstances around the same time Mother Alfreda disappeared. Perhaps they are linked in some way."

"Don't be absurd." She made a scoffing sound. "There is no link between the two. Mother Alfreda left of her own accord, and the baby's records have merely gone missing. There is no mystery and no conspiracy to cover anything up. I don't know what you think magic has to do with anything, nor do I wish to know. I've given you my views on it, and I have no wish to explore the matter further. Good day."

She thrust her sharp chin out and strode off across the courtyard toward the convent. Sister Clare shot as an apologetic smile and trailed after her. The mother superior did not close the door until she saw that we were on our way.

"She's prickly," I said to Matt as we rounded the school building and returned to the street. "Do you think she has something to hide?"

"Hard to say. Sister Clare seems genuine, though."

"I'm glad you think so, because so do I."

"Trust your instincts, India." He scanned the vicinity thoroughly before climbing into the coach behind me.

"Surely you don't think Payne had something to do with that cross falling?" I teased.

"You never know with Payne." He eyed me closely and

took my hands in both of his. "Are you all right? Did you get hurt?"

"I bumped my elbow, but it's fine."

"Sorry," he said, palming both my elbows. "I wasn't very gentle."

"You saved my life."

He tossed me a sheepish smile. "I saved you from getting a bump on the head. I doubt it would have killed you."

I wasn't so sure. The cross looked heavy, and it had required both Matt and Sister Bernadette to lift it. "Tiredness hasn't slowed you. Thank you, Matt."

"Just repaying the favor you've done for me a number of times." He leaned forward and kissed me lightly on the lips. It was deliciously tender and banished the last tremble of my frayed nerves.

It also had the potential to turn passionate. I gently pushed him away before I deepened the kiss. He sat back again with a curiously satisfied smile, as if he'd won a small victory.

Time to return the situation into something less dangerous. "How do you think the cross fell?" I asked.

"The nails were bent."

"But why were they bent?"

"Nails sometimes bend if the weight they bear is too heavy. Those nails weren't strong enough for that cross."

I wasn't quite convinced. The cross fell at the moment I asked about magic. The very moment.

"It wasn't God trying to strike you down, India," he said. "Don't think like that."

"I'm not. I'm thinking how unlikely it was for it to fall right then, and how no one had touched it." I met his gaze. "And how I can make watches and clocks move without touching them."

He looked as if the stuffing had been knocked out of him. Mere tiredness didn't do that. "You think one of the sisters is a magician and made it move? But…no other magician can do that, only you."

"How do we know? Just because Chronos did not know of one doesn't mean another pure-blooded magician doesn't exist. What does surprise me is that it means one of those nuns is a magician. They both looked upset by the discussion and shaken when the cross fell, however."

"The mother superior was just outside," Matt said with a slow nod of agreement. "She could have done it. So could Sister Clare. She wasn't far away either; she could have doubled back to the convent after leaving the meeting room. India, why are you frowning like that?"

"I saw something near the door just before the cross fell. A flap of black fabric, I think. Like a habit or cloak."

"It's too warm for a cloak, unless someone wishes to wear a hood to hide their face. Someone like Payne."

"Surely you're not suggesting he is a magician too."

He dragged a hand over his face and down his chin. "I don't know what I'm suggesting. We can't discount anything at this point, but it's more likely to be a nun. I'm still not convinced the cross moved magically, though. Those nails weren't sturdy enough to hold such a heavy object."

I wished I'd touched the cross to feel if it held magical warmth. Damnation. I almost suggested turning around and sneaking into the hall, but Matt looked too tired.

The first thing I did when we arrived home was use the extending spell on his magic watch. It usually lengthened the time needed between uses. Whether it still did, he didn't say and I didn't ask. He thanked me and retired to rest before dinner.

His condition threw a cloud over the household. Willie, Cyclops and Duke were like caged tigers, too restless to sit still yet unwilling to take their mind off our predicament by visiting one of London's many entertainments.

"Why not see a show?" I said. "There are any number of

theaters around the city, some of them quite respectable. Or you could have a few drinks in a tavern. Some have music or other entertainments."

My suggestion was met with grumbling excuses.

"I ain't going nowhere," Willie said. "Not while Matt's like this. What if he needs me?"

"Why would he need *you*?" Duke asked. "You can't make him better."

"Not needs me then, just…if something happens, I want to be here when it does."

"*If*. If it happens. Don't bury him yet."

She pushed herself out of the chair and shoved her finger in Duke's face. "You wash your mouth out, Duke. You hear me! I ain't saying nothing of the sort, so don't put words in my mouth."

Cyclops groaned and rubbed his forehead. "Help me, India. They've been like this all afternoon."

"We're all tense," I said. "We're all worried about Matt. But please, this is not helping." As the newcomer to their group, I perhaps had no right to admonish them, but their bickering was getting on my nerves and it couldn't go on. "Matt doesn't want to hear your arguing on top of his other problems. Be kind to one another, for his sake."

Cyclops nodded his approval at my little speech. Willie resumed her seat without a grumble, which I took as agreement. Duke got up and poured drinks at the sideboard. He handed one to Willie.

"Sorry," he said. "India's right. How about we call a truce?"

She clinked her glass against his. "Truce. We all want what's best for Matt."

"So what else can we do, India?" Cyclops asked. "Can we investigate the convent more?"

I tapped my fingers on my thigh as I considered what paths were open to us. There were very few. If I was right, and that cross had not fallen of its own accord, then there had been two magicians at the convent twenty-seven years ago—a silk magician and a wood magician. If Abigail had told the truth, and she didn't know that Phineas was magical, then she wasn't the link we were looking for. But if the wood magician knew…

But how could the wood magician know when Phineas was too young to talk, let alone recite a spell?

I told the others of my theory, and talking it over helped cement the idea in my head but it didn't provide any answers. "We'll talk to Abigail again and see if she knew about a wood magician," I said. "She might know which of the nuns had an affinity for it, if nothing else."

"It might not be one of the nuns," Duke said. "Could be Father Antonio."

"The convent could do with some further repair work, and the three of you are bored here. Why not offer to help Sister Bernadette tomorrow and discreetly ask questions."

"Finally, something to do," Willie said.

A fist pounded on the front door, the thumps echoing through the house.

"Someone ain't happy," Cyclops said.

We met Bristow in the entrance hall just as he was about to open the door. Willie put a hand on his arm to caution him. She showed him the gun she held at her back.

His eyes widened and he let the door handle go as if it stung. Duke rolled his eyes and opened it.

Lord Rycroft barged in, brandishing a walking stick with a silver head. "Where is he? Where is my nephew?"

Lady Rycroft followed her husband. Her eyes bore signs of crying and she held a handkerchief to her nose.

"Matthew!" Lord Rycroft shouted up the staircase. "Matthew, come down here at once!"

"Keep your voices down," Willie snapped. "He needs his rest and your bellowing ain't helping."

"Should I fetch him, Miss?" Bristow asked me.

"I don't think there'll be a need," I said. "He'll hear. Madam, what's happened?" I asked Lady Rycroft, even though I dreaded the answer.

Neither Lord nor Lady Rycroft answered me. She stood by her husband and stared tearfully up the staircase where both Matt and Miss Glass now stood. He escorted his aunt down the stairs as if he didn't have a care in the world. She glowered at her brother and sister-in-law.

"Such a racket, Richard," Miss Glass scolded. "The servants will have heard everything. Do lower your voice."

"I don't bloody well care what your servants think!" Lord Rycroft marched off toward the drawing room without waiting to be invited. "Come. We have a serious matter to discuss. A matter for which you must make amends, Matthew."

I watched them go, feeling sick to my stomach.

"Anyone want to take a wager what that's about?" Willie asked as Matt shut the door, excluding us.

"Ain't no point in wagering," Cyclops said. "We know what it's about."

"Payne," Duke said heavily. "He must have told Lord Cox."

"So much for Matt's advertisement." Willie headed across the hall to the library. "I need a strong drink."

As did I. It did nothing to comfort me, however, and I brooded in silence until I heard the Rycrofts leaving only a few minutes later. Matt then joined us. He looked like a man driven to the end of his rope, and Matt's rope was very long.

"You look like dung what's been in the sun a week," Willie said.

"As eloquent as always." Matt cast her a limp smile but his gaze flicked to me. It didn't linger. "As you've probably guessed, Payne has informed Lord Cox of Patience's indiscretion. My advertisement was too late."

"That ain't your fault," Cyclops said.

"I should have done it days ago."

"No, Matt," Willie said.

"Hold your breath," I told them. "He's going to blame himself, no matter how much we protest. How is Patience?"

"Devastated, apparently," he said. "Aunt Beatrice and the girls were going to leave for Rycroft tomorrow to begin wedding preparations there. Patience hasn't stopped crying since she received the letter from Lord Cox calling off the wedding."

Poor Patience. I felt for her. I knew what it was like the first few days after receiving such news. It was like waking aboard a storm-ravaged ship. You did not know where you were, the surface beneath your feet was unstable, and there was no end to the turmoil in sight.

"So what did Lord Rycroft ask you to do?" I said.

Matt sat and rested his elbows on his knees. He dragged his hand through his hair. The silence thinned until Willie could no longer stand it.

"Well?" she barked.

"Lord Cox must be convinced that Patience is still a worthy and valuable bride," he said. "He needs to be made aware of just how virtuous she is, and how deeply she regrets her mistake. If he's a reasonable fellow, he'll reconsider."

"And who is going to convince him?" I asked. "You?"

He frowned. "My uncle doesn't have a delicate touch. I think I'm the better choice."

"Lord Cox lives in Yorkshire! You can't travel for days to reach him then spend days returning. We're in the middle of an important investigation that will save your life."

He said nothing, and that only riled me more.

"Don't you dare even consider leaving London now unless it's to find Phineas Millroy."

"You can investigate very well without me, India. The others will help, but you don't really need it. You're competent and excellent at solving knotty puzzles. You'll be fine."

"Don't try to sweet talk me," I said. "You are not leaving, and that's final."

"Agreed," Duke said. "You're staying here, Matt."

"Aye," both Willie and Cyclops added.

Matt turned an icy glare onto each of them in turn, but saved the extra iciness for me. "I have to speak to him now. My uncle will only make things worse if he blunders in, and time is of the essence. Lord Cox must be convinced to change his mind before anyone finds out. It'll be too late to sweep it under the carpet if we delay. I have to strike now or not at all."

Cyclops, Duke and Willie all crossed their arms over their chests at the same time. They weren't capitulating. Matt lowered his head and raked his hair again.

"What did Lord Rycroft want from you?" I asked, a little gentler. "I doubt it was to suggest you speak with Lord Cox on his behalf."

A muscle in Matt's cheek pulsed. "You know why," he said quietly. "He has the same idiotic notion as Aunt Letitia. That's why I have to speak to Lord Cox myself and do it immediately."

His uncle wanted him to marry Patience. Indeed, he had probably put enormous pressure on Matt to agree to the scheme. The fact that Lord and Lady Rycroft had left quite soon after arriving meant Matt had placated them with an offer they considered reasonable.

I swallowed hard but the lump in my throat remained. "You can't leave now," I said lamely. "Not only is it a crucial time in our search for Phineas Millroy but you can't travel such a long distance alone. Someone needs to be with you if you fall unconscious."

"The alternative is not an option either." Head still bowed, he regarded me through thick lashes. He looked so forlorn that my heart lurched in response.

"Let them solve their own damned problems," Duke spat. "It ain't nothing to do with you."

"Aye," Cyclops said. "You don't have to marry her, Matt. There must be another way."

"Money," Willie said without much conviction. "Either give some to Patience and her sisters, or to Lord Cox to make him marry her."

"Lord Cox is rich and doesn't need my money, and money is hardly compensation enough for my cousins. It's not fair that they have to give up marriage because of my mistake."

"It's not *your* mistake!" I shot to my feet and strode to the door, my skirts snapping at my ankles. There was no point rehashing old arguments and providing the same suggestions. We were getting nowhere. "I'll dine in my room."

I raced up the stairs and threw myself on the bed. Sulking achieved nothing except more frayed nerves, so I took out my watch and opened the casing. I could dismantle it by rote so I didn't need to concentrate. The familiar work soothed me, allowed me to clear my mind and calm my temper.

By the time I put my watch's innards back in the housing, I'd realized there was one way Matt could make it clear to his aunts and uncle that he wouldn't marry Patience. He could engage himself to me.

But he had not proposed, not exactly, and he wouldn't while he was so ill. He was free to marry whomever he chose.

While he said all the things I wanted to hear, I couldn't be sure which path he'd choose. It wouldn't surprise me if his chivalry and sense of duty overrode his love for me. It would be just like Matt to tell his aunt and uncle the things he knew they wanted to hear.

They had, after all, left soon after arriving.

CHAPTER 9

*O*nce again, Matt had already left the house when I went down for breakfast. Once again, no one knew where he'd gone. When Bristow informed me, I got the most awful tightening in my chest.

"I already checked his room," Duke told me, pressing a cup of tea into my hands in the dining room. "His clothes are still there."

"He wouldn't leave London without telling us," Willie said from the table where she attacked a pile of bacon heaped on her plate.

"Or leaving a note," Cyclops added. "There's no note."

I looked to Bristow. "No note that I've found," he added.

That was a relief. I served myself breakfast from the selection on the sideboard but found I wasn't hungry and hardly ate.

Matt still hadn't returned by the time breakfast finished. I retreated to the sitting room, where waiting became extremely trying. I wanted to speak to Abigail Pilcher again, but I didn't want to do so without Matt. If he didn't return soon, however, I would go alone.

It occurred to me that he had gone to see her without me

to avoid my lectures. That was more disheartening than thinking he'd gone to speak to Lord Cox, and I resolved to be more pleasant today and not even bring up Patience's situation.

My resolution didn't extend to Miss Glass. She joined me in the sitting room mid-morning and settled her portable writing desk on her lap.

"What an awful business about Patience," I began.

"Very."

"Do you think Lord Cox can be convinced to change his mind?"

She pulled out a letter from the desk and perched her spectacles on the end of her nose. "No. He's much too proud, so my brother says."

"Has Lord Rycroft even tried to speak to him?"

"He has written."

"A letter isn't enough. He must go in person and try to sway him."

She sighed and lowered the letter. "Richard does not grovel."

"Not even for his daughter's sake? Indeed, for the sake of all his daughters?"

"Not when there is another, more palatable alternative."

She meant Matt marrying Patience. From the sympathetic look Miss Glass gave me, I suspected she assumed that was the path Matt would take. It would do me no good to tell her otherwise. That was Matt's responsibility—and clearly he had not done it.

With a sigh, Miss Glass set aside her writing desk and came to sit beside me on the sofa. "I know it's not what either of you want, India, but it's the way it has to be. Matthew has a duty. He is not free. He must do what is best for his family, his lineage. Do you understand?"

"We've been through this." I looked away to hide the burning tears welling in my eyes.

"But do you understand?"

"Yes."

"Good. Matthew does too."

I whipped around to face her again. "He does?"

"He said so last night, right to Richard's face." Her features softened, and the wrinkles bracketing her eyes and mouth flattened out. "If you love him, you will let him go, India."

I opened my mouth but shut it again. I wasn't entirely sure what I'd been about to say, only that I felt I must protest. But my mind suddenly went numb and the words wouldn't form.

"He'll never be happy with you if he knows he could save Patience and didn't," she went on. "Her sisters too, don't forget. They're all relying on him."

"You put too much pressure on his shoulders."

"He has broad shoulders."

"Yes," I said, sounding rather dull-witted.

"He'll always blame himself if he doesn't rescue them," Miss Glass went on. "You know that, don't you?"

I ought to tell her there must be another way, that we owed it to Matt to find it and free him of his obligations. But I'd spent much of the night trying to find that other way and I couldn't. Short of Matt visiting Lord Cox and somehow convincing him to set aside his distaste of Patience's indiscretion, I could think of no way out. Besides, I suspected Miss Glass rather liked the idea of her niece and nephew marrying. Patience was a more appealing option than me.

"She is not a bad match for him," Miss Glass said as if reading my mind. "She would make a suitable wife. She's good and demure, and knows how to manage staff, host parties and further his career. She'll be a great asset to him."

The unspoken words being that I would only bring him down to my level. I looked away. I couldn't bear to see it in her eyes, mixed in with a little pain for me. She was not unsympathetic, but that sympathy was not enough to favor a marriage between me and Matt.

She picked up her writing desk again and set it on her lap. "My sister-in-law has won. She did look pleased as she left last night." She clicked her tongue. "I wonder how far her preparations are along already. It wouldn't surprise me if she has new invitations made up by the end of the week. There's no point changing the date, after all."

I gasped then choked, bringing fresh tears burning my eyes. I leapt up and would have made my excuses if I could talk without my voice shaking.

I got as far as the door and stopped. Bristow was showing the three Miss Glasses up the stairs to the sitting room. Of all the people I didn't want to see at that moment, they were top of my list. The only saving grace was that they came alone, without their mother.

I resumed my seat. There was no way I would let them see how upset the business of Matt marrying Patience had made me. I would never give Hope that satisfaction.

They filed into the sitting room one by one, led by the youngest, Hope. She was followed by Charity and finally Patience, the eldest. While they greeted their aunt with brisk kisses, Hope and Patience could hardly even look at me. It was understandable perhaps, considering Patience's disgrace and Hope's recent attempts to steal Matt's watch and to trick him into a compromising position. Of the three girls, Hope was the prettiest and cleverest, but those attributes had given her a diabolical precociousness. Her aunt didn't like her, and as charitable as I tried to be toward her, I couldn't either.

Charity, the middle sister, seemed the least concerned to see me. She was too interested in hovering by the door, checking the vicinity. No doubt she was looking for Cyclops, whom she'd taken quite a shine to.

"Is our cousin in?" Hope asked Miss Glass. "My sister wishes to speak with him."

Patience sat with her feet together and her hands in her lap. She bowed her head, a picture of demure respectability. It was almost impossible to think of her having a dalliance, let alone having one with a scoundrel.

"He's out," Miss Glass said. "What did you want to speak to him about, Patience?"

"A...a private matter," Patience stammered.

"Speak louder, girl, I can hardly hear you."

"A private matter regarding..." Her face flushed and she lowered her head further.

"Regarding an arrangement between them," Charity said, finally taking a seat. "For goodness sake, Patience, just say it. She's not going to attack you."

Hope pressed her lips together but didn't completely smother her snicker. It was only then that I realized Charity was referring to me.

"I...I'm not even sure there is an arrangement," Patience said.

"Of course there is," Hope said. "Mama made it clear last night."

"I'd rather hear it from Matt himself so that there's no mistake. It seems...unlikely." She blinked red, swollen eyes at me.

My heart pinched and I looked away. I didn't want to feel sympathy for her, yet I did. Like me, her fiancé had thrown her to the wolves without a care for her wellbeing. It was cruel, and I couldn't blame her for clutching at the lifeline offered now.

Patience cleared her throat. "Do you and Matt have an arrangement, India?"

I gripped the edge of the sofa, digging my nails into the upholstery. A thick blanket of silence enveloped us, stifling me. It was difficult to take a full breath.

"We are not engaged," I managed to say.

A collective sigh of relief banished the silence.

"There!" Hope declared. "See. He's free to marry you, Patience. All is well."

Patience chewed the inside of her lip. "Well…if you're sure, India."

"Of course she's sure," Miss Glass snipped off. "Matthew is a Glass, the heir to the Rycroft title. It's time he married and married well. You're a good match, Patience. Don't let anyone allow you to think otherwise." She shot a glare at Hope. "India is not at all suitable for Matthew. They both know it. You have nothing to worry about on that score."

"Our mother says the same thing," Patience said. "But I wanted to make sure first. If you say there is nothing between you, India, then I'll feel better."

"She already said they're not engaged," Charity blurted out, throwing up her hands. "For goodness' sake, Patience, just accept that he's going to marry you. Forget that boring Cox. Matt is a much better catch."

Patience gave a small nod. "I know. I'd be honored to be his wife." She smiled, but it withered when she turned to me, and she once again dipped her head.

"Since Patience will now be marrying Matt," Hope said with a tilt of her chin, "it seems appropriate that you no longer live here, India. I do hope you understand. We have nothing against you. You seem kind, and as devoted as a pet, but it just wouldn't be decorous anymore."

I wished I'd had the strength in my legs to walk out. I really should have. Better yet, I wished I'd ordered her out of the house.

"India stays here," Miss Glass snapped. "She is my companion."

"But Aunt Letitia." Hope's soothing voice and big eyes did an excellent job at imploring. I imagined it worked on her parents and paramours quite well. "You must see how awkward it is with her here. Think of Patience."

"Do stop, Hope," Patience said with effort. "I don't mind if she stays. Honestly."

"Be quiet, Patience. You don't know what's good for you."

Miss Glass's nostrils flared, her spine stiffened. "India is not leaving, and that is final."

Hope sniffed. "We'll see what Father has to say."

Cyclops wandered in and stopped when he spotted our visitors. For a long moment he stood without moving, as if he couldn't decide whether to stay or go and so did nothing. In the end, his manners won out and he greeted the Glass sisters politely.

Charity sprang up from her chair and grasped his arm. She dragged him across the room and ordered him to sit on the sofa then squeezed herself between Cyclops and Patience, forcing her sister aside. Cyclops squashed himself into the corner, taking up far less space than a man his size ought.

"I'm so glad you're here," Charity gushed. "Your company is sorely needed today."

"It is?" He glanced over her head at me. I merely shrugged one shoulder.

"Everyone is such a bore," she whispered.

Hope rolled her eyes. "We can hear you."

Cyclops cleared his throat. "I should go."

"No!" Charity clutched his arm again and leaned into him. "Do stay a little longer. Talk to me. Tell me about yourself. Your life must be thrilling."

He leaned away and stared owlishly at her through his one good eye. "Not that thrilling."

"It must be! You can't look like a pirate then tell me you sit inside reading books all day." She pulled a face. "That would be awfully disappointing."

"Actually, that's all I do." He cleared his throat. "I sit in Matt's library and read. I read everything. I hate the outdoors." She drew back. Sensing an opportunity to escape, Cyclops warmed to his theme. "There's too much...dirt outside. And fresh air. I prefer stale air and cleanliness."

"But the scar..."

"A childhood accident. My mother dropped me as a baby."

I bit my lip to stop my smile.

"And your size." Charity squeezed his shoulder and giggled. "You're so big and strong. You must be an excellent fighter."

"Charity!" Patience scolded. "Restrain yourself."

"Why should I?" Charity snapped at her older sister. "*You* didn't."

Patience blushed fiercely and stared down at her folded hands.

"I'm not that strong," Cyclops said. "In fact, I'm a coward. I hate fighting. It hurts. And being big means I scare people without meaning to. Do you know what it's like to pick up your baby niece and she starts crying? No matter how many times I play peekaboo, she won't stop. It breaks my heart." He pressed a hand to his chest. "I'm very sensitive. Some say too sensitive. I even cry. A lot."

I tried hard to hold back my laugh, but it escaped as a choke. Poor Cyclops was trying, but Charity seemed more enthused than ever. Telling her that he cried only made her click her tongue and coo at him as if he were a child.

She slid even closer to him, crushing her skirt against his thigh. "So you don't like fisticuffs, but what about knives? Do you carry one? How big is it? Can I see it?"

Her questions shot like bullets, forcing Cyclops to lean back inch by inch with each one. The poor man needed rescuing, and I was only too happy to leave as well.

"Excuse me," I said, "I've just remembered I have something to do in the library. Cyclops—"

"Be glad to help! You know how much I love libraries and books, India. I can't stay away." He extricated himself from Charity's clutches and followed me out. "Thank you," he whispered. "I thought I'd be trapped in there for the rest of the morning."

"Oh?" I said innocently. "You don't wish to be the object of Charity Glass's affections?"

"She scares me. Who asks about knives like that?"

"It could have been worse. She could have asked about guns."

"If she does next time, I'm throwing Willie into her path. They'd get along."

"Probably a little too well," I said. "It might be best to keep them apart. Letting Willie and Charity loose together in the city seems like a recipe for trouble."

He chuckled, and I hugged his arm, feeling some of the heaviness that had been weighing me down lift.

It didn't last long. Whenever I thought about the visit from the Glass sisters, my heart sank a little further. They all seemed set on Matt marrying Patience, as if the entire family had decided it was a foregone conclusion and not open for negotiation. Even Patience had accepted it, exchanging one fiancé for another as if they were as interchangeable as bonnets. Miss Glass, once staunchly opposed to Matt marrying any of the girls, now thought Patience would make a good wife. I felt utterly cast aside, even though Matt told me he had not agreed to the union. How long could he withstand the onslaught from his family? How long could he withstand the onslaught from his own guilty conscience?

That was my greatest concern. If anything convinced him it was a good idea, it would be his own guilt. I knew better than anyone how chivalric Matt could be when he thought himself at fault.

He returned but refused to tell us where he'd been, only saying he had an errand to perform. His secrecy stretched my nerves more.

He used his watch but refused to rest, even though he'd suppressed several yawns over luncheon. "We have work to do. Ready, India?"

I didn't want to sit in the coach alone with him, but I had no choice. He did not invite the others to join us. Inevitably, the conversation turned in a predictable yet unwanted direction.

"Bristow informed me that my cousins called this morning and that you and Aunt Letitia sat with them."

"Cyclops joined us for a while too," I said. "It was quite an entertainment watching him trying to avoid Charity. She doesn't give up easily."

"I'm not interested in hearing about Cyclops," he said darkly. "I want to know why my cousins called."

"Ask your aunt. I'd prefer not to discuss it."

"I'm avoiding her at the moment, as I'm avoiding the rest of my family. They have nothing to say that I wish to hear."

"Then you won't want to know why they visited."

He regarded me a moment. "Did they say anything to upset you?"

I crossed my arms, determined not to speak about it. Unless the situation changed, there was no point. I would only get more upset, and I was already too close to tears.

"India," he purred, "nothing they say can convince me to marry anyone but you."

My throat tightened. I turned to the window.

"Not even if my life depended upon it."

And what if *her* life depended on it, I wanted to say but did not. Patience's *life* may not depend on her marrying Matt, but her future certainly did, and that of her sisters. And as far as everyone else was concerned, I was the only thing standing in the way of them marrying.

That was a rather sobering thought.

"India—"

"Let's concentrate on the task at hand," I said. "Nothing good will come of discussing anything else."

He sighed and sat back. "As long as you know my feelings on the matter."

"I do."

We rounded a sharp corner and I suddenly found myself

face to face with him, his hands planted on the seat on either side of me. He brushed his lips to mine then withdrew and gave me one of his boyish smiles.

"My apologies," he said, sitting down opposite again. "I lost my balance."

The corner would have seen him move to the side, not forward. But his smiles and the twinkle momentarily brightening his tired eyes had me smiling too.

"That's better," he said. "I like it when you blush for me."

"It's hot in here."

His smile turned wicked. "It certainly is."

Fortunately—or perhaps unfortunately—the drive to Oxford Street was short. We could have walked but the coach was ready from Matt's earlier outing and a constant drizzling rain made walks unpleasant. We had to pay Abigail Pilcher's supervisor again before he'd let her speak to us outside the workroom. We didn't retreat outside the shop, due to the rain, but stood in the stairwell. The hum of the sewing machines provided a backdrop to our discussion but wasn't so noisy that we needed to raise our voices.

"We have reason to believe there is a magician at the convent," Matt told her. "Did you know of another there other than yourself?"

She crossed her arms, not as a show of defiance but to hug herself. "No."

"A wood magician," I added.

She shook her head.

"You never felt magical heat in any of the crucifixes?" I asked.

Another shake of her head. "It would be madness to work magic in the convent. Are you sure you felt its heat, Miss Steele?"

"I didn't feel anything. It was simply a theory."

"Then your theory is wrong. I never felt magic there, and

only a fool would use it in a place where magicians would be called the devil's agent and worse."

We thanked her and headed back outside to our waiting carriage. "Do you think she's lying?" I asked.

"Do you?"

"No. Yes." I sighed as I climbed into the coach. "I'm not sure."

"I think she was holding something back from us. The question is, why?" He hesitated before giving orders to the coachman to drive to St. Mary's church in Chelsea.

"You want to speak to Father Antonio again?" I asked as he settled on the opposite seat.

"I want to ask him if he believes in magic."

I tilted my head to the side. "You think he's the magician? Why?"

"If Abigail is holding something back from us, it could be because she's protecting the magician. And who does, or did, she care about?"

"Father Antonio? Do you think she still cares for him, even now?"

"I don't know, but she cared enough once to be with him, and he is the father of her son. She might not love him, but she might not want his name associated with magic, either. It could ruin him."

"I see. Perhaps you're right. It's certainly worth investigating."

Matt stifled a yawn and his eyelids drooped.

"Use your watch," I said, closing the curtains. "Then rest for a few minutes while we drive."

To my surprise, he obeyed without a grumble. His easy acquiescence only proved how tired he was.

I watched him as he rested, his face slackening with every passing second until he fell asleep. Deep purple veins webbed dark eyelids, while the rest of his face sported the pallor of long illness. We shouldn't have left the house so soon after he returned home from his mysterious outing. I resolved to keep the conversation with Father Antonio short and get Matt home as soon as possible.

Fortunately, Father Antonio was in the rectory preparing his sermon for Sunday. He was not pleased to see us but forced a smile for the sake of politeness.

"I'll have my housekeeper bring tea," he said.

"We're not staying for tea," I said. "We only have one or two quick questions, and we'd be grateful if you answered them honestly."

Matt frowned at me and arched a brow in question.

"We're busy," I told him and the priest.

"Yes, of course," Father Antonio said. "I'll answer as honestly as I can, naturally, but I don't know anything of importance to you."

Matt gave a small grunt and pressed his fingertips to his heart. His face turned even paler.

"Matt?" I said. "Was is it?"

"Nothing." He lowered his hand to his side. "I'm fine."

"Do you require smelling salts?" the priest asked.

Matt waved him away and gave a reassuring smile. It did not reassure me. I watched him closely. His lips remained white, pinched, as if he were in pain. Did he need his watch again? Why the pain this time and not mere tiredness? I didn't like it.

"We should go," I said.

He grabbed my hand. "We have questions for Father Antonio."

"Then please sit," Father Antonio said.

Matt sat then frowned at me until I sat too. I clutched my reticule in my lap, prepared to leap up at any moment to extract his watch from its hidden pocket and place it in his hand. I didn't care if Father Antonio saw.

"Who made the crucifix in the meeting hall behind the school?" Matt asked.

The priest blinked at him. "I'm not sure. Why?"

"Was it you?"

"No. Mr. Glass, why do you ask such an odd question?"

"Was it one of the nuns?"

"I don't know. It's been there for years. Since before my time."

"The building isn't more than a few years old and you were here twenty-seven years ago at least," Matt said. "So who made it?"

"I told you, I don't know. The building was built and someone put it in there shortly after. That's all I know. I ask again, why?"

Matt's fingers, resting on his knee, curled up. His eyelids fluttered closed then reopened. "What do you know of magic?"

The priest blanched. "Only what has been printed in the newspapers in recent days. I don't believe it, of course. Utter nonsense."

I couldn't detect a lie but I was somewhat distracted by Matt and not entirely focused on the priest.

"Why are you asking such an absurd question? Surely you don't believe in magic, Mr. Glass. You're an educated, intelligent man. Magic is…is childish fantasy. Now, if you'll excuse me, I have work to do."

Matt scrubbed his jaw and sucked in a sharp breath. He let it out slowly.

"Matt?" I asked. "Your watch?"

He shook his head. "Father Antonio, you must know something about Mother Alfreda's disappearance and that of the babies. *Someone* here must know."

The priest clasped his hands between his knees. "This is harassment. I thought the commissioner was going to speak to you."

"He did," I said. "But he knows it's important to get to the bottom of this mystery. Now, please answer Mr. Glass's questions. What do you know?"

Father Antonio shook his head. "I have nothing to say."

"Is that so?" I snapped. "Because you know nothing or because you're not willing to tell us anything?"

"I beg your pardon! Miss Steele, Mr. Glass, I'm going to have to ask you to leave." He stood and indicated the door.

Matt drew in another sharp breath and both hands formed fists. The pain had returned. We needed to leave—and quickly.

"Matt," I said again. "Let's go."

"Not yet." He uncurled his fists.

Well, if he wouldn't leave without answers, it was vital we got some without delay. I could think of only one way to do that. "Father," I said, "has anyone confessed to the murder of Mother Alfreda?"

"Murder!"

"Yes."

"I wasn't expecting you to be so forthright, India," Matt muttered.

"We have no time for finesse. Well, Father? Has someone confessed to you?"

Father Antonio sat heavily. "Confessions are confidential," he said flatly. "I won't be breaking that trust."

That was tantamount to a yes in my book. In that case, I had no choice but to use the last remaining weapon available to me. "Very well," I said. "If you do not tell us what was confessed to you about the disappearances of the babies and Mother Alfreda, then we will write to your bishop and tell him about your indiscretions with Abigail Pilcher when she was a nun here. Do you understand what I'm saying?" I felt a little filthy for blackmailing him, but I had no choice. Matt wanted answers before leaving and this was the fastest way to get them. Indeed, it was the only way.

Matt did not protest so I suspected he agreed.

"That is...! You cannot...!" Father Antonio spluttered something incoherent and sank further into the chair. "You are unchristian and unfeeling," he said sulkily.

"And you are the father of a twenty-seven year old man," I said. "He's doing well for himself. Do you ever wonder what became of him?"

His face flushed and he looked away.

"Just tell us what you know," I urged him.

"I cannot. I broke one vow when Abigail and I—" He cut himself off. "I cannot break another, after all these years. I will not. But I will tell you something that I observed at the time. Telling you doesn't break any rules of the confessional."

"What is it?" I asked on a rushed breath.

Matt leaned forward, looking a little healthier again, thankfully.

"I happened to be in the convent's grounds the night Mother Alfreda disappeared." Father Antonio blushed and I suspected his reason for being on convent property was to meet Abigail in secret. "I was in the small woods at the back when I saw one of the sisters passing by. She headed into the woods carrying a spade and a box." He indicated the approximate size with his hands, two feet by two. "She emerged some time later without the box. I was curious so went looking for it but couldn't find it."

"Who was the nun?" I asked.

"I didn't see her face."

"Did you see any freshly turned earth when you investigated?" Matt asked.

"No, but it was dark. I never did go back to search in the daylight."

"Can you show us where in the woods?" I asked.

"No, I will not. The woods are still there, however some of it has been cleared away to allow the school children more space. I advise you not to take it upon yourselves to look around. Someone may grow suspicious."

I met Matt's gaze and tried not to show my triumph. Father Antonio's concern meant that the person he suspected of carrying the box—the person who'd confessed to being involved in Mother Alfreda's disappearance—still lived at the convent.

"Thank you, Father," Matt said, rising. "We're sorry to have put you into this position."

"But it was necessary to save a life," I finished.

Father Antonio didn't look as if he believed me. I didn't care. We had something to go on with, only I wasn't sure what to do with the new information and said so to Matt on the way home.

"We have to investigate the woods, of course," he said.

"We can't dig up the entire area without arousing suspicion."

"We have to try. We'll make a start tonight. Between Duke, Cyclops and myself we should cover a large part."

"You are not going anywhere. You need your rest."

"Don't, India."

"What happened in there? You looked as if you were in pain."

He lifted one shoulder. "It's gone now."

"But—"

"I'm fine. Don't mention it to the others. I don't want to worry them."

"If you're fine, there's no need for them to worry, is there?"

He scowled but offered no retort and we traveled in silence back to Mayfair. He took himself off to his room without me prompting, and he remained there for the rest of the afternoon.

I'd forgotten that the others were at the convent, helping with repairs and observing the goings on. Unfortunately, they had nothing to report by the time they came home in the late afternoon. They found me playing cards with Miss Glass in the sitting room. We'd hardly spoken, which was perhaps safer than touching on sensitive topics. Nevertheless, I was glad when Willie, Duke and Cyclops walked in.

"Did you learn anything?" I asked.

Willie threw herself into a chair and sighed. "Only that I hate hammering nails."

"What did you two find out?" Cyclops asked.

I told them what Father Antonio had told us but not how we'd extracted the information. I still felt uncomfortable about our methods.

"Where's Matt?" Willie asked.

"Resting."

"He's been resting for a long time," Miss Glass said, glancing at the clock.

My heart tripped. He had been resting longer than usual. "I'll see how he is," I said as calmly as I could. "And I'll ask Bristow to bring tea."

I left and fortunately no one followed. I didn't want to alarm them. Not yet. I raced to Matt's room and knocked lightly. No answer. With my heart in my throat, I pushed open the door and peered inside. He lay on top of the bed covers on his back, his eyes closed. His chest didn't move.

Oh god.

I touched his face with a shaking hand.

He was warm. Alive. Thank God. Now that I was closer, I could see his chest rise and fall, albeit slowly.

His eyes suddenly opened and I fell back. He caught my hand, steadying me, trapping me at his side. "India," he murmured, drawing my hand to his lips. "India."

CHAPTER 10

I tugged my hand free and backed away from the bed. "You've slept a long time," I said. "I grew worried."

Matt sat up and rubbed his eyes. His hair was delightfully rumpled and his eyes, when he withdrew his hands, still sported the haze of sleep. It took a great deal of control not to reach out and envelope him in my arms.

"What time is it?" he asked.

"Almost six."

"Already?" He scooted off the bed and clasped my face in his hands before I knew what was happening. He planted a kiss on my forehead. "Thank you for checking on me." He let me go and sat on the bed to put on his shoes. He seemed quite unaffected by the little kiss while my nerves sang. It was grossly unfair.

"How do you feel?" I asked.

"Fine."

"Has the pain returned?"

"I feel fine, India." I heard the abruptness in his voice loud and clear. It was my cue to exit.

"I'm sorry I woke you," I said. "We're all in the sitting room."

"India, wait." He joined me at the door and we left together. "I'm sorry I snapped. I don't like to be fussed over."

"I'm concerned, Matt, not fussing. It doesn't help that you won't discuss it with me or allow me to tell the others."

"There's nothing to discuss. I had a pain in my chest, but it went away. Nothing came of it. The long rest did me good. I feel fitter than I have in some time."

I eyed him closely, trying to detect if that were a lie or not, but he noticed and broke into a grin. "Be truthful, India, you were really hoping to catch me without my shirt. That's why you barged into my room."

"I didn't barge in," I said, striding off down the corridor. "I knocked first. And I know what you're trying to do, Matt. You're trying to distract me from inquiring about your health."

Miss Glass met us on her way up the stairs and looked relieved to see Matt. "I thought I should check on you," she said. "But I see India already has."

Matt placed a hand on my lower back and steered me down the stairs alongside his aunt. "She takes good care of me," he said.

"India, can you help me with something, please?"

I silently groaned but allowed Matt to go on ahead of us.

"India, you mustn't encourage him," Miss Glass hissed. "It's not appropriate for you to enter his room alone, now that he and Patience are almost engaged."

There were a thousand things I could have said in response but I chose the most benign one. I did not want to enter into awkward discussions with her. "You're right. It was highly inappropriate. I'll only enter his room if his life is in danger, from now on."

She hooked my arm with hers. "Thank you, India. You're such a good, agreeable sort."

Sometimes I wished I wasn't.

We caught up to Matt in the sitting room where he stood reading a newspaper. From the looks on the faces of the others, I knew it contained something I wouldn't like.

"It's this week's edition of *The Weekly Gazette*," Duke said. "Barratt's latest article is in it."

Matt lowered the paper so I could read too. The article contained no surprises, thankfully. It was a quarter page feature, and it mostly outlined the good work magicians could do when allowed to, such as building sturdy houses, creating beautiful and functional maps, and generally being useful yet ordinary members of society. The word "ordinary" had been stressed with bold type, and Oscar had gone on to say that magicians could be a friend or neighbor but suppress their true nature to go about their daily lives undetected. If they did not, the craft guilds would refuse membership to protect non-magician members. I thought it a tempered article. He could have said the guilds persecuted magicians.

Then I reached the final paragraph. Oscar wrote that magic was fleeting, but it could be extended by combining one magician's magic with that of a timepiece magician. He'd posed it as a theory only and had not expanded on the potential. Even so, he gave away too much for my liking. Where Force's article in *The City Review* had merely alluded to the possibility of extending magic through the experiment on Wilson Sweet, Barratt's article had left nothing open to interpretation.

"Damn it." Matt slapped the newspaper onto a table. "Damn Barratt."

"He always pushes the boundary," Cyclops said with a shake of his head.

"It's his job," Willie said. "He wouldn't be a good reporter if he didn't stir things up."

"Nonsense," Miss Glass said, picking up the paper. "There's no reason he can't write nice, sensible things that don't ruffle feathers. I'd read it. Many people would. There's no need to cause trouble like this." She dropped the paper back onto the table. "No need at all."

Willie rolled her eyes but wisely kept her mouth shut.

"So what do we do about it?" Duke asked. "Confront him? Warn him not to do it again?"

"Ask him to write a retraction," Cyclops added.

Willie leaned forward where she sat, legs apart like a man. "It's too late. The horse has bolted. We need to stop him from writing anything more, and the only way to do that is to threaten him. Make him afraid." She tapped her chest. "Let me do it. I'm the only one with the stomach for it."

"The only one fool enough," Duke muttered.

"Willie," Miss Glass snapped. "Knees together. You're not a cowboy, as much as you dress and act like one. And no one will threaten anyone with weapons. There are non-violent methods to explore first. I propose we find out what secrets he has to hide then threaten to tell his loved ones. If we can't find anything of a salacious nature, we can always make something up. Journalists do that all the time. It's entirely justified to give him a taste of his own medicine."

Everyone stared at her. Then Willie smiled. "I like you more and more, Letty."

"Since Oscar doesn't seem to have any loved ones, there's very little we can do," I told them. "He doesn't even seem like he particularly cares for his brother. We go on as we have been and find Phineas Millroy. That's our priority. This," I indicated the newspaper. "This is not important right now."

"I beg to differ," Matt said. "Barratt may not have mentioned you, but between Force's article and this, you've been exposed as a timepiece magician with the power to extend magic. Every magician who has ever wanted their magic to last will seek you out now. Where Force's article made them wonder, Barratt's has banished all doubts."

"Not *all* of them. Besides, complete strangers won't know

where to find me. And if they do find me, I'll simply send them on their way."

He regarded me darkly but left the matter alone. I suspected he had more to say, but I was glad he kept quiet. There was already too much tension between us, of all kinds.

Over dinner, we discussed plans to return to the convent that night. Matt refused to stay home and rest. I didn't tell anyone that I planned on going too. I would wait for Miss Glass to retire before doing so.

Lord Rycroft visited shortly after we removed ourselves from the dining room and asked to see Matt alone. He even asked his sister to leave. Matt did not protest, and he retired to the smoking room with his uncle.

I spent a restless fifteen minutes in the drawing room, waiting for Lord Rycroft to leave. When I heard movement in the entrance hall, I peered out to see. Bristow handed him his hat and coat. Matt was nowhere to be seen.

Lord Rycroft turned, catching me watching him. A satisfied smile touched his lips, sending an icy shiver down my spine. He slapped his hat on his head, sending a waft of cigar smoke my way. "Farewell, Miss Steele. I know it may not seem it right now, but I do wish you well in your future. I hope Mr. Barratt's latest article doesn't cause you too many difficulties."

I stared at the closed door for some time after he left. Farewell? Not good evening or good day? And why was he wishing me well? It sounded like he expected never to see me again.

Matt emerged from the smoking room only to stop upon seeing me. All the benefits of his long rest had disappeared, leaving him looking haggard and drawn again. His gaze slid to the front door. "What did he say to you?" he asked.

"Farewell. What did he say to *you*?"

He hesitated then said, "He'd seen Barratt's article in this evening's paper and wanted to know if you are a time magician. I told him it was none of his business."

That wasn't all. It couldn't be all. Lord Rycroft's smile implied he'd won a game and Matt's forlorn expression told me he'd lost. "What else did he say?"

"Nothing." He pushed past me and plucked his hat off the hat stand.

"Where are you going?"

"Out."

"Out where?"

"For a walk. I need some fresh air." He didn't look at me as he spoke. He seemed distracted, distant, and I knew him to be lost in thought. A thinking Matt was better than a forlorn Matt, but it still worried me. What *had* his uncle said to him?

"Someone should go with you. I'll fetch Cyclops—"

"I want to be alone." He left before I had a chance to protest again.

At least my worries had company.

"Why didn't you fetch us, India?" Willie wailed after I informed her and the others of Matt's movements. She paced across the drawing room floor, drew back the curtain to look through the window, then continued her pacing. "He's been gone an age."

"Thirty minutes is not an age," I said. "And I didn't fetch you because he didn't give me a chance. He wanted to be alone."

"So he could forget to use his watch!" She threw her hands in the air and continued her pacing.

"He won't forget. He doesn't forget."

"But sometimes he doesn't use it in time," Duke said. "Like when he's being attacked."

"No will attack him," Cyclops said. "Can you both shut your traps? You're frightening the ladies."

Miss Glass did look rather frightened. She sat like a small

statue dressed in black lace. The last time I'd seen her so still, her mind wandered into the past where she felt safer.

"What did my rotten brother say to him?" she asked, proving she was still in the here and now.

"I don't know," I said. "But Lord Rycroft looked...triumphant."

Willie stilled. "Surely not," she whispered, her gaze boring into me. "Surely Matt didn't agree to marry Patience."

My heart plunged. I'd been thinking it too, but I hadn't allowed myself to fully explore the notion. Yet Willie must be right. What else could Lord Rycroft be triumphant about?

More importantly, why did Matt look so troubled?

"That ain't it," Duke said with a shake of his head. "Nope. Not a chance. Matt wouldn't agree to it, no matter what." He got up to pour himself a brandy at the sideboard. He drank the contents of the tumbler then refilled it.

I felt sick.

We convinced Miss Glass to retire at ten. She was half asleep on the sofa, waiting up for Matt to return. My reassurance that he would be fine soothed her enough and she took herself off, stifling her yawn.

The rest of us could not be so easily convinced. By the time the clock struck eleven, I took over pacing from Willie. My jittery nerves wouldn't allow me to sit still any longer. Something must have happened to Matt for him to be away so long. He wouldn't be so cruel as to leave us worrying for hours.

"I can't wait here all night doing nothing," Cyclops said, getting to his feet. "I'm going to look for him."

"Me too." Willie followed him out, Duke at her heels.

I refused to be left behind and asked them to wait while I fetched a coat. I was half way up the stairs when the front door opened and Matt walked in. Indeed, he didn't so much as walk in, but rather stumbled across the threshold. He righted himself before he fell and shoved his hat into Duke's chest.

"Where's Bristow?" Matt asked, frowning at Duke. "And why are you all standing here?"

"We were about to look for you." Duke thrust Matt's hat onto the hook on the hat stand as if he were a medieval warrior ramming an enemy's head onto a spike.

"No need. I'm here. Thank God India's not with you. I don't want to face her tonight."

I cleared my throat and descended the stairs.

"Oh." He plastered on a smile. "What a lovely surprise, India. It's always good to see you."

"Where have you been?" I asked, ever so casually.

Cyclops sniffed. "Drinking's my guess."

"Idiot," Willie snapped. "You know you shouldn't drink more than one, Matt."

"I can hold my liquor," Matt protested. "I'll prove it." He proceeded to walk in a straight line to the base of the staircase where I stood. He took one look at me and tucked his hands behind his back. "Hell," he said. "I was hoping you'd be in bed by now."

"And miss the joy of you walking in straight lines?"

He grunted. "Go on, then. Lecture me for being out drinking." He sighed, half closing his eyes. "I deserve it."

Part of me wanted to walk him up the stairs and tuck him into bed. But I knew now was my best chance of getting answers so I remained standing on the first step where I was the right height to look him in the eye.

"So why don't you want to face me?" I asked.

"Because I'm drunk."

"But you walked in a straight line."

"Not that drunk. Just drunk enough for you to disapprove."

"Have I said I disapprove?"

"You don't have to." His gaze lowered to my mouth and

for one heart-stopping moment I thought he'd kiss me in front of the others. "I can see the disapproval on your lips."

"My lips?"

"They're pinched and hard. I'm considering how best to fix them."

One of the men cleared his throat, and Matt seemed to recall that we weren't alone. He squared his shoulders.

"Excuse me, India. I should freshen up before we go to the convent."

"I'm not sure you should come," I said.

He grunted. "Try and stop me." He took a step to the side and paused, as if he expected me to move and block his way. When he realized I was staying put, he climbed the stairs.

"Well," I said to the others after he'd vanished from sight. "I don't know about you three, but I need something to fortify my nerves before we sneak onto convent grounds. Who wants a brandy?"

* * *

MATT SLEPT for an hour and I must have dozed off on the sofa because I opened my eyes to see him talking quietly to Cyclops and Duke by the fireplace. Willie sprawled in an armchair, her head tipped back and her mouth open. She snored loudly.

"Ready?" I asked the men. It was a little after midnight, the perfect time to head to the convent where the nuns kept early hours. "We need digging equipment, black clothing and something to light our way."

Matt opened his mouth.

"Do not order me to stay behind," I told him before he could speak.

"I wasn't going to. I was about to suggest you borrow some trousers from Willie but changed my mind."

"You're right to change it," I said. "Willie's smaller than me and her trousers wouldn't fit."

"That's not why I changed my mind," he said, voice husky.

I was about to ask him what he meant, but he began giving orders to Duke and Cyclops. Willie awoke and dazedly asked what we were doing.

"Going to the convent," I said. "If you hadn't woken up we would have left you behind."

"Damned lucky you didn't," she growled. "I'm as important to this mission as you are, India. Maybe more, since you can't wield a shovel on account of you being all delicate."

"Thank you, Willie, you are sweet. I've never been called delicate before."

A short time later I sat in the coach with Cyclops and Duke. Matt insisted on driving and Willie insisted on sitting beside him. I knew she wanted to be near him to keep an eye on him, and I suspected he drove so he didn't have to sit with me and risk me interrogating him about the reason for his uncle's visit.

I wasn't sure if he ought to drive so soon after admitting to being drunk, but the horses were well behaved enough that they wouldn't follow any silly orders he gave them, and Willie would be there if he nodded off. And anyway, he seemed quite sober in the few minutes we were together in the stables preparing the coach. He did an excellent job of avoiding me and seemed in control of the situation and himself. The others obeyed his commands when he gave them and didn't seem in the least concerned that he wanted to drive.

We'd brought the stable boy with us and he remained with the horses and coach one street back from the convent. It was a middle class area so he shouldn't be troubled. Even so, Matt told him to whistle if he needed us.

We each carried a shovel, pick or small trowel to the

convent gate, only to find it locked. I swore under my breath, earning a wide-eyed stare from Willie.

"Wash your mouth out, India," she hissed. "This here's a house of God."

"Sorry," I muttered. "I'm having a bad day."

Matt used a pair of slender metal tools to unlock the gate. He held it open for each of us to slip through. While the others walked ahead, I remained behind with Matt as he shut the gate.

"What did your uncle want?" I asked, tackling the question that had been on my mind head-on. I could no longer avoid it, it occupied my entire waking moments, and so it simply blurted out.

"Don't ask me that, India," he said, his voice a low rumble.

I wished it wasn't so dark so I could see his face. But the moon hid behind clouds and we'd shuttered our lanterns. "It was about you marrying Patience, wasn't it?"

He quickened his pace.

"He found a way to convince you to do it, didn't he?"

The silence was so profound it was a tangible thing. It blanketed us as we followed the others to the rear of the convent. "I'll find a way out," he finally said.

My pace slowed. My heart plunged to my stomach, leaving a hole in my chest. I hadn't expected to feel so empty upon hearing him admit it. Then again, I hadn't truly expected him to tell me his uncle was forcing his hand and that he had gone along with it.

Matt stopped when he realized I'd fallen behind. He slung the pick over his shoulder and held out his free hand to me. I took it without a word and together we headed past the convent outbuildings for the small copse of trees that Father Antonio had referred to as woods.

I glanced back at the hulking form of the convent with its chimneys reaching into the inky sky from the razor sharp spine of its roofline. No lights shone, and the dark windows reflected nothing. Yet I felt like we were being watched. I tightened my grip on Matt's hand and passed through the thicket into the trees.

It was even darker in the woods but a dim light dancing between branches ahead gave me something to aim for. We soon caught up to Willie, Duke and Cyclops in a clearing barely large enough for all of us to stand in.

Duke leaned on his shovel, the lamp at his feet. "What about here?" he whispered.

Willie didn't wait for an answer. She thrust her shovel into the bed of leaves and began to dig.

"It's as good a place as any," Matt said, swinging his pick into the ground.

I knelt at the clearing's edge and cleared away the decaying matt of leaves then pushed the gardening trowel into the soft earth. After what I gauged to be thirty minutes, an ache settled into my hand yet I'd made little progress. I looked up, expecting to see much more progress from the others, but despite a few strategically placed holes, they had covered very little ground.

We worked silently for an hour more before Willie flopped onto the ground with a sigh. She leaned back against a tree and stretched out her legs. "My back is broken," she moaned.

"I'd offer to massage it if my shoulder didn't feel like a knife were stabbing it," Duke said, carefully lowering himself to sit next to her.

Cyclops and Matt worked a little longer before Matt declared the task complete. "Unless the box was buried very deep, it's not in this clearing."

"Let's try somewhere else," Cyclops said.

Matt wiped his brow with the back of his hand. "We'll rest here for a little first. India, are you all right? You're rubbing your hand."

"I'm fine," I said, getting to my feet. "Which direction shall we head in?"

We decided to check the extent of the woods before choosing our next location. The woods were bigger than I first thought. Although not wide, the copse of trees stretched deep into the property.

Despite the size, we did not come across another clearing as large as the first. Certainly nothing large enough for all of us to dig without hitting one another with shovels. We had to split up, yet we only had one lamp.

"We'll take it in turns," Matt said. "We each dig in short stints, that way we won't get as tired."

"Except for India," Willie said. "On account of her being delicate."

"Do stop saying that, Willie," I said on a sigh. "I can wield a shovel as easily as you can."

She handed me her shovel. "Go on then."

Digging holes with shovels was more difficult than it looked, and I struggled to make a good dent in the ground. Willie leaned against a tree, her arms crossed, and made scoffing noises at every pathetic pile of soil I dug up. Eventually she gave up and took the shovel off me.

For a small figure, she was surprisingly strong, and the hole I'd begun grew larger quite quickly. I felt useless and slunk to the shadowy edge of the lamplight. As I watched the others take turns, my uselessness became hopelessness. We wouldn't find the box. Father Antonio had seen someone walk into the woods with it years ago. The person who did so could have retrieved it the following night, or any other night in the last twenty-seven years. Even if they'd left it, we could spend every night for the next month and we wouldn't cover every inch of the woods. Then there was the very real possibility that the box contained no evidence relating to the disappearances of the Mother Alfreda or the babies. We were clutching at straws, and those straws were small indeed.

I sat on a fallen log and blinked back my tears. Despite the cool air, I felt warm from the exercise of digging, but over the next few minutes, the warmth began to fade. That is, it faded in all parts of my body except for a small section of my chest. The section beneath my watch. I wore it on a chain as a necklace, knowing I would not carry my reticule tonight, but wanting to have the watch close.

I fished it out from where it nestled against my skin beneath my clothing, and removed my glove. The watch was definitely warm, and not from my own body heat. It was magical warmth.

"India, what are you doing?" Matt asked.

"My watch is warm."

He suddenly straightened and took up the pick as if it were a weapon. He scrutinized the edge of the small clearing. "Stop digging," he hissed at Willie.

"Someone there?" Duke whispered.

"The watch could be warning India of imminent danger," Matt whispered back without taking his gaze from the shadows.

"I don't think it's a warning," I said. "It *chimes* when there is danger."

Matt did not lower the pick, but I could see his shoulders relax a little.

Cyclops sat on the log beside me. "What do you think it means then?"

"I think it's responding to other magic."

"It can feel magic heat like you can feel it?"

I placed my palm on the log. Nothing. No magic warmth, just rough bark and a clump of damp moss. I leaned down and touched the leaf litter.

There. I felt it. A small wave of heat pulsed through me, faint but definite.

"India?" Cyclops murmured.

Matt crouched before me. "Can you feel magic heat?"

"Very faintly." I met his gaze and smiled, not quite believing what I could feel. Not really grasping the significance of it. But I did know it was important. It had to be. Our mystery was tied up with magic and magic had been performed in this area.

No. Not performed. If someone had stood here and infused magic into whatever they held, the magic would leave with that item. So the item itself was still here, buried in the ground. The spell could have been spoken anywhere.

"Whatever was in that box has had magic performed on it," I told them. "And it's buried somewhere nearby. Not in this spot," I said when Willie went to thrust her shovel into the ground near my feet. "It's too faint to be right here."

I got down on my knees and pressed both hands to the earth. I felt outward from the warm spot, changing direction whenever the dirt and leaf matter cooled. I crawled along the warm trail, my excitement growing as the warmth increased. My senses heightened, tuning in to the earth beneath me. Something small rustled near my fingers then scurried off. An insect buzzed near my ear before flying to a nearby bush where it rested, watching me. Behind me was utter silence.

The warmth intensified then, no matter which direction I advanced, it weakened. I sat back on my haunches. "Here," I said, tapping the ground. "Dig here."

Willie pushed in her shovel. Cyclops joined her. Duke had got hold of my gardening trowel and dug out small clumps of dirt. Matt crouched beside me and together we watched on.

Thud. Cyclops's shovel hit something hard. Cyclops and Willie cast aside their shovels and joined us on their knees. We used our hands to dig out the earth while Duke used the trowel.

Slowly the box revealed itself. The more of it we exposed, the more intense the heat became. It shocked me at first, so fierce was it, and I stopped digging. I'd felt magic heat before, but never that strong. My fingers tingled as if a little burned and I wasn't sure I wanted to touch the box again. It reminded me of when Chronos had first touched a clock I'd worked on. He'd been surprised by the heat and retracted his hand quickly.

"Whatever magic is inside that box is strong," I told them. "I think the magician who put it there must have been powerful."

"Something made of silk," Matt said between breaths, "from Abigail Pilcher."

It took some time to dig around the box's sides before it could be wrenched free from its grave. Cyclops hauled it out and placed the box near me. It was indeed approximately two feet by two, as Father Antonio had told us, and made of wood. It was in good condition, considering it had been in the ground as long as it had. Even so, the contents might be damaged from time and moisture.

"It's not locked," Duke said, trying to lift the lid. "But I can't open it. The hinges have rusted."

"Let me try." Cyclops's fingers were like rods of iron but it took him several attempts to pry the lid open. The hinge complained but eventually gave way, and Cyclops pushed the lid back as far as it would go.

Inside were some papers, a little aged but not terribly. Matt pulled them out.

"No silk," I said, peering into the now empty box. "How strange."

But no one heard me. They crowded around Matt. Willie held the lamp so they could read. She gasped.

"What is it?" I asked, trying to peer at the paper. "A letter?"

"Records," Matt said, his voice hoarse. "From the convent. Two sets. One is about Phineas Millroy's arrival here and who brought him. The second references a different baby."

He handed one of the papers to me and I scanned the tight, neat scrawl. The brief account listed Phineas's name at the top, his date of birth and the date of his arrival. A woman's name was listed as bringing him to the convent. I didn't recognize it and wondered if it was Lady Buckland's name, without the title. She was noted as being a friend to the baby's mother. There was no information about who adopted him.

"Who's the other record for?" I asked, indicating the second sheet of paper.

"James John Smith," Matt said. "His date of birth, date of arrival, and who brought him in. That's it."

Willie snatched the papers off him and read through them. She turned the pages over several times, held them to the light, and eventually threw them into the box in disgust.

"God damned waste of time," she said, forgetting her rule of not swearing on holy land.

Duke pushed to his feet and threw the trowel at a tree trunk.

"Not necessarily," Matt said. "India felt magic, so we know Abigail Pilcher infused some silk with magic then perhaps placed those silks inside the box. She probably kept scraps in it and took them out, replacing them with these records. What happened to the magical silk is irrelevant. What is relevant is that this box was either in her possession or contained something precious to her. I'd wager *she* placed these records in there and buried the box."

"She lied to you," Willie said. "She goddamn lied when she told you she don't know what happened to Phineas."

"No. You're wrong." I pointed at the box, not willing to touch it yet. "The magic I felt did not come from something no longer inside. It came from the box itself. It's excellently made and water tight too. These papers are in good condition."

I was met with four frowns. "You mean," Matt said slowly, "that box was made by a magician."

I nodded. "One that infused their magic into the wood. The same magician who caused the wooden cross to fall off the wall and nearly crush me."

$\mathcal{I}$ hoped Matt got more sleep than I did in the few hours of nighttime remaining after we returned home. I tossed and turned, considering what our find meant. While there were a number of possibilities, at least we had a clear focus now—find the woodworking magician.

There was also another issue playing on my mind and banishing much-needed sleep—Matt being forced to marry Patience. What could his uncle possibly have said to back Matt into a corner he couldn't find a way out of?

I managed to fall asleep around dawn, but the house still felt quiet when I awoke. It was only half-past eight, so I spent some time taking my watch apart and putting it back together. It wasn't enough to soothe my nerves, however, so I went in search of a clock. I found Willie, Duke and Cyclops in the dining room, already eating breakfast.

"Sleep soundly?" Cyclops asked.

"Not at all." I poured a cup of coffee and placed a piece of toast on my plate. "Did you three come to a conclusion about the box?"

"Aye." Duke got up and closed the door. "We should ask

the Mother Superior if someone at the convent is good with wood."

"Or we show her the box and ask who made it," Willie countered. "If we ask a general question, we might not get the answer we want. What if the magician is hiding their magical ability by making inferior quality things? No, we ask about the box direct and we'll get a direct answer."

Duke shook his head. "She'll get suspicious and won't tell us nothing."

"She don't know who the magician is!"

"We don't know that. She might."

Cyclops picked up his cup and blew on the steaming contents. "They've been like this ever since they got here. I was enjoying a quiet breakfast alone until they arrived."

"What do you think, India?" Duke asked.

"I don't think we should ask the mother superior anything," I said.

"You want to ask one of the other nuns? Someone who won't glare at you with those icy eyes?" He screwed up his nose. "Good idea. She scares me."

"I don't think we should ask any of the nuns, either. There's a chance they'll all close up to protect the woodwork magician, if they realize why we're asking. I have a better idea, but let's wait for Matt to join us before we discuss it."

They grumbled a little but agreed. We lingered in the dining room for a good hour, but Matt did not join us. Willie didn't hide her frustration at having to wait. She huffed, drummed her fingers on the table, and drank copious amounts of tea. Cyclops merely ate, and ate, and ate. There would probably be nothing left for Matt if he didn't come down soon.

I glanced at the door, as I had been doing every minute or so. Should I worry that he wasn't up yet? Usually he would be, but we'd had a late night so it was understandable that he would sleep late

Then again, what if the pain in his chest returned? What if he needed to use his watch but slept on?

I eyed the door, willing it to open.

Willie cracked first. She pushed her chair back and rose. "I'll see if he's awake."

"Let him sleep longer," I said. "He needs it."

"It's getting on to ten. That's seven hours since we got back. That's enough sleep for him."

"Usually," I said and sipped my coffee.

She frowned. "Something you not telling us, India? Something about Matt's health?"

I sipped and considered whether to lie or not.

"You better not be keeping secrets," Duke said darkly. "Not about this."

"India?" Cyclops managed to put a threat into his tone and his one good eye, even though I considered him the gentlest of the three.

"Perhaps we should check," I said, attempting cheerfulness.

The three of them beat me to the door.

"Slow down!" I snapped. "Remain calm or you'll scare Miss Glass and the servants if we come across them. Now," I said, having gained their attention, "we'll sneak into Matt's room and *quietly* check on him."

Matt did not answer my light knock and Willie wouldn't wait. She opened the door but did not cross the threshold. She was short enough that I could see over her head. What I saw filled me with immeasurable relief. Matt was asleep, not... something worse. He'd opened the watchcase and tied it to his hand with his tie. The watch glowed softly, as did his veins. Too softly for my liking, but it was better than not at all.

I tried to signal to Willie to let him sleep, but he began to stir and opened his eyes. Then his hand whipped out and gripped Willie's arm. She gasped.

"What is it? What's wrong?" he asked, voice gravely.

"Nothing," she said. "We wanted to see if you were…"

"Dead?"

She looked away.

Matt's narrowed gaze focused on me. "What did you tell them?"

"That we're not going to ask about the box at the convent," I said breezily.

His eyes narrowed further. "That's not what I meant."

"I think we should speak with Abigail Pilcher. She has no particular loyalty to the convent and she's a magician. She might be able to tell us who the woodwork magician is. Come along, Matt, up you get and have some breakfast." I hurried out before he had a chance to harden his glare even more.

I heard voices as I descended the staircase, one of them Bristow's, the other belonging to someone I had no wish to see but decided to confront anyway.

"Good morning, Mr. Abercrombie," I said to The Watchmaker's Guild master. "This is a surprise. I didn't think we'd see you here ever again after Eddie Hardacre proved to be a fraud."

"I never trusted him." He sounded smug, as if *I* ought to be humiliated since I had once trusted Eddie. "There was something not quite right about him. Something low born in his nature that couldn't be eradicated, no matter how good the actor. Of course, I wouldn't expect someone like you to notice."

"You're correct. I didn't notice whatever it is you think distinguished his birth from yours. What I did notice, however, was his sycophantic nature. It made me glad our engagement ended, as I wanted nothing to do with him when that side emerged."

"How good of you to put your morals ahead of your future," he said slickly. "A pity you must now stoop to seeking whatever employment you can find."

I bristled but forced myself to smile. "On the contrary. I like being employed by Mr. Glass. I have independence, financial means, and companionship. I'd say I'm the envy of many women trapped in a loveless marriage. Speaking of marriage, how is Mrs. Abercrombie? Do you still live with both your mother and wife? How lucky for you to have two such strong-minded women to run your household."

His face fell, and I felt a measure of satisfaction, along with a little guilt for my biting remarks. Mr. Abercrombie's wife and mother not only bickered incessantly with each other but with him too. It was why he spent long hours at his shop or the guild hall.

"What're *you* doing here?" said Willie from the landing. She came down the stairs, flanked by Cyclops and Duke. All three of them scowled.

"He hasn't yet said," I told her.

"Is Mr. Glass in?" Mr. Abercrombie addressed Bristow, not me.

"He is unavailable at present," Bristow said. "May I leave a message, sir?"

"I'll wait. Show me to your drawing room."

"I'm afraid all the reception rooms are being cleaned, sir. I'll let Mr. Glass know you were here."

Mr. Abercrombie looked as if he'd scold Bristow for his impertinence but backed down when Cyclops, Duke and Willie stood behind the butler. None were in good humor and it didn't take a clever man to realize they would not be trifled with today.

"Please inform Mr. Glass that I'd like to have a word with him about Mr. Barratt's latest article in *The Weekly Gazette*," Mr. Abercrombie said.

"Why not have that word with me?" I asked. "Since I am, after all, the one Mr. Barratt is referring to."

"No." Mr. Abercrombie planted his hat on his head. "I want to speak to Mr. Glass himself."

"Then speak." Matt trotted down the stairs as if he was as healthy as a horse. "What is it you want, Abercrombie?"

Mr. Abercrombie shuffled a little away and presented his shoulder to me. "I want you to consider the implications of employing Miss Steele now that it's clear her magic can be used to extend the magic of others."

The nerve of him! "You are quite the despicable creature," I spat. "You make Eddie look harmless in comparison."

He simply sniffed and lifted his chin. "Do you understand my meaning, Glass?"

Matt strode past him and opened the door. "I am aware of the implications for my household. As to whom I employ, it is none of your business. Good day, Abercrombie. You're not welcome here if you wish to insult my friends, family or staff."

"Insult? No, no, no, Mr. Glass, you misunderstand. I have your best interests at heart. Your loyalty blinds you to the possibilities. Think on it. Not only will she become a target for other magicians, but she'll be considered a person of interest to the government, too. Do you think they want someone walking the streets who can potentially extend someone's life? Isn't that what her grandfather was trying to do with that doctor magician? The authorities will want her for themselves, Mr. Glass. So if I were you, I'd cut her loose and—"

Matt grabbed Abercrombie's arm so hard that Abercrombie squeaked. Matt shoved him through the door and slammed it in his face. "I'm going to have breakfast," he said, dusting off his hands. "India, will you join me?"

"I, er, that is…yes. Thank you. I could do with a strong cup of tea."

We did not speak about Abercrombie, or what he'd said, but of the box and what it meant. The brisk conversation allowed me to shut Abercrombie's words out of my mind, though only briefly. While Matt spoke to his aunt alone in her rooms before we left, and I waited for him in the entrance hall, I could think of nothing else. Abercrombie could not possibly be right. To think the government would be interested in something that I could potentially do but hadn't proven possible, was ludicrous. He was scaremongering in an attempt to alienate me from my friends and employment. It was his newest scheme to ruin me.

And it wouldn't work.

Matt took longer than I expected. After seven long minutes, he still hadn't come down. The coach waited outside, and Bristow hovered nearby to see us off. I was about to see what kept him when Mrs. Bristow, the housekeeper, emerged from the back of the house.

"Excuse me, Miss Steele," she said. "There's a man here to see you. He's waiting in the kitchen."

"To see me? Why?"

"I couldn't say, miss."

"Show him to the drawing room, Mrs. Bristow."

"The drawing room!" The Bristows exchanged glances. "But miss, he's wearing workman's boots." Poor Mrs. Bristow spoke as if workman's boots were made by the devil himself. "He can't wear them into the drawing room. They're filthy."

"I can't speak to a guest in the service area, Mrs. Bristow. This man deserves to be received in the drawing room, just like anyone else. Please show him up."

The Bristows exchanged another speaking glance then Mrs. Bristow disappeared back to the services stairs. I waited for the man with the dirty boots in the drawing room.

Peter the footman escorted in a shoeless man holding his cap in his hand. He couldn't have been more than twenty, with a mass of dark blond hair that curled around his ears and cascaded over his forehead to meet his eyebrows. He dipped his head and smiled tentatively. Peter introduced him as Mr. Bunn before standing by the door with Bristow. They must suspect the young man would run off with the silver.

"Where are your shoes, Mr. Bunn?" I asked.

"Kitchen, ma'am. The housekeeper made me take 'em off before coming upstairs. I didn't want to argue with her."

"Very wise," Bristow intoned.

"I see," I said. "How can I help you?"

"I'm a leather worker, ma'am." He cocked his head to the side and studied me to see what impact his words had.

I made sure not to bat an eye even though my heart sank. I had expected this, but not yet. The article had only been published the evening before.

"Fossett, please leave us," I said, using Peter's surname as was the proper way in the presence of company. "Bristow, you will stay." Although I was certain all the servants knew about my magic now, after reading the papers, I did not want to be the latest downstairs gossip. Bristow would be more discreet.

"You're a magician," I said when Peter closed the door behind him.

"Yes, ma'am." Mr. Bunn screwed the cap tightly in his hands.

"How did you find me?"

"A friend pours drinks at the Cross Keys on High Holborn. Your grandfather used to be a regular there, and my friend remembers when you and Mr. Glass came looking for him. Mr. Glass gave his address to my friend to send your grandfather this way. Course, he didn't know he was a magician 'til later, when he read it in the papers."

"I see. And what do you want from me, Mr. Bunn?"

"I want to start my own shoe factory. I'll make men's shoes first then introduce women's when I've got enough capital. I've experimented using my magic on the leather and it makes the shoes sturdier and last longer, but only for six months. Then they wear out, just like any other shoe." His speech became faster as he became more comfortable expressing his idea. His enthusiasm couldn't be faulted. "I wanted to ask you to use your magic to extend mine, Miss Steele."

"I'm afraid that's not possible, Mr. Bunn."

"Course it's possible. I read about it in the *Gazette*. You're a time magician, aren't you? The granddaughter of the fellow what tried to extend a doctor magician's magic?"

I rubbed my forehead. I'd been a fool to speak to this man. Next time a stranger asked to see me, I'd find out his profession first. Any craftsmen would be sent on their way without an interview.

"I'm sorry, Mr. Bunn, but you've wasted your time. I cannot do as you ask."

I nodded at Bristow and he opened the door. I was glad to see Peter waiting just outside.

"But ma'am!" Mr. Bunn advanced toward me and I stood quickly. In my panic, I skirted the sofa, putting it between him and me. He stopped and had the decency to look ashamed. "You have to try, ma'am," he went on, with a softer voice that was no less earnest. "I know you can extend my magic. I know it!"

"Bristow, will you see that Mr. Bunn is reunited with his boots in the kitchen."

Bristow and Peter took one each of Mr. Bunn's arms and marched him toward the door.

"I'll give you a share of the profits!" Mr. Bunn cried over his shoulder. "Sixty-forty! That's more than fair."

His voice grew further away as he continued making me offers to partner with him. I flopped onto the sofa with a sigh.

"India?" Cyclops came racing in, followed by Duke and Matt. "Everything all right?"

"Fine," I said, giving them a smile.

"You seem rattled," Matt said, eyeing me closely. "Who was that and what did he want?"

"He was a leather magician. He wanted me to extend his magic so he could manufacture better shoes."

He drew in a deep, measured breath. "So it has begun."

* * *

THE ENCOUNTER WITH MR. BUNN, coming so soon after Mr. Abercrombie's visit, overwhelmed me. I felt like I was being barraged by both disappointing and bad news lately. It was difficult to put on a positive front, but I was determined, for Matt's sake.

He was looking particularly unhealthy as we traveled to Abigail Pilcher's place of work. While his face was as gray and pinched as it usually was of late, there was a self-containment about the way he walked and held himself. It was as if he were holding himself together through sheer force of will. I suspected he was as determined to put on a brave face for me as I was for him.

Who would succumb first?

I felt the slight tremor in his hand as he assisted me from the coach, but did not let on how worried it made me.

We found Abigail in the workroom at Peter Robinson's. Her supervisor did not appreciate our visit so soon after the last, and Matt had to slip more coins into his palm than last time to convince him to let her speak to us. Abigail was not pleased to see us either.

"What now?" she grumbled once outside in the corridor.

"You weren't the only magician at the convent," Matt said, his charm nowhere in evidence.

A flicker passed through her eyes but she quickly schooled her features. "Why do you say that?"

"We found a wooden object on the convent grounds. It had been infused with magic."

Her gaze met mine then fluttered away. She lifted a shoulder in a shrug.

"I felt its warmth," I told her.

"So? I haven't lived there for years. A new nun might be the magician."

"This box was made years ago." There was no point telling

her that Father Antonio, her old lover, had told us he'd seen it when he'd been waiting for her one night. She might close up at the mention of him. "Who made it?" I asked.

"I don't know, and that's the truth." She tugged on a strip of old leather fastened around her neck and pulled out a small crucifix pendant from beneath her clothing. It was made of wood. "This was given to me by the reverend mother when I took my perpetual vows. When I became a full nun, after my novitiate was complete," she explained. "Touch it, Miss Steele."

I did. It was no longer than my little finger and considerably thinner, but the workmanship in the figure of Christ was exquisite. I could make out the hairs in his beard and the thorns in his crown. "It's made from a single piece of wood," I murmured. To carve such detail on a tiny canvas like this would require exceptional skill. Or magic. "It's warm," I told Matt.

"Mother Alfreda gave it to you?" he asked as Abigail tucked the crucifix away.

"Aye, but I don't know who made it. It could have been any of the nuns, or none."

"You never asked?" I said. "Weren't you curious when you felt the magic in it?"

"I wanted to forget I was a magician back then. I'd been brought up to believe it was evil, and I thought dedicating my life to God would cleanse me, cure me. It weren't until I left that I realized how wrong I'd been. So no, I didn't ask. I thought the nun who made it mad for exposing her magic like that. It was a big risk in the convent, a stupid risk. If she wasn't careful, they'd excommunicate her."

Perhaps they had. Perhaps it was Mother Alfreda herself who'd made the crosses and the box, and she'd been discovered, along with the baby magicians, and forced out of the convent in secret. Or worse.

Or perhaps she'd left of her own accord, taking the boys

with her when it became clear she couldn't live without her magic. She could have buried their records to obliterate all trace of the boys having been at the convent. She could have taken them to safety and they all lived happily ever after. I liked that notion better.

"Do they still give those crosses to the nuns?" I asked.

"I don't know. I ain't been there for twenty-seven years." She clicked her tongue and glanced over her shoulder. "I have to go. I've got work to do."

We returned to our waiting conveyance on Oxford Street. After Matt gave the coachman orders to drive to the convent, he frowned at something up ahead.

"What is it?" I asked.

He ran off without answering. I leaned as far out of the carriage as I could, clamping my hand down on my hat to stop it blowing away. Up ahead, Matt stopped then returned.

"Did you see Payne?" I asked.

He settled opposite me, wincing as he sat. "I think I saw him about to get out of a hansom, but when he spotted me, he stayed put and the cab drove off."

"So he is following us."

"I think so."

"What do we do now?"

"We go on to the convent. If he follows us, I confront him and render him unable to follow us anymore."

"I see."

He winced again and pinched the bridge of his nose. "Sorry, India, that was uncalled for. My baser instincts are getting the better of me at the moment." He did not retract his statement about rendering Payne unable to follow us, however.

Matt got his watch out, closed the curtains, and drew the magic into his body without me having to suggest it. He looked a little better afterward, not quite so tense across the shoulders, but the pallor of his skin remained the same. I didn't mention that. I didn't mention anything about his health, the use of his watch after so short a time, or any other sensitive topic that would see one or both of us becoming upset. That left only the matter at hand.

"Do you think Mother Alfreda was the magician?" I asked.

"I don't know, but I intend to find out today. Someone at the convent knows who made those crucifixes and the box, even if they don't know that person is a magician. It's time we got answers."

"I agree. I think we should ask Sister Clare. She's the one who approached us about the missing mother superior and babies. She's the only one we can be sure is not responsible for their disappearance or know who is."

Unfortunately, Sister Clare did not collect us from the sitting room. A young novice showed us to Mother Frances's office, and Sister Clare was nowhere in sight. The assistant's outer office was empty.

The mother superior greeted us cordially but coolly. "I do hope your visit has nothing to do with searching for that baby, Mr. Glass," she said. "My stance has not changed. I will not divulge personal information to you." She clasped her hands on the desk and offered what I suspected was supposed to be a conciliatory smile, but it came out strained. She looked overbearing and sour, ensconced behind a large bare desk in the austerely furnished room. Despite several flowers blooming in the garden, she did not have a single one on display. In Sister Clare's outer office, I'd counted three vases full of roses and peonies.

"Who makes the small crucifixes you give to your nuns when they take their perpetual vows?" Matt asked.

She blinked rapidly, the question clearly taking her by surprise. "The boys who attend St. Patrick's charity school. They make them in woodwork class. Why?"

"Is that where yours came from?" I asked, nodding at the heavy wooden cross around her neck. While it appeared well made, it was a simple cross, not beautifully detailed like the one worn by Abigail.

"It is."

"What about the crucifixes given to the nuns years ago?" Matt asked. "Before you became Mother Superior?"

"I don't know. It was so long ago."

"You must remember them. They were small and beautifully made."

"I do remember," she said, not bothering to hide her impatience. "I still have mine. But I cannot tell you who made them. Mother Alfreda issued them. When she left, and I became Mother Superior, Father Antonio suggested we get all crucifixes from St. Patrick's to support the charity. Is that all, Mr. Glass? If you don't mind, I have work to do. Of course, I'd be happy to discuss that donation you've been promising the sisters every time you ask them a question."

"Let's be clear," Matt said quietly. "I will not be donating until I find out what happened to Phineas Millroy. But I think you already knew that."

The mother superior's mouth worked but nothing came out. She stood and directed us to the door. "Then I'll ask you to leave without creating a scene and without speaking to anyone else."

"I can't promise that." Matt stood and held out his hand to me.

I took it but kept my gaze on the cross on the wall above the bookshelf. Like Abigail's crucifix, it was beautiful, the carved figure of Christ depicted in superb detail. I let go of Matt's hand and approached the cross.

"What are you doing, Miss Steele?" the mother superior asked.

"It's crooked. Let me straighten it for you." I reached up and touched the wood. It was warm.

My blood throbbed in response. I opened my reticule and pulled out my watch. It gently pulsed too.

"India?" Matt said quietly.

I turned to face him, but I did not have to say anything. He must have read my expression because he looked pleased.

"Reverend Mother, who made this?" I asked, indicating the crucifix.

I heard her grumble from several feet away. "I don't know. It was put there in Mother Alfreda's day."

Then it was time we found someone who did know. "Thank you for your time, Reverend Mother. We'll leave you to your work now."

"You have a plan?" Matt whispered as we headed for the door.

"Yes. We walk slowly through the convent and back outside," I whispered back. "And we hope we come across a nun who *can* help us."

"It's not much of a plan." He softened the barb with a quirk of his lips. He opened the door and waited for me to go ahead of him.

I entered the outer office and couldn't contain my smile of relief. "Sister Clare. How delightful to see you too."

"Miss Steele, Mr. Glass, it's a pleasure to see you too." Her smile suddenly drooped upon seeing the mother superior behind us.

"Sister Clare has work to do," Mother Frances said briskly. "She hasn't got time for silly questions about crosses."

"Oh, but the one on your wall is lovely," I said. "The person who made it should be applauded. Indeed, I think I'd like to commission one just like it."

"If someone from the convent made it," Matt added, "I'll pay handsomely and all the proceeds will remain here. You cannot object to that, Reverend Mother."

Her eyes flashed. I suspected she didn't want us to find out the maker just so she could win. I doubted she was keeping the information from us for any other reason except sheer stubbornness. She had something against us but not necessarily against us knowing the truth.

"Nobody remembers," she snapped.

"I do," Sister Clare said.

"Who?" Matt and I blurted out.

"Sister Bernadette."

"The Irish nun who does the maintenance work?" I looked at Matt and smiled. He smiled back.

We had our magician woodworker. It made sense. All the pieces fitted together. Sister Bernadette was good at fixing things and knew how to use tools. She also did not want her friend, Sister Margaret, to talk to us about the disappearance of the babies and Mother Alfreda.

She had also been present when the large wooden crucifix fell off the wall and nearly hit me in the meeting room. *She* had made that cross move, just like my magic made clocks and watches I'd worked on move to save my life. Her magic must be strong indeed. Too strong for us to confront her. We couldn't risk another wooden object flying at us.

But Matt was already striding off, his broad shoulders set. He was determined to get answers today. I could only trail along in his wake.

CHAPTER 12

"Wait," Sister Clare called after us. I slowed to allow her to catch up, but Matt did not.

"I'm afraid you can't stop him," I said. "Nor will I allow you to try. We need to speak to Sister Bernadette. It's more important than you can ever imagine."

"I understand." Sister Clare glanced behind her to the mother superior, drumming her fingers on the desk and glaring daggers at her assistant. "You'll find Sister Bernadette in the coach house," Sister Clare whispered. "Promise me you'll tell me what happened to Mother Alfreda if you learn the truth."

I nodded and hurried after Matt. I caught up to him on the staircase where he finally stopped to wait for me. "The coach house," I told him.

Nobody tried to stop us, or even ask us why we did not leave the convent grounds. Not that anyone seemed to trust us either, going by the frowns we received in passing. I suspected the mother superior would soon be informed that we had not departed. We only had a short time.

Thankfully Sister Bernadette was indeed in the coach house. The building also housed the stables, going by the smell of horse. A young nun sweeping out the one and only stall in use directed us to the back of the building where Sister Bernadette knelt beside a cart. She peered up at the cart's underside, one dirty hand resting on the wheel. Her toolbox sat within reach. It was wooden and filled with tools sporting wooden handles that could become weapons if she chose to use her magic against us.

"Sister Bernadette," Matt began, "we need to speak with you."

The fingers tightened on the wheel and for a long moment, she did not move, merely continued to inspect the undercarriage. "I'm busy," she said in her thick Irish accent. "Come back later."

"We know what you are," Matt said quietly.

I glanced back toward the stable area, but the young nun could not be seen from where we stood, nor could the sweep of the broom be heard anymore. "Don't be afraid," I said to Sister Bernadette, who had not moved. "I'm a magician too. That's how we discovered you. I felt the warmth of your magic in—"

"Hush," she whispered, finally emerging. "Be quiet. Don't speak that word here." Her nervous gaze flicked toward the stables.

Matt held out his hand but Sister Bernadette merely scowled at it. His fingers curled up as she stood without assistance.

"Is there somewhere we can speak in private?" I asked.

"No," she snapped. "Leave me alone."

I retraced my steps and informed the nun in the stables that Sister Clare had need of her. I waited until she put away the broom and left the stables before returning to the part of the building where they kept the cart. It appeared to be the only vehicle. I supposed nuns had no need for a second conveyance.

"She's gone," I said. "We can talk freely."

Sister Bernadette snatched up her toolbox and held it in both hands in front of her like a shield. "I will not talk to you about…that. It's foolish to discuss it here. Go away and leave me be." Her cold manner was so different to the friendliness she'd shown us upon meeting her for the first time. That day we'd come to the convent and spoken to her and Sister Margaret she'd been cheerful until we'd asked questions about Mother Alfreda and Phineas Millroy.

"We can't leave without answers," Matt said. "This is too important. Tell us why you buried the babies' records in the woods."

Her lips parted in a silent gasp. "I…I…I don't know what you're talking about."

"Yes you do. The box they were buried in was made using strong magic. The cross on the mother superior's office wall was also infused with strong magic. You made it, Sister Bernadette, and I will *not* stand for more lies."

"Are you threatening me, Mr. Glass?"

Matt looked uncertain, hindered by his own gentlemanly code of honor. He would not use violence against a woman, and coercing a nun to speak against her wishes was a task beyond him. We needed to find another way.

"He isn't," I said. "But I am. If you do not tell us what we want to know, I'll tell Mother Frances that you're a magician."

"She won't believe you. I doubt she believes in magic."

"If she needs convincing then I'll tell her how the cross leapt off the wall in the meeting room and almost killed me."

She clutched the toolbox tighter. "It didn't."

"It came close," I said. "Too close. And you made it fall, just as I can make watches and clocks move with my magic."

Her eyes widened ever so slightly. "You can? How do you do it? I can't control it, it just happens all on its own, and only when I'm desperate."

"I can't control it either." If the circumstances were different, I would have liked to compare my magic to hers, but not now. "So you admit you are a magician."

She gave a slight nod of her head. "Don't tell anyone. Do you hear me? They'll send me away, and then what am I supposed to do? This is my home. All my friends are here. I have no family outside these walls, no friends." Her lips trembled and her eyes watered. I suddenly felt ashamed for forcing her to talk to us. "What do you want from me?"

"We want answers," I said gently. "That's all. We are not your enemy. We don't even care if you are responsible for Mother Alfreda's disappearance."

Her face crumpled and a tear fell from each eye. Matt handed her his handkerchief and she set down her toolbox and took it.

"We just want to know what happened to the boy known as Phineas Millroy," I finished. "Is he alive?"

She dabbed at the corner of her eye. "He's alive."

Relief surged through me. I felt light headed, unbalanced. Matt touched my elbow, steadying me. How could he be so calm? Then I felt his fingers tremble.

"I see him in church, from time to time," Sister Bernadette went on. "His parents still live in this parish. Phineas is no longer his name. His parents, the couple I gave him to who brought him up as their own, gave him a new name. I can assure you he is healthy and happy." She smiled sadly. "I remind myself of that every day. Sometimes it helps to banish the guilt, but not always."

"Where can we find him?" I asked.

"I cannot tell you that. I know why you want to see him, and I sympathize, but it is against God's will to use his magic to prolong life."

"You have no right to decide!"

She looked at Matt with sorrow and sympathy. "I know the man you know as Phineas is a healing magician, and I can see that you're ill, Mr. Glass, but I cannot allow you to ask him to cure you. Indeed, he cannot cure you of grave sickness. It's best to succumb to God's will than fight it."

"Listen to me," I said darkly. "Matt was shot in cold blood. That is not God's will. That was the act of a vicious murderer."

She flinched and covered her mouth with Matt's handkerchief.

"He can live longer when a doctor's magic is combined with horology magic," I went on. "We do not have time to go into the specifics, but I urge you most vehemently to tell us where to find Phineas Millroy. Otherwise your secret will be out." I straightened my shoulders and spine. "I'll tell everyone that you killed Mother Alfreda."

She whimpered and tears spilled, but I was beyond caring. We had confirmation that Phineas was alive and also a medical magician. Desperation replaced relief. We were so close, and I refused to be thwarted now that he was within reach.

When she didn't speak, I tried to think of how else to force her to talk. But it was Matt who spoke next. "Tell us what happened," he said. I thought he deliberately gentled his voice to soothe her, but one look at his pinched face made me wonder if he were in pain again. "Tell us why it was necessary to smuggle him out of the convent."

She swallowed. "I…I can't. It's too painful."

"Mother Alfreda was going to do something to him, wasn't she?" She merely blinked at Matt. "Kill him?" he suggested.

She choked on a sob. "I believe so," she said in a small voice. "He was so tiny and helpless, just an innocent baby, yet she thought of him as evil."

"How did she find out about his magic? A baby couldn't perform a spell."

"He didn't need to. His magic is strong, like mine, and simply touching him improved minor ailments. Headaches would disappear, small cuts healed faster and so on. He possessed enough magic that it simply exuded from him without a spell being necessary. But only in a minor way, you understand. He couldn't heal deep cuts or chronic aches, just temporary ones."

"You touched him?" I asked. "Is that how you knew he was a magician?"

She nodded. "I was fixing a cradle in the nursery one day and overheard Sister Francesca—that's Abigail Pilcher—marvel at how warm he felt. Yet when one of the other nuns touched him, she said he felt cool to her. I already knew Sister Francesca was a magician. I'd touched a silk handkerchief she'd fixed and sold in the shop. I never told her that I was a magician too. I thought it best not to tell anyone. But her comment about the warm baby made me curious, so I touched him. I felt his warmth immediately, and I knew it was magical warmth. I didn't know he was a healing magician, however. Not until one of the other nuns complained of a headache before going into the nursery then came out marveling out how better she felt after spending ten minutes with the baby. He was the only one in the nursery at the time, so it had to be him. She thought it was because he was a content baby and his contentment rubbed off on her, but I suspected it was something more. So I snuck into the nursery and experimented on a bruise." She indicated her thumb. "I touched it to his cheek. The bruise instantly went away."

She handed back the handkerchief but Matt refused to take it. "You didn't speak to Abigail Pilcher about what you'd learned and what should be done?" he asked.

She shook her head. "I was too afraid. I knew my magic would be seen as the devil's work. Growing up in Dublin, I'd witnessed first-hand how magicians were treated by the church." Her chin trembled and she struggled to speak. "And she had her own problems at that time."

"Her pregnancy," I said. "So you decided to smuggle Phineas out of the convent alone?"

She nodded. "If I didn't, he would have died, like the other baby."

"The other missing boy?" I said. "The one whose records you also buried in the woods?"

Another nod. "He disappeared from the convent some months before Phineas. Sister Clare brought it to my attention. According to Mother Alfreda, he'd died in the night and she'd taken his body to the morgue herself. Sister Clare thought it odd that she didn't wait for morning. I also had my doubts about the story, but I thought it plausible that he had died. I already knew the baby was a magician, so I was concerned for him. I'd held him once, when I had to relieve one of the sisters in the nursery. Like Phineas, he exuded magical warmth from his skin. I foolishly mentioned it to the Mother Superior. I didn't mention magic, of course, only his warmth. She touched him and said he wasn't. But a look came into her eyes then. A cold, cruel look that frightened me. She directed it at both the baby and me. She must have known somehow that what I'd felt was the baby's magic. I cannot tell you how deeply I regret bringing it to her attention. If I could go back to that day…" She smothered another sob with Matt's handkerchief.

"Did she accuse you?" Matt asked.

"No. She said nothing, but it was that night that the baby apparently died. Yet he was healthy. Despite my doubts, I kept my mouth shut. She no longer trusted me, I could see. Her attitude toward me changed, and I was terrified she'd expose me and send me away. But I couldn't take my mind off the baby, so I visited the morgue. No one had brought in a baby's body that night. I considered all other possibilities— adoption, placing him in an orphanage—but it didn't make sense. Why would she do that in secret? Why not make it official?"

"Hell," Matt said quietly. He seemed to know something I did not.

"What happened to him?" I asked in a rush of breath.

"I had my suspicion, but I needed to be sure," Sister Bernadette went on. "I didn't want to confront the reverend mother without evidence, so I spoke to Father Antonio instead. I asked him what happens if someone is suspected of witchcraft. I made it sound as if I was interested in the subject from a scholarly perspective. He told me about exorcism."

I placed a hand to my throat. "Oh God. That poor baby."

She blinked back tears and nodded. "Father Antonio explained the process, but it seemed too harsh for a baby to endure. I asked him if there was a minimum age for the subject and he said yes. Suffice it to say, a baby is too young. From the way he spoke freely to me, I didn't think he had performed the ritual on this baby. So I only had one option left to me after all."

"You confronted Mother Alfreda?" I asked.

"No. I said nothing. I thought I would but found I couldn't do it. I just couldn't. She already suspected me but hadn't done anything about it. I was afraid if I confronted her, she'd finally act and…" She swallowed.

"Yes, of course. So what happened then?"

"Phineas came to the nursery. Another magical baby. When I learned what he was, I grew instantly afraid for him. I prayed that Mother Alfreda would never find out. But she did. I know she did. To this day, I don't know how."

"Could she have been a magician too?" I said. "Perhaps she'd kept it secret."

"It's possible."

"There's another possibility," Matt said. "Did you confess to Father Antonio?"

"No. I'm no fool."

"Then perhaps Abigail confessed her suspicions about him and he told Mother Alfreda."

"It no longer matters." Sister Bernadette's tears had dried and her eyes took on a glassiness as she dug up painful memories. "I'll never forget when I saw Mother Alfreda leave the nursery one day with a hard gleam in her eyes and a twisted smile on her face. I knew then that *she* was the one possessed by demons. She was the evil one—not the babies, not me. And she was going to have the so-called devil exorcised from that tiny body too, just like the other one. I couldn't let that happen, not when I had the power to stop it. I suspected the first baby had died during the exorcism, and it was my duty to see that another innocent didn't suffer the same fate. So I stole him. I squirreled him out of the nursery one night when everyone else was asleep."

"And gave him to the childless couple," I said.

She nodded. "I begged them to take him. I already suspected the husband of being a magician, and my suspicion was confirmed when they took the baby in without question after I explained what had happened. The following Sunday, when I didn't see the wife in church, I asked where she was. Her husband said she'd gone on an extended visit to her sister's, to nurse her and her ill infant. A few weeks later, she returned with the baby, claiming her sister couldn't care for him. They raised him as their own, and I've watched him grow up." She drew in a deep breath and gave us a watery smile. "It has been my greatest joy to know that I saved his life. It has made everything worth it."

Matt rested a hand on the cart and leaned into it. "Everything?"

It took her a long time to answer, and for a moment, I thought she wouldn't. But eventually she said, "I've come this far, and perhaps it will ease my conscience to tell you."

"You'll suffer no censure from us," I assured her. "We will not judge you harshly."

"But God may."

"Or he may understand that you did what you could to rescue an innocent baby."

She bit her lower lip. "I killed her. I killed Mother Alfreda." She buried her face in her hands and sobbed. I placed my arm around her shoulders and waited for the trembles to stop before letting go.

"You don't have to tell us," I reminded her.

"I want to." She exhaled a shuddery breath. "Mother Alfreda suspected me of taking the baby out of the nursery and demanded I tell her where he was. It wouldn't have been difficult to work out that it was me, since she knew I was a magician. She came to my cell and accused me of being a witch, of being possessed by a demon, and said I needed to have the devil driven out of me. She wouldn't listen to reason. She didn't care that I was born like this, that magic is a God-given talent. I asked her how she would get rid of the devil and she said it would be exorcised from me by a layman she knew. A man with excellent results whose subjects always became meek and mild when he'd driven the demons from their bodies. She described to me how he did it. His methods were much harsher than Father Antonio described. The body was tied up and nails driven into the extremities to mirror the suffering of Christ. It was sickening. Utterly awful. I asked her if she'd taken the first baby there, and she admitted it and then told me he'd not survived." Sister Bernadette closed her eyes, but it didn't stop her tears streaming down her cheeks. "Mother Alfreda was glad he died. She claimed that the devil was too deep within the baby for the exorcism to work, and that death was the best result for such monsters. She *smiled* as she told me."

She leaned back against the cart as if needing the support. She was pale and shaking, her face red and swollen from crying. "I pushed her. I was so angry and terrified that I pushed her. She fell and hit her head on my bedside table. She bled to death right before my eyes. I watched her die. I did not call anyone for help. I did not try to stop the blood. I simply sat on my bed and waited for her to take her last breath. Sometime after midnight, I wrapped her body in my blanket, carried her to the wheelbarrow stored in the gardening shed, and wheeled her to the river. I found some loose bricks along the way and tied them into her habit. Then I rolled the body into the water. She sank and as far as I know, her body was never recovered. It was easy. There are few people out at that time of night, and those who did see me didn't ask." She huffed out a humorless laugh. "Nobody questions a nun, even one acting strangely."

"And the babies' records?" I said. "You buried them that night too?"

She nodded weakly and slumped against the cart, her shoulders hunched. The strong, fiery Irish nun looked defeated. "There could be no questions asked about either child or the truth might come out. I didn't dare risk it. Sister Clare caused a small stir when she said she couldn't find them, but the convent was a hectic place at that time. Nobody was interested in files when Mother Alfreda was missing."

"You confessed to Father Antonio, didn't you?" Matt asked. "The murder, I mean, not about your magic."

She blinked at him, surprised he knew. "I had to or my soul would bear the stain. I didn't tell him why. He knew nothing about the exorcisms. I simply told him we'd argued, that I'd pushed her and she'd fallen. He said he'd take care of the police and, true to his word, they did not return and ask questions after that first day. Thank God."

"We won't tell them either," I assured her.

While I believed in justice, and I trusted Detective Inspector Brockwell to reach the conclusion of accidental death, Sister Bernadette didn't deserve to go through the traumatic experience and have her reputation damaged. The matter was best left alone now. She believed she would face

God's judgment one day, and worrying about that was punishment enough.

"But please, you must tell us where to find Phineas," I urged. "I know you think that we are playing God in keeping someone alive, but you said yourself that magic is a God-given talent, that he made us like this." I took both her hands in mine and dipped my head to meet her gaze. "If he gave us the magic to keep someone alive, isn't it our duty to use it to save the life of someone who is dying from a gunshot wound?"

I could see the moment my reasoning got through to her. Her eyes cleared, the color returned to her cheeks, and she almost smiled. It seemed as if agreeing with me came as a relief.

"Magic has been given to us by God," she said.

"And murder is not God's will," I added.

She swallowed. "The baby known as Phineas was adopted by the Seafords." She spoke quickly, as if she wanted to get the words out before changing her mind. "They named him Gabriel. They can be found at number six Glebe Place although he no longer lives with them."

I threw my arms around her and hugged her. She laughed softly and patted my back. "Thank you," I said, drawing away. "Thank you."

Sister Bernadette picked up her toolbox and straightened. "If that young man can save one worthy life then it means I have saved two. Perhaps God will take that into account when it comes time for me to be judged."

"I'm sure he will." Matt thanked her and took my hand.

He led me outside where the bright light of day stung my eyes. I felt raw from emotion but full of hope. I overflowed with it. A cure was so close I could taste it.

Matt suddenly put his arm around my shoulders and pressed his lips to my forehead, nudging my hat askew. His breaths sounded heavy, labored, and I drew back to study him.

"Are you all right?" I asked. He looked terrible. His skin glistened and his lips were as pale as his face. I removed my glove and touched his cheek. He felt cold. "Matt?" Panic pitched my voice high.

"I'm fine. But let's not delay."

We wordlessly made our way through the convent grounds and back to the carriage. Matt held his hand out to assist me inside then ordered the coachman to the Seafords' house. He tumbled into the cabin and collapsed onto the seat beside me.

"Do you still have the spell with you?" he asked.

"In my reticule." I'd copied the medical spell from Dr. Mill- roy's diary and kept it with me ever since. It had been the same one Dr. Parsons had used on Matt's watch in Broken Creek five years ago. It had worked for him but not Dr. Millroy. We did not know why the complicated spell had worked for one and not the other, but we would experiment with Gabriel Seaford.

I went to close the curtains as he fumbled with his jacket buttons but paused. We passed another parked conveyance where the passenger suddenly sat up straight, as if he'd been half-asleep and something caught his attention. He looked out the window and straight at me.

Sheriff Payne.

He must have been there for some time, waiting for us, and his driver alerted him to our departure. I looked through the back window as his coach pulled away from the curb and followed us. Hell.

I resumed my seat and watched the faint glow of the magic as it spread through Matt's body. All the hope I'd felt upon leaving the convent's coach house was smashed to pieces. The glow should be brighter.

"Better?" I asked him.

He gave me a small smile and nodded, but I knew it was a lie. Even so I took the watch from him and spoke the extending spell into it. He used the watch again, but the glow was just as faint.

He tucked the watch away, and his hand lingered beneath his jacket at his chest.

I didn't dare ask if his heart pained him again. Instead, I pulled down the window and ordered the driver to go faster. A quick glance behind us proved that Payne still followed. I did not inform Matt. If he knew Payne was on our path, he would bypass the Seafords' house altogether. I wouldn't risk further delay.

Glebe Place wasn't far and we reached number six within minutes. Matt pulled himself up from the corner where he'd slumped, but I gently pushed him back. "Wait here," I said. "I'll find out where their son lives."

"No. They should see me. It'll convince them of my need to see a doctor." It may very well do. He looked like a cadaver. His red-rimmed eyelids drooped, as if too heavy to keep fully open, and the hair at the back of his neck was damp with sweat.

I checked through the windows for Payne's carriage but didn't see it. I didn't doubt that he'd followed us, however. He would be waiting around a corner, watching our every move. I felt sure of that now. He was trying to work out what we were doing so he could use the information against Matt. He had not tried to shoot Matt lately, so that was something at least.

Even so, I kept vigilant and climbed out of the carriage first. Matt sucked in a breath as he alighted and needed a moment to steady himself. Despite wanting to offer a shoulder for him to hold onto, I kept my distance as I knocked on the door of the narrow townhouse. A woman's face appeared at the elegant bay window but it was a different woman who opened the door.

"Are Mr. or Mrs. Seaford in?" I asked the housekeeper. "My name is India Steele and this is Mr. Glass."

She gave Matt an uncertain glance before asking us to wait on the porch.

"Do I look that bad?" Matt asked me as we waited.

"You look fine."

"Fine?" He grunted. "The last time someone told me I looked fine was Willie after Cyclops gave me a black eye."

"Why did Cyclops give you a black eye?"

"I can't recall, which means I probably deserved it."

The elderly woman who'd peered through the window greeted us with as much caution as her housekeeper. I reintroduced ourselves and added, "Sister Bernadette from the Convent of the Sisters of the Sacred Heart sent us. Please may we come in? We have something delicate to discuss with you."

"Sister Bernadette?" she asked in a thin voice. "I…I'm not sure…"

"My friend Mr. Glass is ill from a gunshot wound and requires your son's assistance."

"Gunshot!" She put on the pair of spectacles hanging from a thin chain around her neck and gave Matt a thorough scan. "Oh dear. How awful. But my son cannot offer the assistance you need, Mr. Glass. He cannot perform *miracles*."

"Yes, ma'am, he can," Matt said quietly.

She chewed on her lower lip but did not try to shut the door in our faces. I took it as an invitation to continue pleading.

"Sister Bernadette assured us your son could help. Please, we need to find him. Mr. Glass will die if we don't, and I think you'll agree he's too young to die, particularly from a gunshot fired by a murderous villain."

Matt pressed a hand to his chest, perhaps in a plea or perhaps because his heart pained him again. Whatever his reason, it seemed to work. Mrs. Seaford didn't immediately send us on our way.

"Sister Bernadette would not have told us about Gabriel if she didn't think Mr. Glass deserved the special treatment your son can give him."

She leaned forward. "I'm afraid you'll be disappointed. It's only temporary, you know."

I grasped Matt's hand as hope surged. His fingers curled around mine. "I'll take every extra day with him that I can."

She gave me a sad smile. "You will find Gabriel either at the rooms he rents in Pimlico or at the nearby Belgrave Hospital for Children. He works odd hours there so you may catch him at home now." She gave us the address and wished us well, but it was clear she thought Matt's predicament fatal.

I passed the address on to our coachman and added, "Take the shortest route possible."

Matt settled in the cabin with a heavy sigh. He closed his eyes and tipped his head back. It was a few hours since he'd woken and he badly needed a proper rest.

I sat on the edge of the seat and calculated how quickly I could unbutton his jacket and waistcoat and remove his magic watch if his condition worsened. Even if I managed it in mere seconds, I doubted it would be enough. The watch's magic had weakened considerably. What if it stopped working altogether? It didn't bear thinking about.

The passing of a speeding carriage caught my eye. It stopped outside the Seafords' house and Sheriff Payne got out. We turned a corner so I did not see what he did next, but I didn't have to. I knew he would question Mrs. Seaford about our visit and demand she tell him what she'd told us. If he learned that Gabriel Seaford was a doctor, he would know what we intended to do.

I studied Matt, his eyes closed, his breathing shallow. We could not return to the Seafords' house to confront Payne. There wasn't time. As worried as I was about the sheriff coming after us, I took comfort in Mrs. Seaford's reluctance to give us information about her son. She would not give Payne his address. We'd only convinced her by using Sister Bernadette's name and the evidence of Matt's poor health.

While the distance from Chelsea to Pimlico wasn't much, it felt like it took an age to get there. I breathed a sigh of relief when we turned into Sutherland Row, a short street with few houses and no pedestrians or carriages aside from ours.

And then, through the rear window, I spotted Payne's carriage, taking the corner very fast. How had he got the address from Mrs. Seaford so quickly?

My stomach rolled. I felt sick. *Oh God. Please let her be all right.*

Our coach slowed but Payne's did not. It came directly for us. Was the driver mad? He was going to get himself killed! It kept coming and coming, much too fast.

I changed seats to sit beside Matt and put my arms around him. I didn't know why, only that I wanted to protect him in his weakened state if we crashed.

"Matt!" I shouted. "Wake up! Brace yourself!"

He stirred. "What—?" He spotted the carriage and threw his arms around me, tucking my head beneath his chin.

Several things happened at once. Our coachman shouted and swerved, sending us slamming against the side of the cabin. My watch chimed, over and over again in warning. I removed it from my reticule and clutched it in my hand. It pulsed with every chime, like a racing heartbeat.

We came to an abrupt stop, half up on the footpath. Matt pushed open the door and went to jump out.

"Don't!" I cried, grasping his arm. "He'll have a gun!"

"That I do." Payne stood on the footpath, his gun pointed at Matt, and a cold smile stretching his mouth.

CHAPTER 13

*M*att stiffened. He glared at Payne with icy, calculating ferocity. Payne was too far away for Matt to leap out and knock the gun out of his hand. When Eddie had shot him, Matt had been close enough to stop Eddie firing again, and I'd been able to place his watch in his hand as he lay dying. But Payne was no fool. He stayed at a distance. I doubted Matt's watch had enough magic left to save him now anyway, and I was certain Matt didn't have the strength to survive a gunshot long enough for the magic to try.

"Hands where I can see them, Glass." Payne adjusted his jacket over his gun to hide it from onlookers who might be peering from windows. "You try and play the hero and I'll shoot you. You too," he said to our coachman. "Matter of fact, I should shoot you anyway, Glass. I don't need you."

He cocked the gun and aimed at Matt.

I shouldered Matt out of the way, using my entire weight in the confined space, and angled myself in front of him.

"India," he growled.

"This is madness!" I said to Payne. "It's the middle of the

day. There will be witnesses. You'll risk your own life for revenge? Don't you see the folly?"

"Not revenge. Once, yes, when I first came to England. But the more I watched you, Glass, the more I realized you had something of extraordinary value. Something I can sell to the highest bidder. And believe me, the bids will be extraordinarily high for your device. Now hand over your watch."

"An ordinary timepiece?" I scoffed. "Very well."

"Don't play me for a fool, Miss Steele," Payne drawled in his American accent. "You know the watch I mean. I want the magic one. The one that keeps him alive. The one that's going to make me a fortune."

"You don't understand what you're talking about. The watch is useless to anyone but Matt."

His jaw worked and his gaze flicked between us. So he didn't know. It was a point in our favor, but I wasn't yet sure if it would be useful in saving us.

"She's right." Matt's voice sounded strained, his breaths ragged. "My watch's magic only works on me. So we're back to revenge. I'll come quietly with you if you let India go."

"No!" I cried.

"Nice try, Glass," Payne said. "But I can't believe a word either of you say. I'll just have Miss Steele and Dr. Seaford combine their magic into your watch and see, won't I?"

"Don't touch her." Matt circled his arm around my waist, ready to push me out of the way.

"Your watch isn't working very well, isn't it, Glass? That's why you're here. To get the magical doctor to combine his magic with Miss Steele's and fix the damned thing. Don't try to pretend I'm wrong," he said when I opened my mouth to protest. "I know I'm right. I've asked all the same questions you have, of all the same people, and I've read Mr. Barratt's articles in fine detail. I know what your grandfather tried to do many years ago, Miss Steele, and I know the doctor who lives here is a magical doctor."

"Then you'll also know my grandfather failed," I said. "Nobody alive knows the correct spell."

His thin mouth stretched into a gruesome slash. "You wouldn't be here if you believed that." He nodded at Matt. "He's dying, Miss Steele. From the look of him, he'll be dead before the day is out if he can't use his watch."

"You underestimate me, Payne," Matt said. "You always have."

The door to number ten opened and a sleepy eyed man blinked at us. "What's all this then?" He swept his dark brown hair from his forehead and stifled a yawn. "My landlady's in a right state. She thinks someone has a gun."

"Come here, Dr. Seaford," Payne said without turning around, "or I shoot Mr. Glass."

The doctor went very still, and his eyes sharpened. "What the devil is going on here?"

"You threatened his poor mother to find out where he lived and what we wanted with him, didn't you?" I hissed at Payne.

"She wouldn't give up her son so I threatened the house-keeper. She knew everything I needed. Come here *slowly*," he said to Dr. Seaford behind him. "And nobody will get hurt."

Dr. Seaford took a step down then stopped. "Does he have a gun?"

"Yes," I said. "And he will shoot. We're so sorry."

He looked as if he would ask why *I* was sorry but Payne's barked order had him closing his mouth and coming to stand near the coach.

"You two, get out and stand with Seaford."

Matt and I did as ordered. I hazarded a glance at our coachman, only to realize he wasn't even there. He'd run off, thank God, hopefully to get help.

"Will someone tell me what's going on?" Dr. Seaford asked.

"I'll explain soon," Payne said. "But first, hand over your watch, Glass."

Matt put up his hands. "Come and get it."

Payne smirked. "Seaford, retrieve every watch you find on Mr. Glass's person. If you do not, I shoot him."

"But it's useless to you," I wailed. "It only works for Matt. Let him keep it, please."

Payne simply smiled that ratty smile of his. "Check every pocket, every seam, Seaford. He'll have more than one watch."

"All this for a robbery?" Dr. Seaford shook his head.

"Just do it!"

Dr. Seaford turned to Matt and apologized. He found Matt's first watch, the one we recently bought from the Masons', and held it up for Payne to see.

"Where was it made?" Payne asked.

Dr. Seaford opened the case and read the inscription. "Here in London."

"That's not the one. Keep checking."

Dr. Seaford returned the watch to Matt and Matt pocketed it. It didn't take Dr. Seaford long to find Matt's second watch in his hidden pocket.

My stomach dropped. My blood turned to ice in my veins.

"Where was it made?" Payne asked.

Again, Dr. Seaford opened the case and read the inscription. "New York."

"I believe that's the one. Throw it here."

"No!" I cried. "Dr. Seaford, that watch is keeping Matt alive. If you give it to him, he'll destroy it and Matt will slowly die."

"Keeping him alive?" Dr. Seaford asked in wonder. "Are you suggesting what I think you're suggesting?"

"Magic," Payne told him. "You are a magician, she is a magician…and that watch is mine, now. Throw it here or I'll shoot Glass and he'll die immediately. It's your choice. A slow death or a quick one? One gives hope that Glass can over-power me and retrieve the watch. The other...well." He cocked the gun.

"It's all right," Matt told the doctor. "Give him the watch. It doesn't matter."

"Of course it matters!" I shouted.

Dr. Seaford drew in a breath. "I don't quite understand what this is all about." He held up Matt's watch. "But I do know that he has a gun and that it's pointed at Mr. Glass, here. I can't let him shoot you over a watch, sir."

"I understand," Matt said.

Dr. Seaford threw the watch.

"No!" I cried.

Matt grabbed my arm, stopping me from charging forward. But he could not stop me from throwing my own watch. It sailed through the air and I willed it to wrap itself around Payne's wrist and shock him as it had done on more than one occasion to save me.

But it hit him in the shoulder and fell to the pavement where it lay unmoving and silent. It only worked when my life was in danger and it hadn't chimed since Payne stopped pointing the gun at me.

Payne lifted his foot to crush it.

"Don't!" Matt barked. "It was given to her by her parents."

"You know I'm not one for sentimentality, Glass." Payne brought down his boot heel and twisted and twisted and twisted.

The metal case splintered, the glass inside cracked. My watch gave a single, plaintive chime before falling silent. Payne removed his boot to reveal a pile of pieces so broken they could never be fixed.

Tears burned my eyes. My father had made that watch and I had pulled it apart hundreds of times. I knew the inner workings by heart and could put it back together with my eyes closed. It had saved my life. It was beyond repair now.

Matt's hand found mine and grasped tightly. It was an attempt to comfort me, but the tremble wracking him did nothing to ease the ache in my chest. I met his gaze and saw his heart swimming in his eyes, and his pain. So much pain.

The sheriff smirked. Then he pocketed Matt's magic watch.

I closed my eyes. Every sound was amplified in the dark. The *click clack* as one of the horses took a step, Payne's low chuckle, Matt's labored breaths. I slumped against the coach as hot tears slipped down my cheeks.

"India, my love," Matt purred, his lips very close to my ear. I suspected he was about to say something else so when he'd didn't, I opened my eyes.

Payne pointed the gun at Matt's head. "Don't move, Glass," he said. "Miss Steele, Dr. Seaford, come with me. I have work for you both."

"Me?" Dr. Seaford blurted out. "What do you want me for? What work?"

"Magic work."

Dr. Seaford's nostrils flared and the muscles in his jaw pulsed. "I don't know what you're talking about."

"Of course you do. There's no time to discuss it now. Come with me. Walk ahead of me with Miss Steele. *Now*, Miss Steele," he pressed. "You know what will happen if you don't."

I squeezed Matt's hand then let it go. I took one glance at his face and wished I hadn't. There was real fear and helplessness, and bone-shattering pain carved into the hollows of his cheeks and eyes.

I joined Dr. Seaford and together we walked off with Payne at our backs, his gun still obscured by his jacket. I resisted the urge to glance over my shoulder at Matt. I couldn't bear to see his distress.

"Hell," Payne suddenly muttered. "I want to *see* him die."

"No!" I screamed, spinning around.

But I could not reach him in time. He pulled the trigger and fired. Matt reacted but not fast enough. His body jerked from the impact of the bullet and he fell to the ground.

He didn't move.

CHAPTER 14

The gunshot must have acted as a signal to Payne's driver. His coach came around the corner and stopped beside us. Payne opened the door and bundled me inside. He forced Dr. Seaford in with the gun pointed at his temple.

Noise filled my head. Screaming. *I* was screaming.

Payne slapped me across the mouth and I stopped, dazed, my vision blurred. "Make another sound and I'll hit you again," he growled. "That goes for you too, Seaford."

I stared out the window at the houses rushing past and the trees, and slab of gray sky. Then Payne closed the curtains, plunging the cabin into semi-darkness.

No one spoke. I imagined Dr. Seaford had a thousand questions, but was too scared to ask them. I wished I could offer him an explanation at least, but I couldn't even do that. It wasn't Payne's threat that kept me silent, but the yawning hole in my chest. I felt as if it would swallow me.

I huddled into the corner of the cabin and welcomed my tears. They slipped silently down my cheeks, my chin, onto my arms folded around myself. I felt so cold.

Matt was dead.

If that gunshot hadn't killed him, he'd die anyway without his magic watch. It was hopeless. I'd failed him. My magic had proved utterly useless.

I should have told him I loved him.

"Miss Steele?" Dr. Seaford asked gently. When Payne didn't follow through on his threat and hit him, he added, "Are you injured?"

"No," I said.

He heaved a breath and let it out slowly. "Can you tell me what you want from us?" he asked the sheriff.

"Certainly," Payne said. "We have a little time before we reach our destination. You, sir, are a doctor magician and Miss Steele is a timepiece magician."

Dr. Seaford made no sound. I wondered if he'd guessed. It was likely he'd read the newspaper articles and learned about combining magic and the attempt by Chronos and a doctor to extend a dying man's life. Whether he knew that doctor magician was also his own father, I couldn't be sure, although he probably realized I was related to the Steele mentioned in the article.

"Mr. Glass's watch was indeed keeping him alive," Payne went on.

"Impossible," the doctor said.

"No, not impossible. Isn't that right, Miss Steele?"

I said nothing. I would not help him, even in this minor way.

"I think you can take her silence as confirmation," the sheriff said. "Mr. Glass should have died in America five years ago from his injuries. I wasn't there but I heard he lost enough blood to fill a pail. Two men, one an American doctor, the other an English watchmaker, carried him into a saloon. A short time later, he emerged fit as a fiddle. Witnesses hailed it a miracle. I don't believe in miracles, but I couldn't explain it. Five years later, I follow him here. I observe and ask questions. I see and hear things that don't make sense but make me believe in something. Not miracles, mind. Something else. Then *The Weekly Gazette* published an article that has the whole of London talking. Some more pieces of the Matthew Glass puzzle start to fall into place. Then it publishes a second article and there it is." He clicked his fingers. "Everything makes sense."

"Let me see if I understand you correctly," Dr. Seaford said. "You think the watch in your pocket is keeping Mr. Glass alive because it has magic in it."

"Not just any magic. Two kinds. One is medical magic and the other is time magic."

Dr. Seaford huffed out a humorless laugh. "*Time* magic?"

"Tell him, Miss Steele," Payne said. "Tell him what you can do."

I simply glared at him.

"She's a little upset." Payne shrugged. "I'll explain it then, although I think you've already guessed, Dr. Seaford. I can see you're a clever, educated man. You see, Mr. Glass's watch not only has medical magic in it, but that medical magic has been extended by the watchmaker magician."

"So he's immortal as long as he has access to the watch?" Dr. Seaford asked.

"No," I said. "He'll die of old age one day."

"Thank you for your input, Miss Steele," Sheriff Payne said. "I wasn't aware of that. So he's not immortal, but the magic in his watch keeps him from succumbing to the damage done by the old injury and new ones, yes?" He stroked his chin. "Interesting."

Dr. Seaford rubbed a hand over his face and groaned. I looked at him properly for the first time. He was quite handsome in a roguish way. Having just woken up, he had not yet shaved and wore no jacket or tie. His hair stood on end from raking his fingers through it and he sported a scowl.

"I'm supposed to be at the hospital in an hour," he said with a measure of disbelief. It must be terribly disconcerting to find himself in this predicament. I thought he was holding himself together very well. I would have told him so if I had the will to be supportive, but I found I didn't have the will for anything much at all. I didn't even care for attempting to escape.

Oh Matt.

"You will be free later today, if you and Miss Steele work together," Payne said.

"Work together?" Dr. Seaford snapped. "I will not be a party to extending a person's life in the way you describe."

"Not even to make yourself rich? I'm not an unreasonable man. I'll share the profits with you."

"No!"

"Very well. More for me."

"You can't make me speak a spell against my wishes. Indeed, I don't even know any."

Sheriff Payne smiled a slick smile.

"It won't work anyway," Dr. Seaford went on. "The newspaper article stated that the last time the experiment was tried, it failed and the sick man died."

"Not true. The last time the experiment was tried was five years ago, on Mr. Glass. It worked then so it can work again. I suspect Miss Steele here knows why one attempt failed and the other succeeded. I also suspect she has the required spells."

"I do not," I managed a mumble. "The doctor who performed Matt's surgery is dead. The spell he used died with him."

"Then why seek out Dr. Seaford here?"

"In the hope he knew the correct spell," I lied.

"Which I do not," Dr. Seaford said. "Come now, Mr..."

"Sheriff Payne."

"Sheriff? You're a lawman?"

"Don't be fooled," I told the doctor. "He's corrupt and ruthless. He has murdered before, and has tried to kill both Matt and me."

Sheriff Payne smirked. "This coming from the grand-daughter of a murderer."

"My grandfather wanted to extend that man's life," I shot back.

"Dr. Seaford, do you know that your real father was the doctor who colluded with Miss Steele's grandfather? That makes you both related to murderers."

Dr. Seaford did not look surprised.

"Let us go," I tried again. "There are no living medical magicians who know the spell. Matt is dead—" I choked on my sob. "You have won. You got your revenge on him. Let us go."

"You're lying, Miss Steele," Payne said, sounding bored. "You know the spell. You know both spells. If you wish to be released, you'll do as I say."

Dr. Seaford sat in silence alongside me for the remainder of the journey. I slunk into the corner and stared straight ahead, trying not to think of Matt lying on the pavement, bleeding to death while his watch was in Payne's pocket. It was impossible not to think of him, however. Impossible not to feel overwhelmed by the dark pit of sorrow where my heart ought to be.

We finally arrived at our destination, a dark slit of a lane lined with non-descript tenements that were neither new nor well kept. Women lounged in doorways, their painted faces and low-cut bodices an advertisement for passersby.

"Do not make a scene or ask for help or someone will be shot," Payne said as he forced us from the coach. "Not that I think anyone would answer your call for help here. I've been generous since I arrived in this stinking city." He passed the driver a pouch jangling with coins and ordered us into the nearest door.

The row house felt empty, and smelled of damp and urine. We headed upstairs on Payne's instruction, and into a sitting room. Light speared through the holes in the curtains, revealing a sofa covered in faded green fabric, its stuffing spewing from the split seams. Peeling wallpaper hung in strips like loose skin. It had probably once been sage in color but was now faded and stained. A pile of cold ash heaped in the grate. There was no coal box, no fire tools, nothing that could be used as a weapon.

"Are we to be kept in here like animals?" Dr. Seaford asked, looking around.

"For now."

"For how long?"

"Until you two combine your magic." He pulled out Matt's magical watch from his pocket. "In this."

"I told you," I said. "That watch is unique to Matt." My voice rasped low in my throat. It did not sound like it belonged to me.

"That may be so, but I'd still like to prove it."

"And if it doesn't work?"

"You'll try on this watch too." He tossed me another. It was a simpler style than Matt's with no engraving on the silver case. It was dented on the edge but it kept time.

"And if that doesn't heal anyone?" Dr. Seaford asked. "Then what?"

"Then you try again and again and again until something does work. Is that understood?"

Dr. Seaford's face fell, his brow furrowed deeply. "You're serious, aren't you? My God, man, this is inhuman. You cannot keep us here!"

"I will see that your basic needs are met," Payne said. "I am not entirely without feeling. I'll make tea now. Prefer a bourbon myself, but you English do love tea. I'm sure you'll try and escape in my absence, but let me point out that we are one floor up and there are bars on the windows. I'll also be locking this door. Why not take the time to get to know one another better? You might be spending quite a bit of time together and it will be easier for you both if you are friends."

"You're a fiend," Dr. Seaford snapped.

Payne chuckled. "Fiend? You English are too polite for your own good." He marched up to me and snatched the reticule out of my hand before I realized what he intended. "Can't risk you having a small knife tucked away in there."

He backed out of the room and shut the door. The tumbling of the lock echoed in the near-empty room.

I sat on the sofa, both watches in my lap, feeling small and vulnerable without my own watch to save me. And now Payne had my reticule too. It contained no weapons, but it did contain the medical spell written on a piece of paper. The spell could no longer serve me any purpose, but Payne might realize what it was and demand Dr. Seaford speak it.

Dr. Seaford flung the curtains back, sending a cloud of dust billowing into the room. Coughing, he pulled on the bars covering the windows, but they wouldn't budge. He tried reaching between the bars to tap on the glass, but his hand wouldn't fit. Undeterred, he tried the door next, but it was firmly locked.

I watched as he searched the room for a weapon to use on Payne, but he predictably found nothing. There were no fire irons, no weighty objects, not even a rug to pull out from under Payne's feet. Our situation was hopeless. I could have told Dr. Seaford that, but he needed to learn for himself that Payne was no fool.

Finding no weapons, he stood in the middle of the room and bellowed, "Help! Can anyone hear me? Help us!" He listened. Then repeated his shout.

"No one will come," I said on a sigh. "Sheriff Payne will have seen to that."

"Come, Miss Steele, don't give up without trying."

"There is no *point*, Dr. Seaford." I dug my fingers into my throbbing forehead and squeezed my eyes shut. A tear leaked out and slipped down to my chin.

The sofa depressed beside me. "I can see that you're grieving," he said kindly, "and I am sorry for your loss, but if we are to escape, we have to work together."

I opened my eyes to see him looking earnestly at me. He had warm brown eyes, like Matt, and must have looked like his father because I saw nothing of Lady Buckland in him.

"You're a good man," I said. "I am so sorry to have brought Payne to your door. I shouldn't have, but I was desperate, and that desperation made me selfish."

"Desperate to save your friend, Mr. Glass."

I nodded and clutched Matt's watch to my chest. The magic in it pulsed lightly. It seemed strange that it should feel alive when he was surely dead.

"But you said yourself you don't know the medical spell, that the only one who did is dead." He cocked his head to the side. "Why seek me out if that's true?"

"Your father, Dr. Millroy, wrote it down in his diary. I brought it with me so that you could read it and help me fix Matt's watch. It's in my reticule."

Dr. Seaford dragged his hands through his hair. "Which he now has in his possession. Hell."

"Yes. Hell." That summed up the situation perfectly.

I buried my face in my hands and cried silently. Dr. Seaford's hand clasped my shoulder gently, but it did nothing to stem my tears. I couldn't stop them. They flowed out of me like a flooded river intent on its course.

"I would offer you a handkerchief but I don't have one," he said. "I didn't even have a chance to dress properly."

"I'm sorry," I said through my tears. "I am so sorry, Doctor."

"Call me Gabe. What is your first name, Miss Steele?"

"India." I drew in a breath and managed to quell further tears.

"What an interesting name."

I knew he was trying to lighten my mood so that we could put our heads together and think of a way out. Either that or he didn't want to be cooped up with a sobbing female.

"He'll be back soon," he said. "He will probably have found the spell in your reticule."

"But he cannot force you to speak it."

"Yes, India, he can. If he's as ruthless as you say, he can threaten my parents."

Oh God. He was right. Payne could do that. And to get me to speak my spell, he could threaten Willie, Miss Glass, Duke or Cyclops. I may have lost Matt, but I wouldn't let another die if I could save them.

"So we have to do what he wants," he said, indicating Matt's watch. "We have to speak the spells into it."

"We can, but it won't work. According to Dr. Parsons, the medical magician who saved Matt, the watch has to belong to the person being healed. We cannot simply use one of these watches to save another. Payne's will save him, but no one else."

He held up Payne's watch by its chain and studied it. "If we tell him that, he will keep us here and bring paying clients for us to put magic into their watches."

"Forever," I said heavily.

He jerked the chain and caught the watch. "Then we give him what he *thinks* he wants. We pretend it will work on any old watch, and on anyone."

"And when he discovers that it doesn't?"

He shrugged. "I don't know, but we will have bought ourselves some time." He gave me a flat smile. "Time is a friend to a horology magician, is it not?"

"Time is no one's friend. It's no one's enemy, either. It simply is, and it cannot be stopped or sped up. Not even by me."

The lock tumbled and the door opened. Payne balanced a

tray on one hand and carried the gun in the other. The tray held two chipped cups that had probably once been white but were now stained brown, and a plate of sandwiches. He set the tray on the small table near the sofa and slipped a piece of paper out from beneath the plate. I recognized my own handwriting.

Payne handed it to Gabe. "This is for you, I reckon. I've made several copies, so don't bother destroying it."

Gabe attempted to read it, but stumbled over a few of the words. "What language is this?"

"Magic," I said.

"It's complicated." He tried again and again until he spoke the spell smoothly, without faltering.

Payne nodded with satisfaction. "Now both of you hold the watch and speak your spells into it."

Gabe picked up Payne's watch, but Payne shook his head.

"Try Glass's watch. It already contains some magic."

I removed my glove and held one side of the watch while Gabe touched the other. He read his spell, and I spoke one that was close to mine, but not quite right. I switched the order of two words and mispronounced another.

When we finished, both men studied the watch. I studied Payne.

He clicked his tongue as if admonishing a naughty child. "Again. And this time, Miss Steele, say the proper spell."

"That was the proper one."

"It didn't glow. Glass's watch always glowed when the magic worked. I saw it myself. Try again, and this time, if it doesn't glow, I'll quite happily shoot that annoying little cousin of Glass's."

I didn't know which cousin he spoke of, but I didn't dare ask or risk speaking the spell incorrectly again. I opened the watchcase and we touched the watch again. This time I used the correct extending spell.

The watch emitted a pale purple glow, much weaker than when I'd first witnessed Matt use it.

Gabe reached the end of his spell and gasped. He stared at the watch. "It's warm." It was likely he'd never felt any magic other than what he naturally exuded. I almost managed a smile, thinking back to my reaction when I'd first felt magic.

Payne took the watch, snapped the case closed and stood. "Thank you. I'll be back in an hour."

Gabe shot to his feet. "Where are you going?"

"None of your business."

"You can't leave us here! We did as you asked."

"I cannot be sure of that until I try this out on a dying man."

Gabe charged forward, but Payne lifted the gun and aimed it at his chest. Gabe halted and put up his hands.

Payne left, locking the door behind him.

I went to the window and looked out. A few moments later, Payne walked off down the street. "He's gone," I said, leaning my forehead against the bars.

Gabe shouted for help again. He asked me to step aside then tried to wrench the bars free, all the while bellowing. I even joined in, although I knew it was hopeless. Everything was hopeless. We would be trapped here until Payne decided to set us free, and I knew from Matt's stories that he wouldn't let us simply walk away. We were too valuable.

Gabe perched on the back of the sofa and groaned. I felt terrible for him. I felt terrible for my part in his capture. I really ought to help him try to escape to make amends.

"Help!" I shouted. "Help us!"

He bucked up a little and joined in. Together we shouted until our voices became hoarse and our throats dry. I even sipped some of the cold tea to moisten it.

No one came to our aid.

We both sat on the sofa, sending up a cloud of dust. Neither of us spoke for several long seconds.

"We did it, though," Gabe eventually said, his voice full of wonder. "We combined our spells into that watch. Bloody hell." He stared down at his hands as if they had performed the magic.

"Don't be too excited," I said.

"It only works for the watch's owner, I know."

"And we can't be certain your spell worked until the person who owns the watch tries to use it to heal themselves. And since Matt is the owner of the watch..." I choked back a sob.

"But it *glowed*. My magic *did* work."

"*My* magic caused it to glow. I've used that spell on that watch several times and it has glowed each time. The glow has grown fainter in recent days, however. Faint like it was today. My magic hasn't been enough to revive it."

"So you don't think my spell worked?"

"No."

He studied the piece of paper again. "Should I have spoken it differently?"

"Probably, but I don't know how. You said it the way I would have."

"We'll have to tell Payne that when he returns. If we don't..." He swallowed heavily.

We sat in silence, until I could no longer stand it. All I could think about was Matt, and that started my tears again.

"He asked me to marry him." I didn't know why I told Gabe. The words spilled out before I even realized what I was saying.

"Oh?"

"I said no."

"Oh."

My lips trembled and I fought against a fresh wave of tears. "I should have said yes."

"Perhaps you still can. Perhaps he's all right."

"You saw him, Gabe. In your professional opinion, did he have long to live?"

He picked up Payne's watch and opened the case. He studied the dial, keeping his face averted. "The American doctor who saved Mr. Glass, was he related to...to my father?"

It was a relief to talk about something other than Matt. My own thoughts were too awful and I no longer wished to be left alone with them. "They were cousins."

"Did he have children?"

"No. You really are the only doctor magician we could find. My grandfather searched the globe for years. He was rather obsessed with finding one."

He heaved a sigh. "It would have been nice to have cousins."

"I'm an only child too, with no cousins, no aunts or uncles, only my grandfather now, and I don't know where he is. Matt's friends are like my family." I hadn't known them more than a few months, yet that was how they felt—like a family.

"Do you know the circumstances of my birth, India?"

"Yes."

"Would...would you mind telling me?"

I told him what I knew about his father, including the fact he'd kept a mistress despite being already married. I told him about his mother and how I'd met her, and even how Matt had broken into her house and learned about the convent. His crime didn't matter anymore anyway.

I told Gabe about the mystery surrounding his disappearance as a baby, and how Sister Bernadette had rescued him. I did not tell him that she had accidentally killed Mother Alfreda. I'd promised to keep it a secret, and I would keep that promise.

"She told us where to find the couple who took you in," I said. "Your mother seemed very nice. Mrs. Seaford, I mean."

He smiled. "She is. They're good people, and I haven't

always been a good son." His smile turned sad. "I should have told them how grateful I am for everything. And that I love them."

"I'm sure you don't need to. Parents just know these things. Adopted ones too, I'm sure."

"It was the magic, you see. I grew up feeling out of place, like I didn't belong with them, or around the artless. It led me to say and do things I later regretted."

"Your adopted father was a magician, wasn't he? Didn't he help you understand it?"

"He tried, but it wasn't the same. He's a silversmith magician. He has his own jewelry shop but never uses magic on the creations he sells, only in things he gave me or Mama. He explained about magic, how it didn't last, and how it must be kept hidden or the guild would find a way to exclude him. My parents told me that I have the power to heal minor wounds through touch alone, but without a spell, I can't do more." He stared at his hands. "My father warned me growing up that I would be compelled to try to heal the sick, and they never stopped me from becoming a physician. They never expected me to take over from my father in the shop. I'm eternally grateful for that."

"He understood your compulsion to heal."

He nodded. "Thank you for listening, India. Tell me about your magic. Have you always known you possessed it?"

We passed an hour talking. I told him everything about my magic and how I discovered it, including my recent re-introduction to the grandfather I thought dead. It was necessary to mention Matt, since he had such a big part to play in my magical awareness. That inevitably led to why Matt needed the magical watch and how he'd been shot by his own grandfather, and that led to more tears from me. I didn't think I had any left, but it seemed I had a deep well to draw from.

The rattle of the key in the lock not only instantly cut off my tears, but made my heart thump. It wasn't entirely broken after all.

As I watched Sheriff Payne enter the room, one thing became clear. I did not want to die here. I wanted to be free. I wanted to see Miss Glass, Willie, Cyclops and Duke again. I wanted to see Catherine Mason and even Chronos again. Miss Glass needed me now, more than ever, and I wanted to be there for her.

I rose from the sofa and glared at Payne. "I assume it failed. I told you it would only work on Matt."

Payne regarded me from a distance with glittering, hard eyes. He held the gun but did not point it at me. "Why does it only work for him?" he demanded.

"I don't know."

"Don't lie to me."

"It's not a lie."

Gabe stood beside me. "She said she doesn't know. Now let us go. We can't do what you want."

Payne's nostrils flared. "There is something in the spell that you failed to say. What is it, Miss Steele? What did you leave out?"

"That was the spell my grandfather taught me. Every word was precisely the same, and you saw Gabe's spell written down for yourself. You also saw the watch glow. I don't know how to make the watch work for other people. I truly don't."

"Your grandfather must have taught you, otherwise what's the damned point!" He flung the watch and Gabe caught it. "Do you have to say the subject's name?" Payne snapped.

Gabe put up his hands in an attempt to placate the seething sheriff. "That's enough. We've done our best—"

"You do not tell me when it's enough! I say when it's enough!" Payne leveled the gun at Gabe.

"No!" I cried. "Stop! You need him! You need us both."

Payne did not shoot, but it had nothing to do with my

plea. Footsteps pounded up the stairs and, just as Payne realized he had forgotten to lock the door, it flung open.

Many things happened at once.

Matt lurched into the room, his face bloodless, his eyes wild and unfocused.

Chronos followed behind him. "India!" he cried.

I shouted Matt's name, a riot of emotions surging through me. Immeasurable relief was quickly banished by raw, ferocious fear as Payne pointed the gun at Matt. Matt was in no condition to tackle him or reach him before the gun went off.

But Gabe was. He pushed Payne. The gun fired.

I tried not to scream, but it burst out of me. "Matt!"

The blast of the gunshot reverberated around the room, momentarily deafening me. The smell of metal and smoke filled my nostrils.

Matt lay on the floor, and I found myself praying for the second time that day for him to be alive. I scrambled to his side, not even sure when I'd fallen to my knees. Someone crouched beside me, their arm around my shoulders. When my hearing returned, I realized it was Chronos, saying my name over and over.

But I was too intent on Matt. He was alive, but only just. His shoulder was covered in dried blood from the earlier wound inflicted by Payne. His hair clung to his neck and forehead in damp clumps, and his face was as pale and cold as new snow yet he sported no fresh wounds. The bullet had missed him, but he'd collapsed from sheer exhaustion. He offered a weak smile and tried to sit up but couldn't manage it.

"Lie still," I urged.

His lips formed my name but no sound came out. His breathing came in rattling gasps, each one shallow and labored. His eyelids fluttered closed as if he could no longer keep them open. He was dying.

The watch.

"Gabe! Matt's watch!" I turned toward him, my hand out.

And my heart dove. Payne pointed the gun at Gabe.

Matt made a sound, half gasp, half gurgle. I stroked his face, his throat, his chest, willing him to stay alive, to hang on a little longer until I could devise a way to get the watch—the watch that now dangled by its chain from Payne's fingers.

"Is this what you want?" His lips twitched with his smile, his eyes lit up in victory.

"Give it to me," Chronos said, inching forward. "He needs it."

"Yes, he does, doesn't he?" Payne dropped the watch on the floor.

"No!" I screamed.

Payne crushed the magic watch beneath his boot, grinding his heel into the metal, destroying the inner workings until they were no longer recognizable and certainly not functional.

Just like that, all my hope was crushed too.

CHAPTER 15

*A*nother shot rang out and I glanced up, afraid for Chronos and Gabe. But to my utter surprise, Willie stood holding a smoking gun, her face distorted with rage.

Sheriff Payne collapsed to the floor, bleeding from his leg and spitting expletives at Willie. Cyclops snatched the gun from him.

The room became crowded. Even Detective Inspector Brockwell was there, introducing himself to Gabe. Gabe, however, excused himself and came to my side. He put his ear to Matt's lips and listened.

Willie knelt down, her face ashen, her eyes huge. "India?" she murmured. "Is he...?"

"His watch," I said, unable to stop myself from crying. "It's broken."

Chronos scooped the watch up and brought the pieces over. It was mangled, the springs twisted and cogs dented. Even so, we placed Matt's hand over them. Nothing happened. It did not glow.

I spoke the extending spell, and still it didn't glow.

"It won't work," Chronos said heavily. "I'm sorry, India."

"What if Gabe speaks his spell into it too?" I said in a small voice.

"The watch is broken. It needs to be a functioning watch for the magic to work."

Willie curled in on herself and wailed into her hands. Duke put his arms around her and hugged her to his chest. His eyes glistened with tears.

I slumped over Matt's body, spilling my own tears onto his chest. That's how I heard and felt him breathe his last.

It was also how I noticed his watch. Not the magic one but the one he'd recently purchased from the Masons' shop. Payne had given it back to him outside Gabe's house when he realized it wasn't magic. Yet it was still Matt's watch. He owned it, just like he'd owned the original American one.

We had a working watch, a doctor magician and two horology magicians. Matt would not die today.

I scrabbled at the chain, pulling it out of his waistcoat pocket. Chronos realized what I was doing and ordered everyone to be silent.

"Gabe!" I said, flipping open the watchcase. "Speak the spell. Where is it?"

Cyclops found the piece of paper and handed it to Gabe. But Gabe shook his head.

"I can't," he said. "It's not right. He should be dead."

I slapped him hard across the face. But it wasn't that which changed his mind. It was Willie's gun pointed at his temple.

"If you don't do it, I *will* kill someone you care about." She had never sounded more deadly and more certain.

Gabe did not need any further urging. He took the paper from Cyclops and held Matt's hand as Chronos directed.

"India, hold the watch," Chronos said, placing Matt's lifeless hand over mine, the watch wedged between our palms. "Now both of you, speak the spell."

The room fell silent. Even Payne had stopped moaning.

Gabe read his spell and I recited the extending spell.

Nothing happened. The watch didn't glow.

"Why isn't it working?" Duke barked.

Chronos shrugged. "I don't know. I don't remember the doctor's part, only my own. Try again, but perhaps say the words differently."

"Differently how?" Gabe was shouting. "That's how they're written."

"It is," I said, glancing over the written spell. "But try something different. Anything!"

"Do not fail," Willie said darkly.

Gabe swallowed and tried again. Still there was no glow. We were running out of time! It had been several seconds since Matt's last breath.

"Again!" Willie shouted. "You got to get this right or he'll die!" Her voice pitched high and her accent thickened.

Her accent…

"Say it with an American accent," I told Gabe. "Do it!"

Cyclops leaned over Gabe's shoulder and read the spell, and Gabe mimicked him, word for word, inflection for inflection, in an American accent. I spoke the extending spell. We finished speaking at the same time.

The watch flared with heat and a blinding light hurt my eyes. I clutched the device harder, afraid I'd drop it as the heat surged from the watch up my arm. A purple glow lit up Matt's veins, disappearing beneath his clothes, then up his throat, across his face and into his hair.

His chest expanded. He breathed!

I sobbed.

Someone behind me murmured in wonder.

Gabe touched two fingers lightly to Matt's throat and bent closer to inspect the glowing veins. "My God. I've never seen anything like it. He's alive."

I pressed Matt's hand against the watch to keep it in place. The longer the magic had time to work, the better. Cyclops,

Duke and Willie crowded in, despite Chronos ordering them back.

"Matt?" Willie whispered, dashing away the tears dampening her cheeks. "Matt? Can you hear me?"

The hand holding mine twitched. I pressed my lips together to suppress another sob but it escaped anyway.

Matt's eyes cracked open and the purple glow slowly receded until his veins returned to normal. "Don't cry, India," he said softly. "I won't be dying today."

My lower lip trembled. He let go of my hand and reached up and cupped my face. I smiled. He smiled back.

Then I flung myself across him, pinning him to the floor. He laughed softly in my ear.

"It's almost worth dying if this is the reaction I get," he said.

"Don't you dare," Willie scolded him. "Now get off him, India. It's my turn."

I tore myself away and allowed him to sit up, with help from Cyclops. The color had returned to Matt's face and lips, but his body trembled slightly. I could feel it in our linked hands.

A round of hugs followed. Even Chronos hugged him. Then I hugged Chronos. His arms tightened around me and he kissed my cheek.

"Why are you here?" I asked.

"It's a long story. I'll tell you later."

Payne grunted as Brockwell hauled him to his feet. His right leg still bled. "The watch works for him because it *belongs* to him," Payne said, nodding in understanding. "That's what you weren't telling me, Miss Steele." He indicated his wound. "You have my watch. Use it to heal me."

"No," came a chorus of voices.

"I hope you die from your injuries," Willie spat. "And if you don't, I hope you hang."

"He will," Matt said. "For Bryce's murder."

"And the attempted murders of yourself and Miss Steele," Brockwell added. "You won't be seeing American soil again, Sheriff."

Payne curled his lip in a snarl. "And what of *his* crimes? Glass has lied to you. He has duped you and others, here and back home, he has committed theft and countless other crimes. Arrest *him*."

Brockwell pushed him toward the door. "It seems Mr. Glass lied because I wouldn't believe him if he told me about his watch and...magic."

"And do you believe now?" Chronos asked.

"I believe in what I can witness with my own eyes. In light of what I just saw...I suppose I have to. Go on, Payne, move." He marched a limping Payne out just as two constables pounded up the stairs, both puffing hard from exertion.

"What's going on here?" asked one. "We have a report of a gunshot."

"You're a little late," Brockwell said, punching out each consonant. "Help me get this man into custody. He's a slippery cur."

Matt took my hand and squeezed. "Are you all right, India?"

I nodded and blinked up at him, my eyes and heart full. "I am now. I was a little upset before."

"Only a little?"

"British understatement."

"Ah, the famous stiff upper lip." He skimmed the pad of his thumb along my top lip. "It's selfish of me to want you to be devastated over my death," he murmured. "But I find I can't help it."

I smiled. "You're allowed one fault, Matt."

He chuckled and drew my hand to his lips.

Chronos cleared his throat. "I don't expect *you* to stand for this sentimentality, Willie," he said.

"Matt died," she shot back. "He's allowed to get sentimen-

232

tal. We all are." She threw herself at Matt, flinging her arms around him.

He managed to catch her and steady her, proving he had regained his strength. She could be a fierce little whirlwind when emotion propelled her.

"I think it's time for answers," I said, ready to hear them now that the watch's magic seemed to have worked. Matt had already tucked it back into his hidden pocket. Tomorrow he would purchase another spare from the Masons. I hoped he would never have to use it for anything other than telling the time, but it was a comfort to know it was there as a backup if needed.

"We haven't been properly introduced," Matt said, plucking Willie off and extended his hand to Gabe.

They introduced themselves and I introduced Gabe to the others. "Thank you for saving my life," Matt said. "I know you feel uncomfortable with your role in keeping me alive, but I want to assure you that I'll give you no cause for regret."

Gabe nodded but looked unconvinced. "So what now? Do I return home as if nothing happened?"

"If you like," I said. "If you need anything, we can be found at number sixteen Park Street, Mayfair. You'll always be welcome."

"Always," Matt assured him.

Gabe eyed Willie carefully.

Willie scuffed the toe of her boot on the floor and placed her hands behind her. "I weren't going to really kill someone you loved."

"I'm glad to hear it."

"We'll drive you home," Matt said. "My carriage is waiting."

I finally had my explanations as we drove Gabe to Pimlico. Payne had only wounded Matt in the shoulder, but because of his desperate need for healing magic, he'd been in a "bad way," according to Chronos. Matt had hailed a hack and driven to Chronos's lodgings, and they both traveled to Mr. Gibbons's house in order to find me.

I crossed my arms. "And how did Matt know where to find you?" I asked Chronos.

"I left him a letter the day I departed," he said. "In it was my new address."

"Why didn't you give it to *me*?"

"It was best that way. I knew he'd only come if it was an emergency."

"Best for whom?"

"Let's not start this again, India. Can you not simply be happy that you have him back? You don't want me around too. I'm old and crotchety. Some would call me mad." He shot a smile at Gabe. "If I am mad it's because I've spent a lifetime looking for you."

Gabe leaned back a little and blinked wide eyes at Chronos.

"You are not to go near him ever again," I told Chronos. "Is that understood?"

"Do you know where my parents live?" Gabe asked Chronos.

"No," Chronos said.

Gabe blew out a breath. "Well then, I won't be helping you bring anyone back to life."

Chronos held up a finger. "You can't bring someone back to life if they're dead, only extend their life if they're dying. Matt stopped breathing in that room today, but there must have been enough breath left in him to keep him alive until the magic worked."

"A few seconds longer would have been too late," Gabe agreed.

My stomach rolled. Matt had come close. So very close.

"It was clever of you to remember about the accent, India," Matt said.

"My granddaughter is smart. I'm proud of her." Chronos's

words brought tears to my eyes again. I looked away, not yet prepared to acknowledge that I'd wanted to hear him say those words ever since meeting him.

"So, tell me," Gabe said, "who is Mr. Gibbons and how did he help you find us? And why was it necessary to have Mr. Steele with you?"

"Gibbons is a mapmaker magician acquaintance of ours," Matt told him. "India discovered that a cartography magician can draw a map that reveals the location of a magical object if another magician joins his magic to the process. You had my magic watch," he said to me. "Not only did it have Chronos's original magic in it, but it also had yours. All I needed were the right magicians to find it."

"I chanted my spell while Gibbons chanted his and sketched," Chronos said. "He claims *you* don't need a spell but simply hold the map edge, India."

"Remarkable," Gabe murmured.

Matt watched me from beneath lowered eyelids. "Yes. She is."

"The problem was, it kept moving," Chronos said. "The watch, that is. We thought we had it in one location and were just about to go there when it moved slowly away."

"That must have been when Payne left," I said. "He went to find a sick person to see if the watch would heal them."

"He wouldn't believe India when she told him it only worked for you, Glass," Gabe said.

Matt took up the story again. "When the watch appeared to be returning along the same route, we decided to head to the original location where it had been located an hour before."

Chronos pointed his chin at Matt. "He wouldn't wait any longer."

"If he had, he might be dead," Gabe said.

"If I had, India might have died," Matt added darkly.

"And what about Willie and the others?" I asked. They

were currently outside with the coachman and on the footman's seat at the back of the carriage since we couldn't all fit in the cabin. "How did they know where to find us?"

"Once we'd pinpointed the watch's location, Miss Gibbons, Mr. Gibbons's daughter, fetched them. She had them collect Brockwell from Scotland Yard first, upon my instruction."

Gabe dragged his hand through his hair and huffed out a disbelieving laugh. "I have learned more today about magic than I have in my entire life."

"You are a unique magician," Chronos told him. "If there is another like you, I am yet to find him or her, and believe me, I have searched."

The more earnest Chronos became, the more Gabe looked appalled and uncertain. "I won't combine my magic with time magic again, sir. Do not ask that of me."

"He won't," Matt assured him. "If he bothers you, contact me."

Chronos threw his hands in the air. "What's the point of all that magic if it's not used?"

"He can use it," I said. "He can cure minor ailments as he always has. It's combining that magic with yours or mine that is the problem."

"It's not a problem, it's a gift." Chronos slouched into the corner with a pout on his lips.

Thankfully he said nothing more and we were able to have a pleasant conversation with Gabe for the remainder of the journey. He inspected Matt's shoulder wound and instructed him to simply clean it when he got home. The magic had almost healed it completely. He really was a kind man—and dedicated to his work at the children's hospital. He was keen to get there and complete his afternoon shift, although it grew quite late.

"I also think I'd better visit my parents." He gave me a

sheepish smile. "I'd like to thank them for their love and kindness over the years. I owe them."

"I doubt they'll see it as owing," I said. "Perhaps you could also send Sister Bernadette a letter telling her how you are. Saving you cost her, in a way, and she deserves to know that it was worth it."

We arrived at his lodging house and thanked him again. He was heading up the front steps when Willie called out, "Wait!" She jumped down from the coach and threw herself at him. The poor man staggered under her weight. She spoke some quiet words and kissed his cheek.

"Duke may have a rival," I said, smiling.

"Chronos, you could do with some fresh air," Matt said. "Why not ride outside with the others?"

"No." Chronos crossed his arms over his chest. "I'm not leaving you alone to take advantage of India. Not until I see something in writing that states you'll take care of her for the rest of her life. Mark my words, India, get an agreement first. You've got your future to think of."

Matt looked as if he would argue but thought better of it. He simply gave me a sad smile, reminding me of the situation his uncle had forced him into with Patience. I tried not to think about that. Matt was alive and that was all that mattered for now.

Bristow met us at the door with a beaming smile. "I am very glad to see you looking in such fine health, sir," he said to Matt. "Very glad indeed. On behalf of all the staff, may I say welcome home."

"Thank you, Bristow. I'll thank the staff personally after I clean up." Matt looked down at his bloodied clothing. "If this doesn't come out, salvage what fabric you can and donate it. Otherwise, burn all of it."

"It will come out, sir. Between Mrs. Bristow and me, we've not met a stain that could best us."

"Is my aunt all right?"

"In the sitting room, sir." Bristow leaned in. "She hasn't been herself ever since Miss Gibbons came with your message and the others left. Polly has been sitting with her."

Matt and I headed upstairs to the sitting room, Chronos, Willie, Duke and Cyclops following. They didn't seem interested in going their own way, perhaps because none wanted to let Matt out of sight yet.

"Aunt Letitia?" Matt said gently, sitting down beside his aunt on the sofa.

"Thank you, Polly," I said to the ladies' maid. "We'll keep her company for a while."

"Aunt Letitia, can you hear me?"

"Of course I can," his aunt said, turning glassy eyes onto Matt. "Where have you been, Harry? I've been waiting and waiting." She clicked her tongue. "Look at you; you're filthy. Go and clean up for dinner or Father will be cross."

"I'll go now."

"I'll take you to your room, Miss Glass," I said. "We'll get you ready for dinner. Tonight is a celebration."

"Celebration?" she echoed, taking Matt's hand. "What are we celebrating?"

"Life and living."

She nodded solemnly. "Come along then, Veronica," she said, calling me the name of her maid from years ago. "I want to wear something colorful. I don't know why I'm in this dreary black. Mama has been gone long enough; it's time to wear something other than mourning."

"And you all call me mad," Chronos muttered.

I shot him a glare and followed Matt and Miss Glass up the stairs. He opened her door for us and directed her inside, but stopped me with a hand on my arm. His thumb caressed my elbow. His gaze searched mine, but I wasn't sure what he was looking for. He didn't look as happy as a man who'd escaped death ought.

"India," he said but did not go on.

"How do you feel?" I asked. "Do you need to rest now?"

"I feel better than I have in a long time. A very long time. No resting required."

"So it worked. It really worked." I would not cry again. I would *not* cry again. I managed to keep the tears in check but my eyes watered.

Matt stroked my cheek with his knuckles. "Thank you isn't enough, but it's all I can offer, for now. Thank you, India. You saved my life. Again."

"You rescued me, and Gabe too. We're even."

"Hardly." The corner of his mouth lifted but quickly fell again. "We need to talk. It won't be quite the talk I had in mind—my uncle has seen to that—but your grandfather is right. We need to plan for the future."

A lump swelled in my throat. "Tomorrow. Tonight, I want to drink to your health." I wanted to be happy, and I had a feeling our talk would not end the way either of us wanted it to.

"India!" Miss Glass called from inside. "India, help me choose what to wear."

Miss Glass didn't need my help choosing an outfit, and once she was sure that Matt had left, she dismissed me. Thankfully she didn't scold me for having a quiet conversation with her nephew. I was in no mood for her lecture.

I headed to my own rooms, passing Matt's on the way. Bristow exited, carrying bloodied clothing. I caught a glimpse of Matt standing in his room, bare-chested and looking more masculine than I'd ever seen him. The sight sent quite a thrill through me.

Bristow caught me staring, and although he didn't smile, the brightness of his eyes gave away his thoughts. He was more mischievous than he let on.

* * *

239

I WORE one of my best dresses to dinner, a pale cream silk with yellow spring flowers embroidered into the bodice. Somehow Mrs. Potter the cook had managed to put on quite a feast, considering the lateness of our return. To my surprise, Chronos had not yet left. He must be staying for the food.

Matt had dressed for the occasion too, wearing a double breasted waistcoat and white tie. Miss Glass wore her finest mourning, but everyone else wore the clothes they'd worn during the day. Miss Glass scolded Willie for it.

"Why don't you tell the men to change?" Willie said. "Why just me?"

"Because you're a lady," Miss Glass said.

"No, I ain't."

"Amen," Duke muttered.

Instead of arguing with him, Willie smiled and he returned it.

"You are Matthew's cousin," Miss Glass said. "Therefore you *are* a lady when you associate with him."

Willie answered by picking up a slice of rabbit pie and shoving it into her mouth. Thank goodness she didn't try to talk. Her manners were improving.

Bristow finished pouring the wine, and Cyclops told him to pour another for himself. At Matt's encouraging nod, he did so, and Cyclops lifted his glass in salute. "To your health, Matt."

"To your health," the rest of us chorused.

Bristow sipped before starting to make his exit. "Open a few bottles for yourselves," Matt told him. "Then take the rest of the night off. The cleaning up can wait for tomorrow."

"That's what I like to hear," Chronos said. "Does that mean you're drinking like a proper man now, Matt?"

"Just a glass or two," Matt said. "That hasn't changed."

Chronos rolled his eyes. "Willie'll match me, won't you, Willie?"

"Try and keep up with me," she said, and drank the contents of her glass.

She was drunk before dinner finished, but in true Wild West spirit, she refused to retire and continued drinking afterward in the drawing room. She even took to playing the piano, badly, until Miss Glass pushed her aside. They bickered until Duke suggested they play a duet. It worked out rather well, even when Willie decided to add her singing voice. It only began to dissolve into bickering again when she changed the words of *God Save the Queen* to a version I'd only heard drunkards bellowing.

"Oi!" Chronos added his objection to Miss Glass's. "You can't say that about our monarch."

"She ain't *my* queen," Willie said. "And she is aging and has a face like a sow. Look." She fished out a coin from her pocket and tossed it to him.

He did not catch it and it rolled into the corner of the room. "You should show some respect if you want to live in England."

Willie swung around to face Matt. "Speaking of which." She crossed her arms and swayed a little on the seat. "Now that you're better, when are we going home?"

"I can't go yet," Matt said.

"Why the hell not?"

"Language," Miss Glass scolded. "And he can't go because he's going to live here permanently, that's why. Aren't you, Matthew?"

Matt sighed. "I'm not discussing this tonight."

"Aye," Duke said with a glare for Willie. "Let the man have some peace and enjoy himself."

She turned back to the piano and muttered, "All right."

"Do you really want to leave yet, Willie?" Cyclops said. "Are you sure you've resolved all your personal business here in London?"

"Personal business, eh?" Chronos smirked. "Sounds intriguing."

"Don't you have somewhere to go?" Willie snapped at him. "And you, Cyclops, you oversized one-eyed so-called friend, you got personal business to fix here too. Catherine Mason don't deserve to have you run off on her without a word of goodbye."

"Miss Mason, eh?" Chronos chuckled. "Well, well, her father's in for a shock when he learns that."

"He's got nothing to worry about," Cyclops growled. "I ain't pursuing his daughter." He swallowed the remaining contents of his glass and thumped it down on the chair arm.

"That's enough," I declared. "Tonight is supposed to be a celebration. Miss Glass, please play something uplifting."

"Something we can dance to," Matt added.

Willie whooped and leapt off the piano stool. She helped the men push furniture aside to make space for dancing. Miss Glass played a fast, joyful tune that didn't require intimacy. I suspected she'd done it on purpose to keep Matt and me apart, but I didn't mind. The mood turned happier and there was no more bickering. We danced, drank, and played poker —without gambling for money—until the early hours.

Matt looked healthier and more awake than I'd ever seen him. I'd always thought him handsome, but for the first time since meeting him, he looked his proper age of twenty-nine, not ten years older. The lines that usually fanned from his eyes and scored his forehead had diminished, the color of his skin was normal, not gray, and a smile was never far from his lips. His eyes shone with good humor most of the time, although I occasionally caught him regarding me somberly.

At those moments, I smiled back, determined not to let the question of our relationship overshadow the happiness I felt at him being healthy again.

* * *

THE FOLLOWING MORNING, I insisted Matt purchase a watch before he went anywhere else. We went directly to the Masons' shop, not the neighboring house, but Catherine was there anyway, showing a lady their range of feminine timepieces. She smiled when she saw me.

"Have you spoken to Abercrombie lately?" Matt asked Mr. Mason at the counter.

"No, but a guild meeting has been called for tonight." Mr. Mason set out a range of watches on the counter in front of me, not Matt. He seemed to do it without thinking, concentrating as he was on the conversation.

I picked out the same watch as last time, since it was the best piece there. "To discuss Oscar Barratt's article?" I asked.

"And all that it implies." He regarded me levelly, without suspicion or fear. He had never looked at me like that. When my father was alive, he treated me like a child, even when I kept house and ran the shop. After my father died and the guild grew suspicious of me, he treated me like a creature that might attack at any moment. It felt good to now be looked upon as an adult, and an equal at that. Very good indeed. "Did your grandfather really try to extend the life of Eddie Hardacre's father, all those years ago?" he asked.

"You would have to ask him."

He leaned over the counter and lowered his voice. "And can *you* extend another magician's magic?"

No matter how much I wanted to, I found I couldn't lie to him altogether. "It's a theory that only time can prove or disprove."

"India, Matt," said Catherine, joining us as her customer exited. "You do both look well. Particularly you, Matt."

He smiled. "I had a good night's sleep."

"And how is your family?" I asked before she or her father could question us further.

"Fine," Catherine said. "And your friends?"

"A little bored," Matt said. "You ought to visit. One in particular would like to see you."

Catherine flushed but fortunately her father didn't seem to notice as he wrapped up the new purchase.

I thought it a good time to steer Matt out of the shop before he created mischief. He seemed in that sort of mood. I chatted about the Masons and other safe topics until we reached the convent. Matt joined in and didn't attempt to turn the conversation into something more personal, for which I was grateful. Perhaps he wasn't ready yet either.

We spotted Gabriel Seaford as the coach slowed but did not hail him. He left the convent, his head bowed and pace slow.

"I'm glad he came," I said. "Sister Bernadette needed to see him. It's only fair she knows her actions achieved a good outcome."

"He looks contemplative," Matt said.

"A lot has happened in the last twenty-four hours. It'll take time for it to sink in, particularly the importance of his magic."

"And what he did for me," he said quietly. "I hope he comes to terms with it in the next five years."

"Why?" I hedged.

"I may have need of his magic again, if my watch slows down as it did last time. Hopefully this one will last longer, since your magic is stronger than your grandfather's."

Five years suddenly seemed far too soon. I had never wanted my magic to be strong until now.

Sister Clare greeted us in the sitting room a few minutes later with an uncertain smile and a glance over her shoulder. "I spoke with Sister Bernadette after you left here yesterday," she whispered. "She told me what happened to the baby boys, and how Mother Alfreda..." She touched the cross hanging around her neck. "She has answered to God for her sins. That is all that can be said about her now."

I didn't ask if she believed in magic, and she didn't offer an opinion.

"You look well, Mr. Glass," she added.

"I feel well," he said. "Better than I have in a long time. Will you give this letter to your mother superior, please? You may read it. It's a promise of a donation. My lawyer will contact you with the details."

She read the letter and gasped. "Thank you. It will help enormously."

"I'll send my friends around to assist Sister Bernadette with any repairs she can't do on her own. They're bored at home and getting under my feet, so I'd be grateful if she obliged."

She beamed. "Thank you. She will be pleased to hear it. She works so hard and her back pains her, these days. Why don't you tell her yourself? She's in the meeting room."

We knew where the meeting room was located. It was the room where the cross had fallen off the wall and almost hit me. We found Sister Bernadette standing before the cross that had been re-mounted back on the wall. She was deep in contemplation and didn't hear us enter. We waited until she crossed herself then turned away.

"Sorry to interrupt," Matt said. "We wanted to see how you were."

She smiled and extended her hands to us in greeting. "I'm well, as I see you are, Mr. Glass. You look much better."

"I saw an excellent doctor yesterday."

"So he told me. He was just here. What a remarkable young man he turned out to be. Mr. and Mrs. Seaford must be very proud."

"As you should be," I said, clasping her hand.

She nodded and blinked back tears.

"I see the cross is back where it belongs," Matt said, nodding at the crucifix. "I hope it stays there this time."

"As do I," she said. "I put in extra supports. Gabe—Dr. Seaford—helped me."

I wasn't sure that extra supports would stop it falling again if she used her magic to move it. There was no need to tell her that, however. She knew the power of her magic now and would be more careful.

"You come from a long line of carpenters, don't you?" I asked.

"On both sides of my family." She picked up her toolbox and walked with us back to our carriage.

Matt told her he'd send Duke and Cyclops to help her, and perhaps Willie too. "They need something to do," he said.

"And what will you do now, Mr. Glass?" she asked.

"I have an important matter to attend to."

"Ah, yes, you men of business are always busy."

"It's not a business matter, it's personal. Very personal."

With that pronouncement hanging in the air between us, I expected Matt to raise the issue on the way home, but he did not. Indeed, he had the coachman leave him at the top of Oxford Street and take me back to Park Street alone.

Detective Inspector Brockwell had made himself at home in the drawing room, presided over by Miss Glass. He contemplated a cup of tea in one hand and a plate with cake on the other, as if he couldn't decide which to consume first. He stood when he saw me and greeted me with a slight stutter. Was he nervous? About me? Perhaps he thought I'd use my magic to fling the clock at him.

"The inspector has just been telling me that the nasty fellow who calls himself a sheriff will go before a judge soon," Miss Glass said.

"It won't take long," Brockwell said, once again using a precise clipped manner of speaking. Now that I know he stuttered, I wondered if he spoke with such control to suppress it. "With so many witnesses of impeccable reputation," he went on, "the defense has no case."

"I'm glad to hear it," I said. "Is there any way to keep the element of, er, fantasy out of the proceedings?"

"I'm not sure that's wise. Hear me out, Miss Steele," he said when I began to protest. "Since I suspect Payne will mention magic as his motivation for the kidnap, purely to cause you difficulty, why not go along with it? Then it can be presented as fact that the magic didn't work."

"But it did. Matt's living proof."

"That part will be denied. We can say he was never ill to begin with, or merely had a fever that he overcame with bed rest. I'm sure Dr. Seaford will agree to such a diagnosis. What we *can* present is the fact that Payne tried to get the magic watch to work on an ill man, and it failed. I have some men searching for the poor fellow now, or witnesses who may have seen Payne attempt to cure him with the watch. Evidence of the experiment's failure will end rumor and speculation about medical magic once and for all."

"I suppose it's the only course open to us," I said. "As you say, Payne will mention it. It won't set him free, but he'll use it as a last ditch effort to cause Matt problems."

"I will be glad when he hangs," Miss Glass said, peering innocently at me over her teacup rim.

"It will cause a sensation, naturally," Brockwell said. "But acknowledging medical magic then refuting its power will dampen the enthusiasm *The Weekly Gazette* has drummed up. It's my belief that the public's enthusiasm *must* be dampened, for your sake—and Dr. Seaford's."

"I agree," I said. "You'll have our support in court."

He set down the teacup and considered the cake from all angles before biting off the corner. He took delight in eating it and did not speak again until he'd finished.

"I almost forgot to mention, in all the excitement," he said, not sounding the least excited. "Eddie Hardacre, otherwise known as Jack Sweet, changed his plea to guilty, so you won't be required to appear in court for his case."

I blew out a breath. "That is a relief."

"Excellent," Miss Glass said. "Perhaps now it will be easier for you to get your shop back, India."

"My grandfather's shop. But yes, I hope so."

"I must go," Brockwell said, rising. "Tell Mr. Glass I'm sorry I missed him."

I walked him to the front door where Bristow handed him his umbrella.

"I know you and I have not always found one another agreeable," I said to the inspector, "but I want you to know that I appreciate your honesty and determination to get to the truth."

His face fell. "I can assure you, Miss Steele, I have always thought you agreeable. Just because we do not see eye to eye on every matter doesn't make us enemies. Indeed, I found our conversations stimulating."

Then he was a better person than me.

"It hasn't been easy for you, bearing the burden of your secret and worrying about Mr. Glass's health," he went on. "He is your employer, is he not?"

"He is."

"Good. Good." He placed his hat on his head and gave me a curt bow. "I look forward to the next time we meet, Miss Steele."

It wasn't until he was gone that I wondered if his curious little smile had meant something more than simple politeness. "Why do you think he was pleased that Mr. Glass is my employer, Bristow?"

"I would not want to speculate, miss. But I'll be sure to tell Mr. Glass that the inspector made a particular point of asking."

* * *

MATT ARRIVED HOME a little while later bearing gifts and a

somber mood. He handed out the gifts to each of us in turn, and then disappeared to deliver some to the servants before we could thank him.

"Matthew, my sweet boy, come here," his aunt said when he returned. "Thank you for the tickets and necklace. I do love the opera, and now I will have something to wear with my favorite evening dress. You will attend with me, won't you?"

"Of course," he said. "That's why there are three tickets. India and I will both go with you. I doubted the others would want to attend."

"You know me well," Willie said, holding up her gift of a new leather gun holster. I didn't think it wise to encourage her to carry her weapon, but didn't say.

He'd bought Cyclops a new hat and a *Baedeker's* travel guide to northern France, since it was "easy to get to from London."

"You trying to get rid of me?" Cyclops asked.

"No, but I thought you might want to travel while you're in this part of the world. If I wanted to get rid of you, I would have purchase two one-way boat tickets."

Cyclops narrowed his good eye at Matt. "Two?"

Matt simply smiled.

He'd also bought Duke a set of pencils and a sketchbook since he used to enjoy drawing back in America. Matt even bought Chronos a gift, but he was nowhere to be seen. According to Bristow, he'd left while we were out after sleeping the night in the guest room.

My gift was a gold pocket watch with a moon face and chronometer. It would have cost a considerable amount. "I returned to Mason's after I left you," Matt told me. "According to him, it's the finest piece he has ever made." He arched his brows. "Is it?"

"It's beautiful," I said, inspecting the back. "And I'm sure it keeps perfect time and uses only the highest quality parts. Mr. Mason is an excellent craftsman."

"Good, because I didn't want to give my custom to Abercrombie, but if you told me his watches are better—"

"They certainly aren't. He only has a reputation thanks to the patronage of princes, back in his father's day. If those princes had ever visited Mr. Mason, they would have purchased *his* watches instead." I rubbed my thumb over the smooth gold. "It's far too good for everyday use."

"I want you to use it every day," he said quietly. "I want you to think of me every time you look at it. I know it will never replace the one your parents gave you, but I hope it will become special."

"Thank you, Matt. I'll treasure it."

He watched me with that intense stare of his, as if he were trying to learn something from me without asking a direct question. It was both unsettling and yet sent a thrill through me.

"What is it?" I asked carefully, unsure I wanted to know the answer.

"Something has changed," he said quietly. "I can see it in your eyes, the way you look at me now. Do I have reason to hope?"

I clutched the watch tightly in my fist. "If you ask...I won't say no."

His smile began as a small tug of his lips then it widened, but only briefly before disappearing. He sighed heavily. "I am not in a position to ask. Yet."

"Because you're supposed to be marrying Patience?"

He scrubbed his hand over his jaw and could no longer look at me. "I'll find a way out. A way that won't hurt Patience. I just need time."

"What are you two whispering about?" Miss Glass demanded. "I need to know."

"The weather, Aunt," Matt said with an attempt at cheerfulness that didn't ring true. "Just the weather."

Her lips flattened. She didn't believe him but she wouldn't challenge him.

"You English call this spring?" Duke said with a nod at the window. "It's raining again."

Bristow entered, carrying the mail. It included another invitation for me to dine with Lord Coyle.

"This time he has included you, Matt," I said, showing him.

He set aside his own mail to read it. "Perhaps he thought your previous refusal was because you didn't want to attend alone."

"Will you accept?" Cyclops asked.

Matt handed the invitation back to me without making a suggestion either way. He was allowing me to make a choice without interference. While I appreciated it, I would have liked his opinion. I was torn between my desire to leave magic well alone and being proud of my skill with timepieces.

"He probably just wants me to donate a watch to his collection," I said. "And perhaps ask me questions about my magic. Not all of which I will answer, of course," I added to reassure Matt who did not look entirely pleased with my response.

"Then we'll see what he wants," he said.

Willie suddenly crumpled the letter she'd received and raced from the room. Duke rose to go after her but thought better of it.

"Will you go, India?" he said. "She won't talk to me, but she might to you."

I hurried after Willie and found her lying face down on her bed, sobbing into the pillow. She quieted a little when I sat beside her but didn't acknowledge me for several minutes. I didn't speak either, just let her have a good cry.

Eventually she mumbled, "What do you want?" into the pillow.

"I want to see if you're all right."

"Well I'm not. I'm damned miserable. Go away."

"Was the letter from your nurse friend?"

She sniffed. "I said go away."

"I'm not going away, so you might as well answer me. A problem shared is a problem halved, as they say."

"You English have got a stupid saying for everything."

"Oh really? Even more stupid than 'beat the devil around the stump'? I heard Cyclops say that to Matt once, and I still don't know what it means. Or 'nailed to the counter'. I do know what 'hot as a whorehouse on nickel night' implies, but it hardly requires an active imagination."

She rolled over and wiped her sleeve across her red, swollen nose. "I sent her one final letter saying I'd never bother her again if that's what she wanted." She uncurled her hand and showed me the ball of paper. "She wrote that it's what she wants."

"Oh, Willie. I am sorry."

Her lower lip wobbled and I drew her into a hug. She cried against my shoulder.

* * *

I LEFT Willie when her tears dried and went in search of Matt. We hadn't been able to say much to one another with the others around earlier, and I wanted to make it clear how I felt. I also simply wanted to be with him, alone.

I heard his voice coming from the drawing room and went to see who he was having a quiet conversation with. I paused outside the door when I heard Patience speaking.

"Don't try to deny it," she said with more vehemence than she'd ever used in conversations with us before. "I know my father is forcing this marriage on you."

I ought to leave but I could not. I wanted to hear their

conversation very much. I would deal with my guilt over my eavesdropping later. For now, I stepped closer.

"I know you are in love with India," Patience added.

"I am."

My heart rose to my throat.

"And that she is in love with you."

Matt took a long moment before he answered. "Do you wish to be free?"

"I...I want to be married."

Did she mean that she didn't care whom she wed? That any man would do, and since Matt was on offer, she'd take him? I suddenly felt unbalanced and leaned against the wall near the door for support.

"I cannot refuse you, Matt, even though I know you don't love me," Patience said. "My parents have seen to that. My sisters will suffer if I do not agree to this union."

"Then you should agree to it. Don't give them any cause to be angry with you."

She sighed heavily. Clearly she was finding the conversation perplexing. I wished Matt would tell her what he'd told me—that he would find a way out, somehow.

Perhaps he didn't tell her because he knew he wouldn't find a way. My stomach rolled at the thought.

"I know there will be consequences if you fail to follow through with the wedding," Patience said. "Although I am not entirely sure what those consequences are."

There was a long pause and I wished I could see Matt's face, to try to understand his thoughts and emotions.

"Please say something," she added, sounding tearful. "I feel awful about this. It's not what I wanted but...but for my own selfish reasons, I will go through with it. I want to be free, you see, I want to get away from my parents and my sisters. I'm so sick of being teased and told how ugly I am, how pathetic and dull. And...and I know you will be kind to me, Matt, and I have decided that marrying a kind man who doesn't love me is better than living the rest of my life as a spinster under my parents' influence."

Again, he did not tell her he would look for a way out. He must feel some sympathy for her plight. I certainly did. She had nowhere to go, no means to support herself. Marriage was her only means of escape. I, at least, had the cottage and the income its rent gave me, and I would likely soon be in possession of my grandfather's shop. I was not without means. Patience, despite all her family's wealth and privilege, had to rely on others.

I ought to walk away from Matt. I ought to do the right thing and stand aside so they could marry.

But I could not.

"Well," she said, rallying, "marriage between people like us is not about love, is it? Perhaps you and India can come to some sort of arrangement. I won't mind. People do it all the time."

My jaw dropped open. She wouldn't *mind*? People did it all the time? Perhaps people in her circle did, but not in mine. Sometimes, I wondered if we lived in the same world with the same rules.

Masculine footsteps thudded across the carpet then stopped abruptly. "Patience, let me explain two things to you." I had to strain to hear Matt, his voice was so quiet. "Firstly, I believe in the sanctity of marriage. When I do marry, I will not take a mistress. Secondly, India will be no man's mistress. Not even mine."

My heart pinched and tears burned my eyes.

"You would rather not have her at all?" Patience asked, incredulous. "Have you asked her what *she* wants?"

I thought he wouldn't answer, at first. "Her responses have been open to interpretation. I've been living in hope, more than anything, and trying to guess her feelings." He grunted. "As any man can attest, it's not easy to guess what is in a woman's heart."

But I told him I wouldn't say no if he asked me to marry him.

Oh. I was beginning to see his point. I'd been clear that I would marry him, but not that I loved him. To him, one did not equal the other.

"You don't deserve this, Patience," he said, "any more than India or I do."

"And yet it must be," she said heavily. "I will try to be a good wife. Perhaps, in time, you can accept me as a fair substitute."

"Christ," I heard him mutter then apologize for his language.

Fabric swished as Patience moved. "Thank you for seeing me, Matt. Perhaps the next time we meet will be at the altar."

I moved into the shadows behind a tall urn. Matt and Patience emerged, but instead of going to the front door, they went upstairs. I took the opportunity to sneak through the hidden door the servants used to travel between floors. I remained there, however, unsure what to do next.

A moment later, I heard both Lady Rycroft and Miss Glass, along with Matt and Patience. So the elderly sisters-in-law knew about this meeting. Indeed, they'd sanctioned it. I felt entirely on the outer and somewhat betrayed by Miss Glass. Although I knew her feelings on the matter, it still hurt that she chose Patience over me.

The front door opened and closed, and I heard Miss Glass tell Matt it was for his own good.

"No, it's not," he growled back. I'd never heard him raise his voice to her before. "Don't bring this up with me again, Aunt. I don't want to argue with you."

His footsteps raced up the stairs. I climbed the narrow service stairs to the floor that housed Matt's study. I knocked lightly on the door, only to receive a curt "Come in."

"Am I disturbing you?" I asked.

He slumped back in his chair and smiled. "I thought it was my aunt. Is Willie all right?"

I nodded and closed the door. "I have a confession to make."

He arched a brow. "Am I to be your confessor?"

I skirted the desk and stood beside his chair. He peered up at me through long, dark lashes, an uncertain smile on his lips.

"I listened in to your conversation with Patience."

The smile vanished. "India…" he purred, low in his chest. "I'm sorry you had to hear that."

"Why? Because now I know for certain that your uncle has forced your hand? Because I also know that Patience will accept you? Or because I know that you love me?"

He lifted a hand and stroked my jaw. "You didn't know? I'm sure I told you."

"It's not simply a matter of telling me you love me or buying me gifts. You told Patience that you would never make me your mistress. It may sound strange to most people, but it shows me that you love and understand me."

"I see," he said thickly. "So what happens now?"

Feeling brazen, I sat on his lap and cupped his face in my hands. "Now I show you that I love you too."

"You do? Love me, I mean?"

"Yes. Very much."

His eyes turned smoky. "And how are you going to show me?"

I kissed him, deeply and completely, and he responded by thrusting his fingers into my hair, dislodging the pins. My heart soared. I felt as though I would burst from my skin it was so tight and hot. We had kissed before but this time there was no hesitation, no testing or teasing, just unadulterated desire. I'd never felt more alive. This was how magic should feel, like my veins were glowing and I was alight from within.

We only parted when we both needed air.

"I am yours, India," he murmured against my lips, "and I *will* marry you."

I pulled away to look at him properly. He was flushed and rumpled and oh so handsome. Yet his eyes held a measure of sadness as he regarded me with an intensity that penetrated to my bones. "You'll tell Lord Rycroft that you refuse?" I asked.

"I can't do that."

"Because your uncle will confine Patience and her sisters to the estate? Are you worried she'll never have a chance to find a husband?"

He looked away. "She needs to escape her family." It wasn't the entire reason he was agreeing to the union. It *couldn't* be.

"I do feel sorry for her," I said. "But there's something else, isn't there? Something your uncle has threatened to do that's worrying you more than Patience's future?"

Still he would not meet my gaze. "I can't tell you that. Not yet. But I can tell you that I won't marry her. I *will* get out of this arrangement."

I sighed. "So what happens now?"

"I don't know yet." He finally looked at me. He smiled. "Perhaps another kiss will help me think of something."

Of course, I could not deny him.

THE END

LOOK OUT FOR

THE INK MASTER'S SILENCE
The 6th Glass and Steele novel by C.J. Archer.

Follow the continuing adventures of India, Matt and their friends as they try to make sense of their magical world.

Sign up to C.J.'s newsletter via her website WWW.CJARCHER.COM to be notified when she releases the next Glass and Steele novel plus get exclusive access to a free short story featuring Matt and his friends, set before THE WATCHMAKER'S DAUGHTER.

A MESSAGE FROM THE AUTHOR

I hope you enjoyed reading THE CONVENT'S SECRET as much as I enjoyed writing it. As an independent author, getting the word out about my book is vital to its success, so if you liked this book please consider telling your friends and writing a review at the store where you purchased it. If you would like to be contacted when I relcase a new book, subscribe to my newsletter at http://cjarcher.com/contact-cj/newsletter/. You will only be contacted when I have a new book out.

GET A FREE SHORT STORY

I wrote a short story for the Glass and Steele series that is set before THE WATCHMAKER'S DAUGHTER. Titled THE TRAITOR'S GAMBLE it features Matt and his friends in the Wild West town of Broken Creek. It contains spoilers from THE WATCHMAKER'S DAUGHTER, so you must read that first. The short story is FREE to my newsletter subscribers so subscribe now via my website if you haven't already.

ALSO BY C.J. ARCHER

SERIES WITH 2 OR MORE BOOKS

Glass and Steele

The Ministry of Curiosities Series

The Emily Chambers Spirit Medium Trilogy

The 1st Freak House Trilogy

The 2nd Freak House Trilogy

The 3rd Freak House Trilogy

The Assassins Guild Series

Lord Hawkesbury's Players Series

The Witchblade Chronicles

SINGLE TITLES NOT IN A SERIES

Courting His Countess

Surrender

Redemption

The Mercenary's Price

ABOUT THE AUTHOR

C.J. Archer has loved history and books for as long as she can remember and feels fortunate that she found a way to combine the two. She spent her early childhood in the dramatic beauty of outback Queensland, Australia, but now lives in suburban Melbourne with her husband, two children and a mischievous black & white cat named Coco.

Subscribe to C.J.'s newsletter through her website to be notified when she releases a new book, as well as get access to exclusive content and subscriber-only giveaways. Her website also contains up to date details on all her books: http://cjarcher.com She loves to hear from readers. You can contact her through email cj@cjarcher.com or follow her on social media to get the latest updates on her books:

Printed in Great Britain   .
by Amazon